The F

Neil S. Plakcy

Copyright © 2012 Neil S. Plakcy
All rights reserved.
ISBN: 1468135716
ISBN-13: 978-1468135718

The Russian Boy

Copyright 2011 Neil S. Plakcy

This book is a work of fiction. Names, characters, places, and incidents either are products of the author's imagination or are used fictitiously. Any resemblance to actual events or locales or persons, living or dead, is entirely coincidental.

All rights reserved, including the right of reproduction in whole or in part in any form.

Thank you to Miriam Auerbach, Mike Jastrzebski, Christine Kling and especially Sharon Potts, for their help in bringing this book together.

The Restorer's Studio

Paris, Friday night

By ten o'clock at night, as Dmitri Baranov was cleaning the floor of the painting studio at the Institute des Artistes in Paris, the building was deserted, the classrooms and studios dark. The cold winter air snuck in through the centuries-old walls, making Dmitri shiver as he scrubbed a stubborn spot of dried paint on the ancient marble floor.

Or perhaps he shivered because he realized this was the last studio he had to clean before ... well, better not to think about it. Just do it.

The institute was housed in a rambling four-story building with mansard roofs and tall windows, located just off the Place Pigalle in Paris, a few blocks from Sacré Coeur. Through one tall window he could see the glowing spire of the Eiffel Tower. The Institute was halfway up the hill of Montmartre and during the day offered commanding views of the grimy streets and leafless plane trees that surrounded it. He loved Paris with all his heart, and he felt at home there in a way he had never felt back in Odessa.

When the marble shone in the sharp overhead light, he stood up and stretched his back. He was only twenty-two, but hours hunched over an easel during the day, then the effort to clean studios used by dozens of messy art students, wore him down.

It did not help that he was short and slim, either. At barely five feet six, he had to work twice as hard as a taller man might to reach paint splattered on the walls, use twice as many strokes to mop the floor. But he was strong and determined.

He carried his bucket down to the second floor, careful not to slosh any dirty water on the grand staircase. He emptied the bucket in a bathroom sink, then carried it, his mops and brushes, to the janitorial cabinet on the first floor. On an ordinary night, he left the building as soon as he had everything put away.

But that night, instead of turning and walking out the tall front door with the glass fanlight, he removed a long cardboard tube from the closet, carried it back to the grand staircase and climbed back up to the third floor. The central atrium was gloomy in the darkness, the only light coming from the skylight above. It didn't matter; Dmitri had walked these stairs and corridors so often he didn't need light.

He had been a student at the Institute des Artistes for nearly two years, studying under a fellowship from the Russian government that

The Russian Boy

barely covered his tuition. But his fellowship would run out in May, and when it did he would lose this job. Without it, he couldn't afford to stay in Paris. And he needed to. He had entered one of his paintings, a nude study of his boyfriend Taylor, in the Grand Concours, a highly prestigious citywide art show. His painting professor was one of the judges, and he had assured Dmitri that his painting was one of the most assured debuts he had ever seen. He was confident that when judging was complete in a month, Dmitri would win one of the top prizes, which came with a gallery show.

That would shoot him from impoverished student to recognized painter. But once the show's results were announced, in about a month, it would still take perhaps until the end of the summer to sign with a gallery that would advance him money against the future sale of his paintings. He had to find enough money to stay in Paris through the summer, and the fat Russian, Yegor, had given him the chance to earn what he needed.

At the third floor, Dmitri veered off to the right, traveling down a long corridor without bothering to turn on any lights. At the end of the hall, he turned right, then made a quick left to a stairway door that led to the annex building where the private studios were.

He did not know this area as well; he only cleaned there once a month, while he mopped and swept the classroom studios daily. He climbed the stairs, then hesitated in front of the fire door to the fourth floor.

This was it, he thought. His last chance to back out. Crossing this threshold was making a choice, a deliberate one, to do whatever he had to do to stay in Paris and keep painting.

He pushed the door open into a small foyer, with four doors that led to small rooftop studios. The locks were old and simple; he didn't even use his keys when he cleaned up there. All it took was a jiggle of the handle, a little pressure against the door, a slight lift, and the lock slipped.

He thought it was foolish that there were so often fabulous works of art up here, being restored, with so little security. But the Institute had focused on protecting only the exterior of the building with an alarm and a wrought-iron fence. He had overheard the director of the institute speak disparagingly about insurance companies, and how money should be spent in support of artists rather than in protecting them.

As the door swung open, he saw floor to ceiling windows that faced the back courtyard and washed the room in moonlight. Along the left wall, he saw the painting he had come for, an oil called *The Russian Boy*. His heart jumped at the sight of this painting, one he had studied in class. He was moved by the boy's beauty, but more by the subtle emotion the painter had expressed through his technique.

He smiled at the irony—a Russian boy himself, he was liberating one of his countrymen from a sort of imprisonment, allowing the handsome, naked boy in the painting to live freely in France, just as he wanted to do himself.

At least he assumed that the painting would stay in France. He had no idea where it would end up after he handed it off to the fat, sweaty Russian who had hired him to take it. He just knew that it wouldn't be going back to New York, where it had been hung on a museum wall.

He slipped on a pair of the rubber gloves he used for cleaning, pulled his Swiss Army knife from his pocket, and walked up to the painting. His fingers trembling, he lifted it from its easel and placed it faced down on a work table. He took a deep breath, steadied himself, and began to take the frame apart.

It was as if time stopped for him as he worked. He worshipped art, and it would devastate him if he did anything to damage such a beautiful piece. When he had removed everything holding the frame together, he lifted the pieces away, leaving the canvas flat, resting against the tabletop.

He rolled the canvas carefully and slid it into the tube, turning the plastic cap to seal it. He slipped his arm through the shoulder strap, slung the tube over his arm, and left the restorer's studio.

On his way out, he used the knife to gouge out the inside of the ancient lock. He hoped that might deflect suspicion from him.

The theft wouldn't be noticed until Monday, at the earliest, if the elderly restorer even came in to work that morning. By then, Dmitri would have handed the painting over to Yegor, and received his payment. He would protest his innocence to anyone who asked, and there would be no evidence to connect him to the theft.

He went back down to the first floor, punched the alarm code in by the front door, and then stepped out the door, closing it gently behind him. He tightened his scarf around his neck and hurried around the corner of the building before the exterior light winked off.

He stayed inside the tall wrought-iron fence and circled to the rear of the building. A year before, he had accidentally discovered that a window in an unused storage closet was not connected to the alarm

The Russian Boy

system. He leaned the cardboard tube against the stone wall and wrapped his hand in his scarf. Then he used the butt of the folding knife to smash the window.

He didn't realize he'd been holding his breath until the window shattered without triggering the alarm. He took a couple of deep breaths and then slung the tube over his shoulder. He went back to the front of the building and let himself out the iron gate, locking it behind him with a heavy skeleton key.

The streets were narrow and dark. He started when a pigeon fluttered past him, almost in his face, and looked around nervously when he heard the pulse of a police siren blocks away. He was relieved when he reached the door to the dank, winding staircase up to the tiny, fifth-floor studio he shared with Taylor, an American student a year behind him at the Institute.

Taylor was already in bed, reading a textbook on Impressionism. He was six feet tall, blond and broad-shouldered, with a long, slim dick that was easily aroused.

They had met a year before, when Taylor began his fellowship at the Institute as Dmitri was entering the second year of his. There was an immediate attraction between them, and they'd gone to bed together the night of their first date, screwing each other behind a curtain in the living room of a rundown flat where Taylor was staying.

Within a month they had found the studio and moved in together. It was tiny as a closet, barely large enough for their double bed and a rickety wardrobe they shared. Taylor thought it was romantic, living like that, but Dmitri had seen the way the wealthy lived and he longed for space and luxury.

"You're late," Taylor said in French, closing the book and setting it on the floor next to the bed. "Lot of mess to clean up?" Dmitri's English was limited, and Taylor's Russian non-existent, so they spoke to each other in the language they had in common.

"Yes, much work." He considered himself lucky to have the job. Other students at the Institute waited tables, moved furniture, or worked outdoors in the cold Parisian winter, freezing their fingers sometimes so that they had trouble holding brushes in painting class.

His job was indoors, and there was no commuting time between class and work, no need to pay a Metro fare or waste time on buses or trains. He often rescued nearly-new brushes with a few bristles missing, and not-quite-empty tubes of paint, from the trash. On a good day, he found a discarded energy bar that had slipped under a table, or a half-empty bottle of Evian water, to supplement his meager food budget.

He placed the cardboard tube against the wall, and then began peeling his clothes off. The room was cold, and he wanted to huddle under the covers and warm up next to his boyfriend.

"What's in the tube?" Taylor asked.

"Just canvas." Taylor had been in the Café SiSi when Yegor approached Dmitri, and he'd been vehemently opposed to any contact with the fat Russian. But Taylor had the luxury of morality. If he needed money, he could call his mother in the US, while Dmitri wouldn't waste the cost of a call on his alcoholic mother—if she was even still alive. He hadn't spoken to her since he left Odessa two years before.

"What kind of canvas?" Taylor asked.

Dmitri could tell his boyfriend was suspicious. There was one way to short-circuit this conversation. He kicked off his shoes, then dropped his jeans and peeled off his briefs. "Forget about canvas. Let's fuck."

He pulled the covers back; Taylor was naked beneath them, and Dmitri hopped into the bed next to him, pressing his mouth to Taylor's. With his lips open, he snaked his tongue into Taylor's mouth, rubbing his nose against Taylor's.

Beneath him, he felt Taylor's body reacting to his own. Taylor kissed back, his own tongue dueling with Dmitri's. His cock rose and pressed against Dmitri's abdomen.

Taylor reached down and grabbed Dmitri's erect cock, stroking it roughly up and down as they kissed. Because Dmitri was so much smaller, he was almost always on top, Taylor below him like a pile of Christmas presents just waiting to be enjoyed.

Dmitri grabbed Taylor's cock just as roughly, squeezing it until Taylor shuddered and winced under him. They both enjoyed this kind of rough and tumble love, though sometimes Taylor complained that he wanted to take things slower. Dmitri didn't care; to him, sex was a power struggle, the chance to vanquish a stronger man by appealing to his deepest needs.

He gnawed on Taylor's lower lip, inhaling his lover's breath, which tasted like stale wine. Taylor reached up and pinched Dmitri's left nipple, and Dmitri squirmed at the roughness, but loved it. It made his dick even harder.

Each of them jerked the other as they kissed. It was a fast and furious kind of lovemaking, a way to release the sexual energy that

The Russian Boy

accumulated in them both. Taylor began to whimper and squirm as his body tensed, then he ejaculated into Dmitri's hand.

That was enough to send Dmitri over the top, too, and he came on Taylor's hand and his belly. He wiped his hand on Taylor's chest, then sunk down on top of him, their sweat and cum mingling together. "Clean up on aisle seven," Taylor mumbled in English, one of those strange expressions Dmitri, with his limited command of the language, could never figure out.

Though he enjoyed sex with Taylor, Dmitri did not respect him. His American boyfriend was too commercial in his art—and Dmitri didn't just think that because Taylor always sold more paintings, for more money, to the tourists. He, Dmitri, had the greater artistic soul. Taylor was a cute boy with a dick and an ass, and it worked out that they shared expenses and got along so well sexually. But it wasn't love.

Both of them supplemented their income by drawing and painting outside Sacré Coeur, just a few blocks away through the steep, narrow streets of Montmartre, and selling their work to tourists.

People thought Dmitri cute and charming, and they liked the way his heavy Russian accent colored his French. He flirted with young women—and a few men, too, usually older ones. He made the middle-aged parents think of him as a son. With his mop of dark curls and cherubic face, he was a great contrast to Taylor, who worked next to him.

Taylor had an innocent American quality, and handled all transactions that needed English language skills. Dmitri could speak a little English—enough to negotiate a price, for example—but he preferred to leave the business to Taylor.

Next to him in bed, he heard Taylor drift into sleep, his slow, rhythmic breathing mixing with the creaks and groans as the old building settled around them. Dmitri himself was just dozing as the ring of the disposable cell phone that Yegor had given him startled both of them with its shrill tone.

"What the fuck?" Taylor groaned in English, as Dmitri scrambled out of bed and searched for the phone in his discarded pants.

"*Allo?*" Dmitri said, finding the phone.

"There has been a change of plan," Yegor said in Russian. "I must leave Paris immediately. You will have to bring the painting to me in Nice."

"Nice?"

"Yes. Write this down. The Bar Les Sables, 18 Rue du Vieux Fort.

It's in the old part of the city. Be there Sunday afternoon."

Dmitri tried to argue, but the phone went dead in his hand.

"Who was that?" Taylor asked in French, sitting up in the bed, his blond hair and pale skin shimmering in the light from the dormer window.

"Nothing. Wrong number."

"Don't lie to me, Dmitri. You don't even have a phone. Where did you get that one?"

"Don't bother yourself." Dmitri felt dirty and sticky, from the sex and his work and the theft. There wouldn't be any hot water until morning, but maybe he could take a cold shower in the stall one floor down.

"It was that Russian guy, wasn't it?" Taylor asked. "Yegor. The one who came up to you in Bar SiSi. The one who wanted you to steal the painting. *The Russian Boy*."

"You don't know my life," Dmitri snapped. "I can't go back to Odessa when fellowship runs out. I won't."

"I told you, we'll find a way to work it out," Taylor said. "All it takes is for one gallery to accept some paintings from either of us, and we'll have our start."

Taylor was a skilled mimic—he could paint in the Parisian streetscape style of Maurice Utrillo, or with the Impressionist flair of Claude Monet. He painted the church in the watery light of Frederick Constable and the dark shadows of Edward Hopper. The tourists ate it up, often buying several canvases in different styles.

Dmitri could only paint in his own manner, heavily influenced by the German expressionists like Edvard Munch and Kathe Kollwitz. His pictures were not as much in demand as Taylor's, but both of them knew that Dmitri was the more talented. Not that Taylor was a hack; he had a perceptive eye and excellent technique. But he had yet to find his true artistic voice, which was why he painted in imitation of the masters.

"You go back to America when your fellowship finishes. You paint your boring commercial paintings and make pots of money. And I am in Odessa struggling to paint from my heart and shivering in lousy shithole like this one."

"You did it, didn't you?" Taylor nodded toward the cardboard tube. "You stole the painting for Yegor. And that was him on the phone."

"Like I say, do not bother yourself." It was as if the future had

x

The Russian Boy

opened up for him in a flash of lightning, and he knew that his relationship with Taylor was over. He got down on his hands and knees and pulled his cheap suitcase out from under the bed. Then he began throwing clothes and art supplies into it.

"Where are you going in the middle of the night?" Taylor asked. "Nice? Is that what you were talking about on the phone?"

"I leave. That's all." As Taylor sat on the bed, Dmitri finished packing, threw his clothes back on, and stalked out the door.

The Kramer Agency

New York, Monday morning

Just after six, Rowan McNair woke to a phone call from his son Nick. "Hey, Dad, did I wake you?"

"Yes. But it's OK. What gets you up so early?"

As far as Rowan knew, his son was a college senior majoring in sleeping late and having fun, to the dismay of his mother, Elizabeth, and her second husband Bruno, an investment banker. But as Bruno was paying the boy's tuition, Rowan had kept his mouth shut.

"Haven't gone to sleep yet. Listen, I need to tell you something, something I've been hiding for a long time."

Rowan inhaled deeply. "Whatever it is I'll still love you."

Nick laughed. "I'm not gay, if that's what you were thinking. I'm a hundred percent straight."

"Then what is it?"

"I've been painting."

"Ah," Rowan said. "Let me guess. Your mom doesn't approve."

"She and Bruno want me to go to work on Wall Street, like him. That'll kill me, Dad. You know that."

Rowan sat up in bed, fumbled for his glasses. It was the first time his son had called him in – well, he couldn't remember how long. Usually he called Nick's cell, checking in with him every couple of months. Ever since the divorce relations had been strained between Rowan and his children, though Nick's sister, Cassidy, two years younger, didn't seem to have the same resentment Nick did.

"How long have you been painting?"

"Pretty much since I went to college."

"Are you any good?"

"The art department has a contest every year. I won the oil painting prize four years in a row."

"And you never told your mother or me?"

Nick hesitated.

"Let me guess," Rowan said. "You were afraid your mother would say you were like me."

"Not like in a bad way, Dad. And not like I was scared she would think I was gay, either. It's just…. Well, you know."

Rowan knew. Elizabeth had been devastated when he lost his teaching job, even more so when she realized that Rowan was gay and

The Russian Boy

that her marriage had been a sham.

He didn't think of it that way. He had loved Elizabeth, still did. At the time they married, he didn't feel like being gay was an option. He loved the kids they had produced, and if it hadn't been for his indiscretion he might still be married. Miserable, but married.

"So what do you need? Want me to talk to your Mom?"

"I want to go to Italy and study painting. I found this great program but it costs five grand and they don't have any scholarships or fellowships for first-year students. You know I can't ask mom and Bruno for the money. I've been saving, I swear, Dad, but life is just so expensive. In a year all I've put away is a grand. And I don't want to have to wait four more years."

"Slow down, Nicky. When do you need the money?"

"You'll help me? Really?"

"Nick. I'm sorry, I don't have that kind of cash sitting around. But if you know when you need it I can see what I can do."

"The program starts July 1. They need half the money to secure my place as soon as possible. Then they need the rest by June 1."

"June first? It's already March. That doesn't give me much time to raise the money." He sighed. There were a couple of things he could do, a few favors he could call in. And he had an appointment later that day with Ron Kramer, a private eye who had hired him to do some investigation in art theft cases. Maybe that would help.

"Get some sleep, Nicky," Rowan said. "I'll see what kind of cash I can put together and I'll call you."

"Thanks, Dad. Listen, I'm sorry I've been, you know, pissed at you. I have some gay friends at school now, and I can see how shitty you must felt being married to Mom."

Rowan was about to protest that his life hadn't been that bad—but in the end, Nick was right. He only hoped that this new understanding would allow them to be father and son again, the way they'd been when Nick was a boy and Rowan spent endless hours with him shooting baskets, playing catch, and teaching him to ride a two-wheeler.

Nick yawned. "G'night, Dad."

He disconnected, and Rowan sat back against the bedding. He had been divorced for six years, and he couldn't remember Nick ever asking for something during that time. Nick was fifteen when Rowan walked out, Cassidy thirteen. Elizabeth was an attorney, and she'd declined any offers of alimony or child support. She was determined to cut him out of her life as cleanly as a tumor, and though she hadn't forbidden him contact with the kids, she hadn't encouraged it either.

He loved his children and the rift between him and his first-born tore at his soul. He was so pleased that Nick had come to him for help, and he was determined to do whatever he could to make things better between them.

He yawned and stretched. If he got up, he could go for a jog in Central Park before his meeting with Ron Kramer. He didn't like the idea, but he knew he needed the exercise. The run rejuvenated him, and by the time he showed up at The Kramer Agency for his appointment he was ready to take on any assignment, as long as it would provide the cash Nick needed.

Ron was a bluff, round-faced man in his early sixties, a former New York cop turned private eye. "How's your French?" he asked, after exchanging greetings.

Rowan shrugged. "Good enough. I studied in high school and college, and had to read a lot in French for my Ph.D. I haven't been back to France in years, but I can still get by." At fifty, he was at least ten years younger than Kramer, a few inches taller and about fifty pounds lighter. But he knew Kramer could take him in any fight. Though Rowan had consulted with The Kramer Agency on several art thefts in the past, he'd never had to do anything more strenuous than walk through museums and stake out galleries.

"You ever hear of a painting called *The Russian Boy*?" Kramer asked.

Rowan felt like his finger had been put in an electric socket. He knew the painting, by Russian artist Fyodor Luschenko, very well. He'd even written an article about it, years before, when he was a practicing academic.

Luschenko was a figurative painter who specialized in portraits, and his paintings hung in the Hermitage in St. Petersburg, the Louvre in Paris, and the New York Museum of Fine Arts, among many others. *Le Jeune Homme Russe*, or *The Russian Boy*, was his most famous, though, because of the scandal that surrounded it.

"It's a nude study of a young Russian count named Alexei Dubernin," Rowan said. "Pretty scandalous when it was painted, because of the overt sexuality. The boy was barely seventeen at the time, and Luschenko painted him like he was ready for sex, with a stiff dick and a dab of precum at the end."

He could see that description made Kramer uneasy. Straight guys

The Russian Boy

always squirmed when it came to talk about stiff dicks. But just the thought of the painting, the way the boy's eyes were glazed with lust, gave Rowan a hard-on. He swallowed deeply and went on. "It turned out that Luschenko had an affair with the boy in his studio in Nice in the years just before World War I."

"It's been stolen," Kramer said. "From a studio in Paris where the NYMFA sent it for restoration. Our client's the insurance company, and they're steaming. Apparently security was pretty lax at this place called the Institute des Artistes. Both the insurers and the Institute want the painting back ASAP."

"Any idea where it went?"

"A curator on the French Riviera called Interpol with a tip that the painting may be there. Interpol is swamped with drug cases and can't promise any follow up in the near future, though. My contact at the NYMFA gave our name to the insurance company, and they want us to look into the theft. Assuming you're available."

"I'm available," Rowan said. Since losing his teaching job, he'd been getting by with occasional work editing for an art history journal, helping out at a gallery, and a couple of investigative jobs for Ron Kramer. This job would provide the money he needed for Nick's deposit. He'd worry about the rest of the cash later.

"Good. I need you on the ground there ASAP."

They negotiated the details, including a $5,000 bonus if Rowan was able to return the painting to the NYMFA. Handily, that five grand was just what Nick needed, and Rowan would be happy to let him use the thousand dollars he'd saved himself for his expenses during the year.

Kramer's secretary found Rowan a red-eye that night to Paris, with a connecting flight to Nice. Walking back to his tiny studio apartment on the Upper West Side, Rowan lost himself in thoughts of *The Russian Boy.*

Rowan had first seen the painting on postcard in a seedy bookstore just off Times Square. Six months into his marriage to Elizabeth, he knew he had made a mistake. Though he was able to perform with her, he was most excited by thoughts of sex with men. He thought he could satisfy those urges with occasional visits to X-rated movies, with books and magazines he destroyed as soon as he was finished with them.

But something about the expression of sexuality in the painting was different. He was working on his dissertation in art history at

xv

Columbia; he spent his days looking at paintings and writing about them. But none of them excited or moved him the way this postcard did. He bought the card, stuffing it as a bookmark in a cheap paperback that purported to be true stories of sex between sailors and Marines.

He had gone to see the painting itself the next day, standing before it in the Russian gallery at NYMFA, and if anything, the real painting moved him even more than the postcard. The Russian teenager was naked, reclining on a velvet chaise longue in the classic pose of an odalisque. The term originally meant an extraordinary beauty from the Sultan's court, but by Luschenko's time, Ingres, Delacroix and many others had painted women in that pose, and the term had come to mean a mistress or prostitute.

Count Alexei Dubernin was Luschenko's apprentice, a painter himself, but only with a very small talent. He was a beautiful young man, with wavy blond hair and perfect skin. He had only a hint of hair under his arms and a small bush of dark blond pubic hair. His right arm rested languidly on the back of the lounge, while his left was splayed open on his thigh beside his erect penis.

His eyes were heavy-lidded, and he stared directly at the painter, and the viewer, his mouth slightly open, exposing just the tip of his tongue. A few droplets of sweat glistened on his perfect chest, and the cowl of his uncircumcised dick had slid back, revealing the tip and the tiny bubble of precum that glistened there. That was a work of magic in itself, capturing the essence of sexual desire. The boy stared openly, lustfully, at the painter, with a smoldering sensuality like the young men in Abercrombie & Fitch magazine ads.

But there was something more, something deeper than sexual attraction. There was love in that gaze as well, and it moved Rowan's heart. Had he given up the chance that a man would ever look at him that way by giving in to convention, and practicality, and marrying Elizabeth? She had paid his graduate school tuition, as well as their living expenses, from the income on a family trust. His parents had beamed at the wedding, happy to see their son settled and financially secure. When Nick and Cassidy came along, they were finally be proud of him.

But things hadn't worked out the way any of them had planned. Now he lived in a small studio apartment on the Upper West Side, met a few friends for brunch occasionally, and struggled to make ends meet with a collage of part-time and freelance jobs. He'd lost the prestige of his academic appointment when his scandal was uncovered, and he'd lost the safety and security of family life as well.

He was determined to stay positive, though, and the idea that this job might bring his son back to him energized him and put a spring in his step as he marched up Broadway.

A Matter of Money

Nice, Monday evening

Dmitri paced the broken sidewalk of the old city, sweat pooling under his arms and dripping down his chest. He had arrived on the overnight train that morning, and gone directly to the bar. Yegor wasn't there, and the bartender said he couldn't stay in the bar all day unless he drank. The man did take pity on him and let him leave his duffle bag in the back room, though.

He called Yegor on the cell phone the Russian had given him, but got no answer. All day long, Dmitri walked up and down the Rue du Vieux Fort, keeping the entry to the bar in sight. It was hot and close in Vieux Nice, with no chance of a cooling ocean breeze. The cobbled streets smelled like stale food with an overlay of salt water, and someone in an apartment on an upper floor kept playing American rap music which gave Dmitri a headache. The Bar Les Sables was in the middle of a block of stores and doorways leading to upper-floor apartments, so there wasn't much room to hide. All he could do was keep moving. Every time he called Yegor, the phone just rang and rang.

The houses here were on top of each other, a crazy quilt of windows and different colored shutters above him. The occasional satellite dish protruded from a wall, while some balconies overflowed with flowers and others were as empty as Dmitri's pockets. Old-fashioned carriage lamps extended from the buildings on wrought-iron arms; T-shirts and other tourist trinkets spilled out of shop doors, and the narrow streets were crowded with people young and old.

At least that's what it was like in the daytime. As evening fell and the stores closed, Dmitri began to feel more out of place. The crowds dispersed, and an awful smell of day-old fish rose from a nearby square and wafted down the street.

Where was Yegor? The fat Russian should have been here already, and every hour that Dmitri kept the painting, the danger increased.

The Russian Boy, still rolled into the shipping tube Dmitri had carried onto the overnight train from Paris, was in a locker at the Gare de Nice. He didn't want to take the chance of having it on his person in case Yegor had anything crazy planned.

And yet, where was he? The instructions had been clear. Meet at the bar called Les Sables in Vieux Nice, just a block away from the

The Russian Boy

Marché aux Fleurs. Yegor would bring the money, and Dmitri would bring the painting, and then everything would be over.

But Yegor was nowhere in sight.

Yegor had overheard Dmitri speaking Russian in the Café SiSi, a hangout for Russian expatriates in Montmartre, and approached him. "You are a painter," he had said. It was a statement, not a question, so Dmitri assumed that Yegor had seen him painting for tourists outside Sacré Coeur. It wasn't completely legal for either of them to be selling paintings; they were both on student visas. But money was always tight, so they staked out a corner with a dramatic view of the church and painted.

Sitting at the bar, nursing a single café crème, Dmitri had admitted that he was, indeed an artist. "Then you must be starving," Yegor had said, ordering him a *croque monsieur* and a *salade verte*.

Dmitri was nervous. What did this fat, sweating man want from him? Surely not sex? He was no prostitute, to have his favors bought for a ham and cheese sandwich and a green salad. And he already had a boyfriend in Taylor.

The man, who introduced himself as Yegor, began to talk about art, and Dmitri relaxed. Yegor had a passing familiarity with the modern Russian masters-- Wassily Kandinsky and Natalia Goncharova and of course, Marc Chagall.

"To me, it is a matter of patriotism, to love the Russian painters," Yegor said. "You know Luschenko?"

Dmitri's sandwich arrived, and he nodded as he began to wolf it down.

"You know his famous painting, *The Russian Boy*?" Yegor asked.

Dmitri's senses went back on alert. Yes, he knew the painting, he said, though he had only seen it in textbooks. Back in Odessa he had giggled over the young nude, the overt sexuality in his gaze. When he was first beginning to paint, he thought he would eagerly lick away that dot of precum on the boy's dick if offered the chance.

But was Yegor making some kind of sideways sexual play? Dmitri did not know, though the man seemed as straight as any.

"What would you say if I told you the painting was being restored, in a studio right here in Paris?" Yegor asked.

Dmitri finished his sandwich and speared a forkful of lettuce. "I would ask why that would matter to me."

"Because the refinisher's studio is at the Institute des Artistes, where you study. And where you clean the studios each night."

Dmitri put his fork down. "And you think I might want to see this painting, while it is here in Paris?"

Yegor grinned, showing a gold tooth at the back of his mouth. "I think you might want to do more than see the painting, if you had the proper motivation."

You could not grow up in Odessa without walking occasionally on the wrong side of the law. Dmitri and his school friends had crossed the line a few times, and as a result he was keenly aware that the conversation had taken a different turn.

"Exactly what kind of motivation?" He pushed the remaining salad away; he had lost his appetite. But at the same time he felt an eager curiosity rising in his chest.

Yegor lowered his voice. "Twenty thousand euros. Ten thousand when you deliver the painting to me, and another ten thousand when my client verifies the painting is authentic."

"You make it sound so easy," Dmitri said.

"It can be. You enter the studio after hours, remove the painting from its frame, roll it up, and secure it in a mailing tube. Then you make it appear that the studio has been burglarized, to protect yourself. Then you deliver the painting to me."

Dmitri's pulse raced. Twenty thousand euros. He could live for years in Paris on a sum of that magnitude. Not like a prince, of course, but by remaining in student digs, living simply, he could complete his studies, begin to establish his career. Pick and choose which gallery would represent him, instead of having to take the first offer. Never have to go back to Odessa.

"Tell me more," he said, pulling the salad back to him. His appetite had returned.

***

Walking the streets of Vieux Nice, Dmitri went over the meeting with Yegor again and again, as the night deepened around him. He was lost in thought when a man in his early thirties asked him, in French, "Have you been waiting for me? Because it seems like I have been waiting all my life for you."

The man had black hair brushed back from his broad forehead and curled back over his collar. His face was saturnine, long and thin. He had a dark tan, which he accented with a white polo shirt.

Dmitri looked at him. "Yegor send you?"

"Yegor? I do not know a man of that name. But I do know that you are very handsome." The man smiled and raised his right eyebrow.

The Russian Boy

Dmitri was tired and cranky. He had been waiting outside the Bar Les Sables for hours, and Yegor was nowhere to be found. His first impulse was to shoo the man away. It was a stupid pick-up line, and Dmitri had no patience for it.

But then he reconsidered. It now nearly eleven o'clock at night, and he had been waiting, inside and outside the bar, since eleven that morning. His feet ached, and he didn't have the money for a hotel room.

He smiled at the man. "You think I am handsome?" he answered in French.

"But of course. Too handsome to be left standing all alone on a street."

Dmitri leaned back against the stone wall and smiled. Maybe he wouldn't need a hotel room at all.

At the urging of his new friend, Dmitri retrieved his duffle from the bar, and followed the Frenchman across the street. They climbed four flights of stairs to a small apartment with a balcony that overlooked the narrow street below, and the entrance to the Bar Les Sables. "I am watching you," the man said, taking Dmitri's hand and leading him to the balcony. He pointed down. "Finally, I can watch no longer and I must speak to you."

Dmitri understood most of the French. "I'm glad you did." He took the Frenchman's hand and squeezed. "My name is Dmitri."

"I am Albin." The Frenchman leaned down to kiss Dmitri, who at five foot six was at least three inches shorter. Up close, Albin smelled like dried sweat with a quick overlay of lemon cologne, but Dmitri didn't care. His lips tasted like red wine, and Dmitri sucked on his lower lip as his eyes met the Frenchman's.

"It is my pleasure to meet you," Albin said, when they pulled apart.

"*Au contraire, mon frere,*" Dmitri said, smiling. "The pleasure is very much mine. Or ours together."

Dmitri had been using sex to get what he wanted since he was fourteen, when he first let the butcher on Irinskaya Street blow him in exchange for a half pound of ground beef. He was determined to taste an American hamburger, though he had no idea what to do with the meat once he had it. He went to the library and searched online, discovering that the meat had to be formed into a patty and cooked on a grill, then served with lettuce, cheese, pickles, onions, and special sauce, on a sesame seed bun.

He had no idea what a special sauce was, or how to get a sesame-seed bun, but while his mother was still at work, he crept back into their apartment and turned on the kitchen stove. He flattened the beef into two patties and fried them with some chopped onions, then layered the beef with *tvorok*, a chunky, semi-liquid Russian cheese, and a few shreds of lettuce and a large slice of a sour pickle.

He put it all between two pieces of rye bread, and the taste was heavenly. If he closed his eyes, he could almost feel like he was in America.

So sleeping with Albin to have a place to stay was no big deal. The man was a few years too old for Dmitri's taste, and it smelled like he had not bathed in days. But he had a dick like any other man's, and Dmitri enjoyed getting down on his knees on the threadbare carpet in Albin's bedroom and fondling the Frenchman through his pants.

Albin groaned, unhooked his belt and opened his trousers, and pulled his dick out the side of his tiny white bikini briefs, studded with blue and black dots. Dmitri began kissing Albin's dick lightly, starting with where it burst forward from a bush of wiry pubic hair. He kissed his way up the dick as Albin moaned with pleasure. When he reached the tip he took it in his mouth, licking and nibbling.

Albin whimpered and pressed Dmitri's head down farther onto his dick. But Dmitri resisted. He grasped Albin's shaft, now slippery from those kisses, and began to jack him as he sucked the tender dick head. In his experience, older men had little staying power when confronted with a master cocksucker, and Albin was no different. Quickly he was whimpering and muttering incoherent words, and then he shot off down Dmitri's throat.

"You are amazing," Albin said, gasping for breath. "You have the face of an angel and the mouth of a devil!"

He lifted Dmitri up from the floor and kissed him. "I would like to see you pleasure yourself," he whispered into Dmitri's ear. "Will you do that for me?"

Dmitri turned to Albin's ear, licked his tongue around the outside and said, "Of course, my friend."

He pushed Albin gently to the bed, and the older man stumbled as his pants fell to the floor, but he scrambled into bed, tossing them and his polka-dot bikini to the side. He unbuttoned his striped shirt and let it fall loosely to his sides as he watched Dmitri.

The young Russian slipped a hand up his T-shirt and began to play with his nipples with one hand, and stroke his flat stomach with the

The Russian Boy

other. Albin sat back and watched as his own personal porno film played out before him.

Dmitri pulled his T-shirt off over his shoulders, then unbuttoned his jeans and let them fall to the floor. He kicked off his trainers and stepped out of the jeans, leaving him wearing only a tight nylon bikini even skimpier than Albin's. He began stroking his dick through the nearly transparent nylon, feeling it stiffen and strain against the fabric.

Albin's mouth hung open as Dmitri skinned down his bikini and began jerking himself in earnest. He closed his eyes, leaned his head back, and tried to imagine himself somewhere else. Back in Odessa, on a beach by the Black Sea, all by himself on a hot, cloudless day. He felt the sun on his shoulders, and smelled the tang of the seawater. His hand worked his dick faster and faster, and then with a shudder, he ejaculated a stream of milky white cum.

Albin sighed deeply. "You are so gorgeous," he said. "Come here, sit by me."

Dmitri slid into the bed next to Albin and rested his head on the Frenchman's chest. Albin was asleep within minutes, but Dmitri stayed awake, considering his next move.

Neil S. Plakcy

It's in His Kiss

Nice, Tuesday morning

The red-eye from New York to Paris was tough on Rowan. At six-two and fifty years old, he was too tall and too old to sleep in an uncomfortable airplane seat. His connecting flight to Nice was delayed for hours by heavy winds at Charles De Gaulle. When the small plane did take off, it was knocked about like a pool ball hit by a cue with a wicked spin. All around him, toughened fliers were vomiting into air sickness bags.

The woman next to him recited the Hail Mary in French over and over again. *"Je vous salue, Marie, pleine de grâce. Le Seigneur est avec vous.* If he hadn't given up on organized religion years before, he would have joined her. But at least he had flight insurance, and if the plane went down in some vineyard in central France, Nick would have the money for his art program, and Cassidy's college tuition would be assured.

But thinking of college only reminded him of his lost teaching career, so he struggled to return his thoughts to *The Russian Boy*. The stolen painting was, after all, the reason for his trip. As the flight smoothed out, he pulled the postcard, now old and worn, from his briefcase, and stared at it.

He was always surprised when a well-known work of art was stolen. You couldn't sell a painting like *The Russian Boy* on the open market. It had to have been a commissioned theft. Who would want it? The client was most likely gay; despite the painting's value, it was hard to imagine a straight man wanting it badly enough to have it stolen.

Was that why Kramer had put him on the case? Because he was gay? That was stupid; Rowan McNair was an art historian who knew the painting, and his sexuality didn't matter when it came to art theft. Or did it?

As the plane approached the airport, Rowan saw the green and gold onion domes surmounted by crosses atop the Russian Orthodox Cathedral, a tiny glimpse of Moscow on the Mediterranean.

Landing just before noon, Rowan took a cab along the oceanfront Promenade des Anglais into Nice. He had never been to the Riviera before, and he was surprised by the brilliant sunshine, the fifty-plus degree temperatures and the overt sensuality of the sun-worshippers clustered along the beachfront walkway. A handsome young man with a tawny mane of shoulder-length hair, tanned skin and tight-fitting shirt

The Russian Boy

and slacks made Rowan's dick stand to attention, and he had to adjust himself in the cab.

His hotel, the Negresco, was right on the Promenade in the center of modern Nice, a Belle Epoque masterpiece with a grand tower topped by a pink dome. He checked in and carried his own bag up to a large, high-ceilinged room with elegant moldings and period furniture. His window looked out at the multicolored beach mats on the rocky shore, and at the blue-green water stretching to the horizon. He could not linger over the view; he had an appointment at the Musée des Beaux Art Jules Cheret to consult an art expert there.

His jet lag was gone, replaced with excitement and interest. From the hotel, he walked purposefully along the inner lane of the Promenade des Anglais, past gleaming hotels, upscale shops and crowded sidewalk cafés. Two short, dark North African men in blue maintenance uniforms leaned against the wall of the Credit Lyonnais, talking animatedly between short drags of strong French cigarettes. Rowan skirted a downed palm frond on the sidewalk and turned inland at the Avenue des Baumettes.

He stopped on the street in front of the museum's iron fence, looking around him at the expanse of blue sky and the palm trees swaying in the light breeze. To think, the day before he'd been mired in the cold of a New York winter. But in January Nice was sunny and bright. He understood why the rich and famous had been wintering on the Cote d'Azur for more than a century.

As he often did when approaching a new museum, he wanted to appreciate the building first, down the long walkway from him. The Musée des Beaux Arts Jules Cheret was a two-story stone edifice with classical columns and pediments surmounted by half-moon arches. Several of the windows on the second floor had been broadened to provide natural light for the collection, but otherwise the building looked as it might have when it was a private residence in the 19th century.

A stone staircase with balustrades led up to the main entrance. Rowan walked up to the building, appraised it straight on, then stepped to the side of the building. He was admiring its proportions as a handsome young man with close-cropped blond hair came rocketing out the front door and down that half staircase. He was in his twenties, wearing khaki slacks and a knit polo shirt.

The young man caught Rowan's glance and their eyes locked. Rowan felt a thrill of sexual longing course through his body. His mouth opened, and his tongue hung out a bit, like a thirsty dog. It had been two years since he'd had any physical contact with another man, and he felt all that desire well up in him as he stared at the handsome young man.

In a flash, the young man had rounded the corner and dashed up to Rowan. Behind him, a uniformed security guard appeared at the top of the stairs. The young man grabbed Rowan and tugged him into the shadow of a pillar.

Before Rowan had a chance to react, the blond had wrapped his strong arms around Rowan, pulling him close. Rowan felt the man's biceps flexing against his back, the way his stiff young cock rose to the occasion. His lips were rough and dry as they pressed against Rowan's, but the sensation was amazing.

Rowan closed his eyes and let himself melt into the embrace, and the kiss. The mystery man smelled of sweat and lemon cologne, and Rowan felt all his pent-up desire rush to his head and his dick, which swelled against his pant leg.

He hadn't kissed a man in so long, he'd forgotten how marvelous it felt. The young man's cheek was smooth, his body so lithe and vibrant.

By looking around from behind the pillar where the young man had pulled him, Rowan could see the guard standing at the top of the stairs. "Don't come back!" the guard yelled in French, shaking his fist at the empty air.

Then the guard turned and went back inside. The young man pulled back from Rowan. "*Merci, mon vieux,*" he said, in an accent even Rowan recognized was atrocious. "*C'etait magnifique!*"

He turned to run away. "Wait!" Rowan said in English. "What's your name? What's going on?"

"Sorry, bud, gotta run," the young man said over his shoulder, in a flat Midwestern accent. He dashed down the pavement toward the street, disappearing out the museum gates as Rowan stared after him.

My god, he's just a kid, Rowan thought as the man ran away. And suddenly he realized why kissing him had felt so good—it reminded him of what he had done with Brian Wojchowski. And remembering how badly that had ended wiped all sense of desire away. He'd already lost his job, his career and his marriage from an inappropriate attraction. Was he doomed to screw up once again?

He wiped his hand across his lips, and the young man's scent rose again. But Rowan ignored it and turned to go into the museum.

Apprenticeship

Nice, 1912

On a crisp morning in November 1912, Alexei Dubernin looked from his canvas to the view outside his window, then threw his paintbrush down in disgust. "I will never be able to paint what I see," he said in Russian, crossing his arms over his chest. "I just don't have the talent."

Alexei was nineteen years old, the younger son of the Count Dubernin, who had extensive landholdings outside St. Petersburg. He had grown up hearing how the Dubernins could trace their lineage back to a daughter of Mikhail, the first Romanov tsar. As the spoiled, beautiful younger son, Alexei had no responsibilities other than to entertain his grandmother and serve as her traveling companion.

That summer, in Paris, he had studied the works of Claude Monet, particularly his "Jardin á Sainte-Adresse" and "The Cliffs at Etretat." He wanted to achieve that same effect of light and color, but he couldn't manage it.

His grandmother, the Dowager Countess, looked up from her needlepoint. She had a rheumatic cough and pain in her joints, and her doctors had told her that the balmy climate of the Cote d'Azur was better for her than the cold of a Russian winter. "You need a new teacher," she said. "Someone better than that man you studied with in St. Petersburg. I have told you this again and again."

"Perhaps you're right, Babushka." He turned to her. "When you were speaking to Madame Stichnayeva yesterday she mentioned she was having her portrait painted by Fyodor Luschenko. I have seen his paintings and I think they are wonderful. Do you think he would take me on as a pupil?"

He didn't mention that he had seen the painter at a party the week before at the home of another Russian family, and been taken with the older man's handsome, knowing face, and the lascivious way he had gazed at Alexei, who had turned away shyly.

While he waited for his grandmother to consider his request, he looked out the window at the sparkling blue water of the Baie des Anges, noticing the way the light seemed to glance off the tips of the waves. Two tall, narrow pine trees framed the view from the villa. The dark green of the trees, the brighter green of the lawn sloping down to the water, the azure blue of the sky—he struggled to get each color just right, to master the strokes necessary to portray the way the light hit them.

He knew his father had purchased the Villa des Oliviers twenty years before, though this was the first time Alexei had accompanied his grandmother there. He had finished his education in a St. Petersburg academy for the sons of the nobility, and he had been taking private painting lessons from an elderly man who specialized in miniature portraits. The lessons bored him to death, and he grabbed at the opportunity to leave the drab gray streets of St. Petersburg and his foul-smelling old teacher for the sunny skies and freedom of the Riviera.

An icon of Saint Nicholas hung on the wall, over a brass samovar on an ormolu tray. Alexei could smell cabbage cooking in the kitchen just the way he remembered from their home in St. Petersburg. If not for the weather, Alexei could imagine he was still back in Russia, so surrounded as he was with the food, language, and ornaments of his people.

The villa was one in a collection of large, rambling homes surrounded by a fragrant olive grove on the slopes of the neighborhood where the Russians congregated. The main salon opened onto a lawn that overlooked the ocean. The Russian Orthodox Cathedral, opened earlier that year, was just down the street.

He turned back to his grandmother. He could tell from her pictures that the Dowager Countess had been a beautiful young woman, the belle of St. Petersburg, and the years had been kind to her—along with a host of face creams and exercise regimens. She was still slim, though her hair had gone gray, and her skin glowed, especially in gentle light.

"I will ask Olga to arrange an introduction," she said, nodding. "Perhaps this Luschenko will take you on as his apprentice."

Alexei turned back to his painting, thrilled at the chance to see the handsome older man again, and perhaps to be working side by side with him. Two days later, a letter arrived by messenger indicating that the painter would be delighted to receive the Dowager Countess and her grandson at his studio in Vieux Nice.

That afternoon, she arranged for the valet, Leo, to take them down into the narrow streets of the old city in a horse-drawn carriage. For Alexei, it was an adventure. His grandmother rarely left the villa, preferring to entertain at home, and so he had little experience of the city. They navigated the narrow streets with difficulty, and Alexei saw

The Russian Boy

his grandmother pinch her nose in disgust. But the rich aroma of fish, flowers and horse piss didn't bother him at all.

They stopped in front of an unimposing building near the Cours Saleya, a few blocks inland from the Mediterranean. "You are sure this is the address?" the Dowager Countess asked, leaning forward to speak to the valet. Though the building's paint was peeling and there were piles of horse dung in the street, Alexei's pulse quickened. A real artist's studio!

"Yes, Madame," Leo said. "And there is a sign." He pointed to the door, where a hand-lettered note directed visitors to Luschenko's studio on the third floor.

"Very well," the Countess said, as Leo stepped to the side of the carriage and extended his hand to help her out. "But do not go far. I am not sure how long we will stay."

"Yes, Madame." Leo extended his hand to Alexei, who disdained the help and jumped lightly from the carriage himself. And even as he did, he regretted the chance to touch the handsome if rough-looking young man who had recently joined the Dubernins, coming from the family's country estate.

Alexei had seen him naked once, coming out of the bath, and was in awe of Leo's strong, muscular body. He longed to run his hands over the curvature of the man's biceps, down his stomach... But there he stopped. He had noticed Leo's thickens hanging limply against a bush of pubic hair, but he could not understand why that sight had excited him so.

Leo nodded his head as Alexei passed him, but Alexei caught the slightest hint of a smile on his face. He hurried past his grandmother, leading the way up to the top floor, where he stepped through an arched, wooden door into the studio. It was suffused with clear, bright light that streamed in through a wall of French doors that opened onto a narrow balcony.

The room smelled of paint and turpentine and salt water. Through the French doors, Alexei saw the Mediterranean glistening in the sun. From down below he heard the horse whinny and stomp its hooves on the cobblestones.

The other three walls were hung with Luschenko's canvases of beach scenes along the Cote d'Azur and pencil sketches of Russian notables who had posed for oil paintings. Alexei was enthralled by a series of studies obviously painted from the studio windows. They reminded him of Monet's liquid light, as they moved from the breaking dawn through the height of the brilliant Riviera sun, to the lavender shades of evening falling over the beach. "I want to paint like that," he said, pointing at the row of paintings.

"And good afternoon to you, my young count," Luschenko said, bowing his head slightly. "And to you, my dear lady Countess."

Luschenko was an older man, the age of Alexei's father, with a pointed goatee that gave him a wolf-like look. His body was slim and fit, his fingers long and delicate. He wore a paint-splattered shirt and canvas overalls. Alexei wished his grandmother hadn't made him dress so formally for the visit; he would much rather wear the kind of simple clothes the painter did.

Looking at him and the sensual grin on his face, Alexei experienced a heated flush, one he had felt when observing the young men who bathed in the sea in their bathing costumes. He'd felt the same thing when he stumbled that day on Leo, naked in the hallway. His loins tightened, and his cock stiffened. He saw the painter look down at the bulge that protruded against his tight white pants and smile, and that shocked Alexei and made him want to flee the studio.

His grandmother sat on an overstuffed chair that the painter had provided for her, and Alexei perched on a low stool next to her.

"I understand you paint," Luschenko said to Alexei. "You have brought something to show me?"

Alexei nodded shyly, and opened the flat leather portfolio he had brought with him from St. Petersburg. He pulled out a few pencil sketches and handed them to Luschenko, who took them over to the windows to examine them.

"You have a talent," he said, nodding. "But come here, let me show you something."

He placed one sketch on an easel and beckoned Alexei to him. Alexei stood up and walked over to the window, where Luschenko leaned in close to him. "See this stroke here? It should be stronger." He pulled a pencil from his pocket and darkened the line.

Alexei felt his heart skip a couple of beats. Was it being so close to Luschenko? Or the way the older man had violated his sketch?

"Then you shade it, like so," Luschenko said, turning the thick pencil on its side and rubbing it along the paper.

With wonder Alexei watched as his drawing came alive under Luschenko's hand. It was a curiously intimate feeling, made even stranger by the feel of Luschenko's body so close to his, sensing the man's breath on his neck as he leaned over Alexei's shoulder. Alexei's

The Russian Boy

cock throbbed relentlessly inside his tight pants and he felt a bit faint.

Finally the artist stepped back and admired his work. "Yes, much better. Do you see?"

Alexei nodded, unable to speak.

"You will come to the studio mornings," Luschenko said. "Monday through Friday, from eight until noon. We will see how you work out."

"Of course Alexei's family must compensate you for your attentions," the Dowager Countess said. "I will arrange to have my son send you an appropriate amount."

Luschenko bowed. "I am sure he will be most accommodating."

Alexei felt the older man's eyes on him and noticed the hint of a smile.

Luschenko offered them tea from a bright brass samovar in the corner of the studio, and served it in tall glasses encased in brightly colored metal sleeves. Alexei was so nervous that he fumbled his, spilling the scalding liquid on his white pants.

"Forgive my clumsiness," Luschenko said. "You are not hurt, I hope?"

"No, just embarrassed," Alexei said.

"That tea will stain unless it is cleaned quickly. Come, there is a water closet down the hall. "He tugged Alexei's hand, forcing him to rise. "My apologies to my dear Countess for leaving you unattended. Come, come, my boy."

Luschenko led him down a dark, narrow hallway to a small room at the end of the corridor, with a toilet and a sink. He stepped inside, and motioned Alexei in behind him. "Close the door and take off your pants."

"I am sure I can clean myself."

"You are a silly, spoiled boy," Luschenko said. "You will ruin your pants more quickly than you can clean them. Now, off!"

Alexei was mortified that his erection would be that much more evident with only his linen undershorts, but he felt he must obey the older man. He stepped out of his leather shoes and unbuttoned his pants, pulling them off. He had to lean against the wall to do so, feeling an uncomfortable sensation of cold and damp against his back.

Luschenko took the pants from him, and began running water in the sink and scrubbing the fabric with a rough bar of soap. He let water pool in the sink, then dropped the pants in. "Now, we wait," he said to Alexei. "And I help you with your other problem."

The older man placed his hand directly over Alexei's stiff dick, and Alexei nearly fainted from the pleasure. Luschenko rubbed his hand gently up and down over Alexei's dick, then leaned forward and kissed him lightly on the lips.

Alexei was startled by the pressure of the older man's lips on his, but he returned the kiss greedily as Luschenko slid his hand between the linen fabric and Alexei's smooth belly. His hand was warm and strong over Alexei's dick, and just the faintest pressure caused him to explode, spewing hot cum into the older man's hand.

Alexei blushed.

"We will have to work on your ability to control yourself as well as your facility with painting," Luschenko said. As Alexei watched, the painter brought his hand to his mouth and licked Alexei's cum from it. When they kissed again, the salty taste remained on Alexei's lips.

He lent Alexei a pair of rough overalls, splattered with paint, to wear back to the villa while his own pants dried. "I will see you tomorrow morning," he said. "Come dressed to work, yes?"

Alexei nodded dumbly, and all the way back to the villa he smiled at the thought of his apprenticeship.

The Story of a Painting

Nice, Tuesday morning

Taylor Griffin ran down the Avenue des Baumettes, away from the Musée des Beaux Arts, the taste of the stranger's kiss still on his lips.

That was a stupid move. On the run after tipping his hand to the museum curator, he stopped to kiss a cute guy. A handsome man, even if he was old enough to be Taylor's father.

There was a chilly thought. Taylor's father was a grizzled alcoholic who had walked out when Taylor was five. His mom said his dad had been an artist, too, which did nothing for Taylor. He didn't want to hear that he had anything in common with the man who'd done little more for him than donate sperm.

The man by the museum, though, was dead handsome. Dark brown hair, going gray at the temples and sideburns, dimpled chin and laughing eyes. Something about him floated Taylor's boat from the moment they locked eyes. But he had to stay focused on *The Russian Boy*.

After Dmitri left, Taylor had researched the painting's history. He knew that it had once hung at the Musée des Beaux Arts in Nice, and that the curator there, Bruno Desjardins, was an expert on it. As soon as he got off the train at the Gare de Nice, he dumped his backpack in a locker and made his way to the Musée.

He thought luck was with him when Desjardins agreed to speak with him. "I'm an art student in Paris," he said in his rough French, shaking the curator's hand. "I'm interested in *The Russian Boy* and discovered that it used to hang here."

"Yes, that is true," Desjardins said. "You have seen the painting?"

Taylor shook his head. "Only in reproductions. I've only been to New York once and the painting was already at the restorer's by then."

"How can I help you?" Desjardins glanced at his watch, as if he had better things to do than chat with a scruffy American art student.

"I read your monograph on the play of light and shadow in the painting," Taylor said. Thank god for the free wireless internet at Café SiSi in Montmartre. "I was hoping you could tell me more about it."

"You know it has been stolen?" Desjardins asked.

Taylor tried his best to feign surprise. "No. From New York?"

Desjardins shook his head. "From a restorer's studio in Paris."

"I had no idea. What a strange coincidence."

Desjardins eyed him, and Taylor smiled blandly. Finally Desjardins shrugged and said, "Fyodor Luschenko had a studio in Nice from 1906 to 1914. Many wealthy Russians came to the Riviera in the winter during those years, and Luschenko painted their portraits, and sold them seascapes for their grand salons. In November 1912, the Dowager Countess Dubernin came to Nice for the season, bringing her grandson with her, the Count's younger son, Alexei. He was nineteen and fancied himself an artist."

Desjardins leaned back in his chair, enjoying the story he had obviously told many times. "The Dowager Countess arranged an apprenticeship for her grandson with Luschenko."

Taylor struggled not to snicker, because he already knew what Luschenko had taught the boy—and it wasn't painting technique. "I didn't know that Alexei Dubernin painted."

"If you can call it that," Desjardins said. "We have a few of his oils in storage. They are interesting only because of his connection to Luschenko."

"So *The Russian Boy* was painted here in Nice?"

Desjardins nodded. "The Dowager Countess returned to St. Petersburg in May, 1913 with her daughter-in-law, but Alexei remained in Nice. Luschenko offered to keep the boy on as his apprentice, provided that his father continued to pay. Soon after Alexei's family left, Luschenko began working on the painting, beginning with a number of charcoal sketches. We have several of them here—mostly of Alexei's head. Nothing lascivious."

"How did the painting end up at this museum?"

"Luschenko finished it at the end of the summer of 1913, but he kept it under wraps because the Dowager Countess and her family returned, including Alexei's father. But it was a real breakthrough in technique for Luschenko, and he couldn't help bragging about it to his friends. Word got back to Alexei's father, who stormed into the studio and demanded to see the portrait of his son."

"Wow," Taylor said. "That must have been some scene."

"I'm sure it was. The Dowager Countess fainted, and the Count dragged the whole family back to St. Petersburg. The Russian community, which had supported Luschenko with painting sales and commissions, shunned him and he began drinking heavily. He decided to leave for the United States, and when he closed his studio, Princess Elisabeth Vassilievna Kotschoubey, whose home this once was, bought

The Russian Boy

several of his canvases, including *The Russian Boy*. Even when the museum opened in 1928, no one knew how good it was. It was not even hung in a gallery until 1948."

Desjardins looked at his watch again. "I expect an appointment," he said. "I must be brief. An American critic saw the painting and wrote about it, and soon after that the New York Museum of Fine Arts made an offer to purchase it. The curator at the time did not appreciate it, and was happy to see it go."

Taylor knew his time was running out. "Is it possible that whoever stole the painting has brought it back in Nice?"

"Why do you ask?" Desjardins leaned forward. "If you know something about this theft you must speak to the gendarmes." He picked up his phone.

"Wait, wait," Taylor said. "If the painting is indeed back here, can you suggest anyone who might know what someone could do with it? Surely there must be a collector somewhere who would want it, even with a cloud on its ownership."

"I believe you know more than you admit," Desjardins said. He began dialing the phone.

Taylor jumped up. "I have to go. Thank you for your time. "He turned and rushed from the office.

Desjardins called after him, and then a security guard took up the chase as Taylor scrambled down the marble stairs at the front of the building.

That's when he saw the older man, the one who made his heart jump and his dick stiffen.

It seemed he had made one stupid move after another all morning long. He was no closer to his goal, and had already made himself persona non grata in the one place that might have been able to help him. Well, if he couldn't trace the painting he would have to look for Dmitri instead. If he could find his boyfriend, maybe he could convince him to return to Paris and give back the painting. Then things could go back to the way they had been, and they'd find a way to keep Dmitri in Paris after his fellowship ran out.

Dmitri's final words had stung Taylor. He knew his work was more commercial than Dmitri's, but that didn't mean he was a sellout. And Dmitri was wrong about his ability to get money from home; his mother barely made enough to support herself, and he was burdened with student loans he'd have to start paying back as soon as he finished his fellowship.

The extra expense involved in this trip to Nice only made things worse. He sighed, and walked through the sunlit streets to the Syndicat d'Initiative, the local tourist office, a free-standing building in the middle of a square of Belle Epoque buildings, each one more elaborate than the next.

It was incongruous to see a line of young backpackers waiting on the cobblestones for help securing a hotel room. He got at the end of the line and pulled out his sketch pad. While he waited he drew the buildings around him, shuffling his pack forward as he moved up in line. When his turn came up, he accepted a free map, and wrote down the names of a dozen hostels and cheap hotels where Dmitri might be staying.

The closest was just a few blocks away, a narrow three-story building with a tiny lobby that smelled of abrasive cleaner. "I am looking for my friend," he said in French to the elderly woman at the desk. She had a faint mustache over her upper lip, and she sneered at the picture he held out to her. It was a Polaroid of himself with Dmitri taken outside the Sacré Coeur by a tourist with an old camera.

"I am supposed to meet him at a hotel in Nice, but I have forgotten the name," he said. "Is he staying here?"

She shook her head, never saying a word, but her hoop earrings jangled.

"Thank you," he said, then muttered "for nothing," under his breath in English.

The light outside the hotel was just too bright, and he had to step into the shadow in order to focus on his map. He wished he had brought sunglasses with him, but January was so cold and gray in Paris, he'd never considered that the light in Nice would be so much stronger.

Taylor walked a few blocks, got confused and backtracked, then found a street name and oriented himself to the map. A young North African girl with a deeply tanned face sat on a blanket on the pavement in front of a tobacco shop, holding one baby to her breast while another played on the blanket next to her. There was a pitifully small pile of coins on the blanket, and the girl looked beseechingly up at him.

He had no money to give away, though, and he hurried to the next stop on his list, a youth hostel. He had to wait while a group of German backpackers asked endless questions about the lavatory facilities, and by the time he reached the dark-haired young woman behind the counter, he was irritable and ready to give up his search.

The Russian Boy

The girl didn't seem to speak much French, or at least she pretended so, and he understood why the Germans had taken so long. He resorted to pointing to the picture of Dmitri and pointing at the desk.

The girl looked at him like this was a new experience for her. She pointed at Dmitri and smiled, then said, "*Che bella*," in what he assumed was Italian.

They went back and forth for a few minutes, and finally she seemed to understand what Taylor was asking. "No," she said, shaking her head. Then she held up a key to him and tilted her head in a question.

He shook his head back at her and turned away. At this rate, he figured, it would take him all afternoon to cover the hotels and hostels on his list. Doggedly, he continued, bumping into people on the street, getting lost, sweating in the bright sun. But no one recognized Dmitri.

By the time evening fell, Taylor had run out of hostels and cheap hotels. No one recognized Dmitri and he didn't know what else to do. He bought a baguette and a round of soft cheese, and ate in a small park along the Promenade des Anglais, overlooking the pebbled beach.

It was chilly down by the water, and Taylor shivered and rubbed his upper arms. The landscape to his left reflected his mood—dark and foreboding. The black sky faded to gray where it met the waves, and shards of moonlight highlighted the rocks on the beach. To the right, harsh neon and the bright glare of street lights created dark spots where a young Russian carrying a stolen painting could disappear, never to be found.

Shadowy figures hurried past him, tourists returning to their hotels after Mediterranean dinners, teenagers with skateboards, dark-skinned men with gold teeth. The Bay of Angels curved ahead of him, streetlamps reflecting on the ocean, spheres of white light dotting the hillsides.

An overweight middle-aged man in jogging shorts toiled past him, sweating and grunting. Two elderly ladies, wearing white gloves and small hats, sat talking on a bench. One of them played with the clasp on her handbag as she completed a long and obviously complicated explanation to her friend with a typically Gallic sigh.

A young blonde with a Swedish flag on her backpack passed Taylor and smiled, then descended a stairway to the beach, heading toward a group of young people who had set up camp on the hard stones there. The air smelled of mist and the mountains.

Looking back at the city, Taylor began to see an image forming, something very different from the tourist crap he painted in Paris. Light and shadow fought for balance in the landscape in his mind. The palm trees were eerie sentinels, the globes of the streetlights like alien ships.

He pulled out the pad he'd been writing hotel and hostel addresses on, turned to a new page, and began to sketch.

A Russian With Soul

Nice, Tuesday morning

After the young man kissed him, then ran away, Rowan McNair stood outside the museum for a moment or two. Was his lack of sleep was making him imagine things? But the taste of the young man's lips lingered on his own. He couldn't have imagined that, could he?

He straightened his button-down shirt, which had come untucked in that moment of passion, and went up the stairs and into the lobby of the museum. The glass doors and the fanlights above them spilled warm sunlight onto the marble floor, with its sunburst just in front of a half-round visitor's desk. The same guard Rowan had seen at the top of the stairs was standing next to it, speaking in voluble French to the dark-haired beauty behind the desk, a ringer for a young Audrey Hepburn, with a heart-shaped face and wide brown eyes.

They stopped speaking as Rowan approached. "I'm here to see Bruno Desjardins," he said in French. "I have an appointment."

The receptionist directed him to an office at the rear of the building. The door was open, and a man of Rowan's age was on the phone. His dark curly hair was a bit wild and streaked with gray. "*Eh, bien,*" he said, finishing his call. "*A bientôt.*"

He hung up and stood to welcome Rowan. He wore a dark gray business suit, the jacket hung over his chair, with a white shirt and a tie in a red and blue geometric pattern Rowan recognized as influenced by the Dutch painter Piet Mondrian.

"My apologies," Desjardins said in a clipped British accent overlaid with French. "We had a disturbance earlier. I believe it may be connected to your inquiry."

"Really?" Rowan asked, sitting across from an ornate wooden desk with gilt molding.

"Yes, a young man was here asking questions about *The Russian Boy*."

"American? Rumpled slacks and a green polo shirt?" Rowan asked.

"Yes. Do you know him?"

"I saw him as he was rushing away. What kind of questions was he asking?"

"He knew the painting was back in Nice," Desjardins said. "He knew it had originally hung here, and he wanted to know who might be interested in buying it."

"You think he was the thief?" Rowan asked. To think, he'd kissed the man, and aided his escape. What would The Kramer Agency think of that? Ron Kramer would never know, of course, but the idea that perhaps he'd kissed an art thief gave Rowan a thrill. Wouldn't stop him tracking the thief down, though.

"He certainly knew a great deal," Desjardins said.

"I have the same questions. I hope you won't suspect me." He smiled.

"Ah, but I have checked your provenance and know you work for The Kramer Agency," Desjardins said. "I also read the article you wrote about the painting. It was very perceptive."

"Thank you. You notified Interpol you believed the painting was here on the Riviera?"

Desjardins nodded. "Yes. A man I know named Rene Scarano overheard a man bragging about the painting. He passed the word to me, and I called a contact I have at Interpol."

"How can I get hold of Scarano?"

"Interpol has already spoken with him. But you will find him most easily at a bar called Les Sables in Vieux Nice, any afternoon." Desjardins wrote the man's name, and the address of the bar, on a piece of museum letterhead. "Tell him you have spoken with me."

"Does this Scarano often deal on the wrong side of the law?"

"He himself is honest," Desjardins said. "As far as I know. But he has many contacts."

Rowan remembered his thoughts on the plane, and the interest of the young man. "Any idea on who would want this painting? Because of its frank approach to gay male sexuality, not to mention the age of the subject, it's got to be a specialized audience. It seems like a crime of opportunity—a theft for a particular buyer, rather than for the chance to sell the painting on the black market."

"You think someone wants it for its erotic potential?"

Rowan laughed at the idea that someone would use *The Russian Boy* as a piece of pornography, to generate an erotic response. "You must admit it would take a certain collector to appreciate the ... unique characteristics of the painting."

It was Desjardins' turn to laugh. "You should have been a diplomat, my friend. You have a unique way of saying what could be otherwise crass." He steepled his fingers and considered the question. "There are several gentlemen who collect such art. It is possible that

The Russian Boy

one of them is the ultimate buyer."

Rowan pulled a pen and small notebook from his pocket. "Names?"

"I will make some inquiries for you. You understand I must be discreet."

"As you just pointed out I can be diplomatic."

"Yes. But these tastes… the men involved would not appreciate having a stranger know of such things."

"Even a stranger who shared those tastes?" Rowan asked.

Desjardins looked Rowan in the eye. "Even so."

Rowan put his pen and notebook away. "If you insist. I understand that the painting was stolen from a restorer's studio in Paris. Do you know anything about the security there?"

"Apparently there was little. An alarm system on the building, but little in the way of interior locks." Desjardins shook his head. "If the painting is not recovered, the insurers will be very unhappy."

"So we could be looking at an amateur thief as well as a professional," Rowan said. "Perhaps even a man who would like the painting for his own enjoyment."

"I do not envy you this investigation," Desjardins said. "There are many avenues." He stood, and Rowan followed his lead, shaking his hand and thanking him.

It was late morning by then, and Rowan discovered, as he left the museum, that he was starving. He looked up and down the Avenue des Baumettes for the handsome young man with the interest in *The Russian Boy,* but without success. He gave up and found a dark café on a side street and ordered a lemonade and a *pissaladiére*, a white pizza topped with onions, olives, garlic and anchovy paste, and devoured it quickly.

Once his hunger was sated, his exhaustion caught up with him, and he stumbled back to the hotel and collapsed in bed. When he awoke it was after four. He showered, changed, and set off on foot along the Promenade des Anglais, west toward the old city.

He was charmed by the profusion of colorful flowers under blue and white striped awnings, and lured into the open-air market by piles of miniature melons, marigolds in tiny pots, and clusters of carrots with dirt still clinging. Plastic-wrapped bunches of pink carnations, red roses and stalks of lavender crowded the tables of flower vendors. There was a faint smell of fish, mixed with the tang of salt air.

He had done some painting himself, in college, before abandoning the creation of art for the study of art instead. For the first time in years he had the urge to paint what he saw, from the colonnaded porticoes overhanging the market to the profusion of bright colors from the flowers and produce. He stood for a moment, observing the scene and trying to construct a painting in his head.

Then he shrugged and hunted for the bar called Les Sables, moving back and forth from the open, sunny market to the narrow, dark alleys that led from it. On the third try he found the right street, and the words "Les Sables" in curling neon above the door. The cobbled street in front of it smelled of piss and cigarettes.

He walked inside and looked around. The room was long and narrow, with a wooden bar running along one wall. Three solitary men were nursing drinks. Rowan stepped up to the bar and ordered a *pastis*, a licorice-flavored drink popular in the south of France.

The air was cool and musty after the heat and humidity of the streets. The bartender poured a shot of Ricard into a small glass, and served it with a small ewer of water and a larger glass. Rowan poured water into the large glass, then dumped in the shot, mixing the two together with a long-handled spoon. As he contemplated the cloudy liquid in his glass, he said, "I'm looking for a man named Rene Scarano."

"Who's asking?" the bartender answered.

"Bruno Desjardins, the curator at the Musée des Beaux Arts, told me I could find Scarano here."

"I am Scarano," the man at the far end of the bar said. He, too, was drinking pastis, and Rowan picked up his glass and moved toward him. The man was small and wizened; his skin was the color of weak tea and his black hair was sparse. He wore a plaid sports shirt over dark slacks.

"Your glass is almost empty," Rowan said. "Another?"

Scarano shrugged, and the bartender poured another shot of the Ricard.

"What is your business with Desjardins?" Scarano asked, after he had mixed his drink.

"He said you spoke with someone about *The Russian Boy*."

Scarano eyed Rowan. "You are an American *flic*?"

Rowan sipped his pastis. "Not a cop. A private detective. Hired by the museum that owns the painting."

"I already spoke with the *flics*," Scarano said. "I know nothing more."

The Russian Boy

"Probably not. But you know how it is, eh? One must earn a living. I have to show my boss I am working here, not just enjoying my pastis."

Scarano shrugged. "Not my problem."

Rowan opened his wallet and pulled out a 50-euro note. He laid it on the bar.

Scarano covered it with his right hand, and Rowan noticed part of his pinky finger had been cut off. Rowan shivered, not wanting to know what had happened to the fingertip, as Scarano said, "He was a Russian."

"Who was that?"

"This is my usual spot, you know," Scarano said. "Here, this stool. You can learn many things simply by staying in the same place." He looked at Rowan. "Americans, they do not understand this principle. Staying still. Always on the move, you people are."

Rowan nodded and sipped his pastis, relishing the licorice tang.

"Sunday afternoon, I was here, as usual. A Russian was sitting where you are, drinking vodka." The way he said it, he could have been saying horse piss, Rowan thought. "The vodka, it loosens the tongue," Scarano continued. "His phone rang, and he answered in French, but with a horrible Russian accent."

The small man paused to sip his drink. "I heard him speak about a Russian boy, and having no interest in boys myself, I made to ignore him. But he spoke so loud and crudely that I could not help but overhear. And gradually I realized he was not speaking of a Russian boy, but of *The Russian Boy*."

"The painting, you mean," Rowan said.

"Yes. He said he would need a frame. That was when I understood."

"You are perceptive. Most men would not have made the connection."

"Ah, but I have an artistic soul." Scarano raised his pastis to his lips and sipped.

"Do you know who he was speaking with?" Rowan asked.

"I know only one man in Nice who would consider creating a frame for a stolen painting," he said.

Rowan pulled out another 50-euro note. "You know his name?"

"I can see you are a man who appreciates the finer things in life." Scarano reached for the note, but Rowan held on to it.

Scarano glared, but said, "Pascal Gaultier." Rowan released his grip on the note, and Scarano pocketed it. "There is only one problem. As far as I know, Gaultier has been dead for three years."

Rowan put down his glass hard on the bar. "Do you take me for a fool? An American with an open wallet and an empty head?"

"No, Monsieur," Scarano said. "But I tell you the truth. The Russian spoke with Pascal Gaultier. I am sure of it. It appears that Gaultier is not as dead as he wished people to believe."

"You know how I can reach this resurrected man?" Rowan asked.

"When he lived, he lived in St. Laurent du Var, a town near the airport. I can give you the address, but I doubt you will find him there."

"But it's a start." Rowan pulled out his small notebook and wrote down the address. "Can you describe him?"

"We were at school together," Scarano said. "So he would be an old man, you see, like me. The last time I saw him his hair had gone completely white. He had a hook nose, and a mole right here." He pointed to the right side of his chin.

"Did you give this information to the flics?"

Scarano shook his head. "They did not ask. And I was not going to tell them I thought the Russian spoke to a dead man."

"You know anything more about the Russian?" Rowan asked. "He ever say his own name?"

"No, Monsieur."

"Can you describe him to me?"

"Your age, perhaps, but quite fat. Dark hair, with a little beard here." He motioned to his chin.

"A soul patch," Rowan said. "That's what we call it in America."

Scarano laughed. "Yes," he said. "You look for a Russian with soul. I wish you luck finding him!"

Yes, Rowan thought, he would need some luck. He needed to find this painting so he could give his son the money he needed. And it wasn't just about the money; he needed to prove that he could be there for Nick, and to restore the relationship they had once had. After so many years of distance from his kids, that was the most important thing of all.

Waiting

Nice, Tuesday morning

Tuesday morning, Dmitri woke up to bright sunlight streaming in through an open window. Albin stood by the rickety wooden bureau, buttoning his shirt.

"My sleeping angel awakes," Albin said.

The hard, narrow bed had not been comfortable, but it was better than sitting up all night on the train, and Dmitri had slept gratefully.

"You are here on vacation?" Albin asked, tucking in his shirttail.

Dmitri hesitated. "I am painter, and I come for inspiration." He smiled lazily up at Albin. "I find it last night."

"And the man you were waiting for? This Yegor?"

"A contact, merely. He will show me places I can sell paintings."

"You would paint me?" Albin asked.

"I would love to paint you. If you will let me stay with you."

Albin looked doubtful. "You would like to stay here while I go to work?"

Dmitri's brain raced. "Yes. I love the view from your balcony. I sit here and paint."

Albin looked out at the view. "But all you can see is the street."

Dmitri got up, found his briefs on the floor, and pulled them on. Walking to the balcony, he said, "Look at the different colors of the buildings. The play of light and shadow. The way that blue shutter across the way hangs loose." He was inspiring himself as he spoke, recalling the language of art he had learned at the Institute. There was a fascinating interplay of color, light and shadow. And if he set up an easel on the balcony, he could watch for Yegor as he painted.

"I have to leave for work." Albin stared at Dmitri, confusion and doubt etched on his face, which was less handsome in the light than it had been the night before.

Finally he sighed. "*Eh, bien,* if you steal from me, I will recover." He reached into the top drawer of the bureau and pulled out a key on a plastic key chain with a miniature Eiffel Tower attached. "Here is my extra key. If you go out, just remember to lock the door downstairs behind you."

Dmitri dashed over and hugged him. "You are super!" he said. "I have wonderful painting to show you when you come home."

They kissed again, and Dmitri dressed hurriedly so he could walk out with Albin, and see how the lock on the street-level door worked. There was no food in Albin's apartment, so Dmitri treated himself to a baguette, which he nibbled as he walked back to Albin's. Back on the fourth floor, he put up his easel on the balcony and began to sketch the street scene in charcoal.

He spent the morning on the little balcony, alternating between sketching the street and watching the Bar Les Sables, so that he would not miss Yegor if the Russian showed up. Hours passed, and Yegor did not appear. Dmitri pushed away his easel in frustration as the sun rose high in the sky, washing out all the interesting shadows.

He could not have gotten the message wrong, he thought. So where was Yegor? He thought back to Albin's suspicion that Dmitri might rob him. If Albin only knew how foolish an idea that was. While he was stuck waiting for Yegor to arrive at the Bar Les Sables he could do nothing to draw suspicion to himself. And besides, the man had been good to him, and there were few around Dmitri could say that about, beyond Taylor.

He thought about emailing Taylor, trying to find out if the police had discovered the theft and were looking for him. But the way he had left things, he was afraid that Taylor would as soon turn him over to the cops as help him.

Throughout the afternoon he found it difficult to concentrate on painting, alternately sitting on the balcony, and leaning against the railing. Where the hell was Yegor? Why hadn't he shown up? Though the afternoon was hot, Dmitri shivered. He had a stolen painting, no money, and no idea what to do.

Soon after five o'clock, Albin returned from work, delighted to find Dmitri still there. After a quick kiss, Albin insisted that they go to dinner. Luckily, there was a good Italian restaurant just down the block, and Dmitri sat with a view of the street. But Yegor never showed up.

Albin drank too much wine at dinner, and Dmitri had to help him back to the apartment. The Frenchman kept mumbling the whole way up the stairs, and then fell like a stone into his bed, asleep and snoring almost immediately.

Dmitri went back out to the bar. The same bartender who had let him store his duffle behind the bar was serving customers, and Dmitri had to wait until he was free.

"No Russians have come," the bartender said. "You are sure he told you to meet here? There are many bars in Nice."

"He say Bar Les Sables."

The Russian Boy

"We are the only bar by that name in Nice. Could your friend have meant another town? Cannes? Menthon?"

Dmitri shook his head. "He say Vieux Nice."

"Then you can only wait," the bartender said. "Wine? Beer?"

Dmitri felt the few euros in his pocket. He had no idea how long he would have to wait, or if he would be able to keep staying with Albin. "No, thanks."

He turned back toward the glass front door. "You are not the only one looking for a Russian," a man said, from the shadows of a booth across from the bar.

Dmitri stopped. The man who had spoken to him was French, and he looked at least a hundred years old, with sparse hair, mottled skin, and a beaky nose.

"Someone else is looking for Yegor?" he asked.

The man motioned across from him, and Dmitri slid into the booth. There was a bottle of cheap red wine on the table, and one half-filled glass in front of the old man. "You would like some wine?" he asked.

"Tell me who ask for Yegor."

"Have a glass of wine with me."

"Eh, bien," Dmitri said, shrugging. The old man flagged down the waitress as she passed and demanded another glass. He did not speak again until she returned with a glass and poured some of the rich, ruby-colored liquid into the glass for Dmitri.

"You are a very beautiful boy," the old man said. "It does my heart good to look at you."

"Yegor," Dmitri said. "Who ask about Yegor?"

"An American." He smiled, showing missing teeth. "A man like you and me."

Dmitri picked up his glass and sipped. "What do you mean?"

The man reached his leg out toward Dmitri's under the table. "You know." He smiled again, then held out his thin, bony hand. "I am Marcel."

"Dmitri. You say this American was..." He struggled for a polite word to use in French. "Pédé?"

Marcel laughed. "Yes, though much too old for a sweet young boy like you."

Dmitri couldn't help flirting. "And you? You're not too old, are you?" He pressed back against Marcel's leg, though he couldn't imagine even kissing the wrinkled lips. And the dick? What a horror it must be!

Marcel cackled. "I was too old for you fifty years ago. But I can still look, can't I? Like admiring a great work of art."

Dmitri blushed. He thought of his work as the art, not himself.

"What else?" he asked Marcel. "Did the American say more about Yegor?"

"He spoke to another regular here at the bar, a criminal type. He said the Russian was fat, with a small beard. That is the man you seek?"

"Yes, yes, that's him. Do he say where Yegor is?"

Marcel shook his head. "This American looks for the Russian, just like you do. What does this man have that everyone seeks him?" He leaned in close. "The fat ones, sometimes they have very big dicks. Is that it?"

Dmitri sat back against the booth. "Not for that. It is business."

Marcel nodded. "A bad business, if you ask me. You would be well advised to steer clear of it."

Dmitri picked up his glass and drained it. "Thank you for the advice, and the wine." He stood up. He didn't know why, but he leaned down and kissed the old man on the top of his bald forehead. Then he walked back out to the street.

Who was this American searching for Yegor, he wondered, as he walked over to Albin's building. Was he the one who was to buy the painting? Had Yegor screwed them both somehow? He tried to recall who had come and gone at the bar, but he had only been looking for Yegor and didn't remember anyone else.

He slumped against the wall, leaning back and watching the entrance to the bar, as if he could will Yegor to show up just by trying. A pair of men in leather jackets moved slowly down the street toward him, but Dmitri didn't feel fear—he had nothing left to lose by then.

The two young toughs cruised slowly past him, and one muttered, "Cocaine? Hashish? Marijuana?" in a low voice.

Dmitri nearly laughed. He barely had money for food. Instead he just shook his head, and the men walked on. He gave up waiting, and climbed the stairs back to Albin's apartment. The man snored so loudly it took Dmitri hours to fall asleep, and his dreams were restless and disturbed.

The Russian Boy

Lessons

Nice, November 1912

Alexei had learned to ride at his family's country estate, and each morning, he rose at first light, and took a basket of fresh-baked rolls from the kitchen. Then he saddled a trim young pony from the stable at the back of the Villa des Oliviers and rode down into the old city. He loved the fresh morning air, redolent with an ocean breeze, and absorbing the light and color of the place as he met servants climbing the hill to the villas of the wealthy Russians.

Working with Luschenko, Alexei was gradually seduced by the smell of the paint, the glorious light coming in from the ocean, and Luschenko's charm. He treated everyone in the same manner, from the highest Russian noble to the woman who cleaned the toilet. He made flattering observations, he smiled and charmed.

It was only when it was just the two of them that his passion shone through. He painted like a madman, attacking the canvas with his oils and brushes, creating great swoops of color that illuminated his ability to represent real life on the canvas. His subjects were always amazed at how vibrant they appeared in Luschenko's work.

Alexei noticed a change in himself, a reaction to being around the maestro. Where before painting had been a hobby, it became an obsession. Luschenko had forbidden him to touch paint until he mastered drawing, so he spent his afternoons sketching angles of the villa, the faces of the staff, his grandmother. By the end of the week Alexei asked the Dowager Countess if he could spend the entire day with the painter.

"If he'll have you," she said. "He has his own work to do."

"But I help him, Babushka," Alexei said. "I clean the brushes and I prepare the canvases, and I open or close the shutters to adjust the light."

The Dowager Countess raised her perfectly manicured eyebrows. "But surely he has servants for such work?"

"No, no servants," Alexei said. "It is important for me, to learn how to take care of the brushes and the canvases. The maestro is always talking to me about why I do things. He says I will understand the composition of the paint from working with it before I even pick up a brush myself."

"Well, if you would like I will arrange the details with your father.

It is good to see you so happy."

Each day, Luschenko combined attention to Alexei's developing eye and technique along with a lesson on the work of being an artist. "I live here in Nice all year, but I make most money when winter strikes Moscow and St. Petersburg and the wealthy take refuge here," he said, one morning, as Alexei set up an easel by the window so that the maestro could put the finishing touches on the portrait of a young Russian noble.

"During the winter, I sell the landscapes I paint during the summer, and I work on commissioned portraits. Sometimes you will see people come here to the studio in the afternoon, when the southern light is most favorable to those no longer in the bloom of youth."

Alexei brought the nearly finished painting to the easel and set it in place. Luschenko stood up and stretched. "In other cases, I will go to their villas or hotels to paint them *in situ*. That is a Latin term which means in the place where they are most comfortable."

Luschenko crossed the room to the easel, and looked toward the window, then back. He adjusted the position by an inch in one direction, a half inch in another, always considering the angle of the light and how it hit the subject and the canvas.

It was a process Alexei saw over and over again. Luschenko fussed over everything, from the layout of the palette to the consistency of the paint. He adjusted the subject's position, tweaking the way a sleeve hung, turning a subject's face a bit one way or the other.

He talked endlessly while he sketched, keeping his subjects entertained with innocent gossip, with tidbits of news or announcements of arrivals or departures. Somehow he knew all the latest news of the Russian community, though he was careful to save the most salacious details only for Alexei's ears.

"You have seen the handsome valet Madame Ostrovsky employs?" Luschenko asked Alexei one afternoon just after the lady had completed her portrait sitting and returned to the sumptuous villa her late husband had left her in Cagnes-sur-Mer.

"Yes," Alexei said. "He was dreamy looking, wasn't he? Those dark eyes, the way they smoldered?"

Luschenko laughed. "He is not for you. I have it on good authority that his sole duty is to pleasure Madame Ostrovsky."

"No! How do you know?"

"The girl who does the laundry for the Madame is the sister of

The Russian Boy

Leona, who works at the tailor shop in the Rue Lantine. She tells me everything."

He looked up from his canvas, where he was using Prussian blue to shade in the evening sky behind Madame Ostrovsky's portrait. "The Baron Pshkov? He employs not one, but two young boys to provide his pleasure. One for buggering, the other for fellatio. It is like a sandwich, I am told, with the Baron the meat and the two boys his slices of bread."

Alexei's mouth gaped open. "You mean... there are other men who like..."

Luschenko laughed. "Did you think you and I were unique? Of course, there are many men who enjoy the pleasure of other men. Why, when I was your age, and I was in the Czar's army, I had intimate relations with many of my fellow soldiers, sometimes two or three at a time. How do you think I became such an expert?"

Alexei's hormones were in full rage by then. Just the thought of the Baron's two young aides was enough to make his dick as stiff as one of the maestro's prized horsehair brushes. And then to think of Fyodor being intimate with soldiers!

Luschenko noticed his discomfort and motioned him over. "Open your pants," he said.

Alexei's grandmother had commissioned the tailor to make Alexei several pairs of the canvas pants that Luschenko preferred, with pockets for brushes and large, easily opened buttons at the fly. With trembling fingers, Alexei undid his pants and they fell to the studio floor, leaving him only constrained by his linen undershorts. With a quick motion, Luschenko yanked them down as well.

Alexei yelped as his dick was dragged down, then bounced free. A tiny pearl of precum already oozed from his tip, and with his index finger Luschenko reached out and oh so gently smeared it down the length of Alexei's shaft. The boy shivered at his touch, his heart palpitating as he anticipated the pleasure to come.

With that same index finger, Luschenko traced his way back from the root to the tip, his fingernail etching the faintest line in the boy's skin, and Alexei hiccupped with desire. "Maestro," he breathed.

"All in good time, my boy." Luschenko used that same finger to caress Alexei's milk-white, hairless thigh, then burrow into the patch of wiry black pubic hair at the base of his dick. Alexei felt like his dick was going to explode at any moment, just from his maestro's touch.

He closed his eyes and thought of painting the sky at the moment just before the sun rose, when the deep black of midnight was fading toward the pastel blue of the morning. Though his insides were churning and tears were welling at the corners of his eyes, he tried hard not to give in to the pressure of the maestro's hand.

Then Luschenko flicked his tongue at the tip of Alexei's dick and Alexei thought he would pass out from the pleasure. He grabbed the table behind him to steady himself, and Luschenko laughed. "Mmm," he said, licking the mushroom cap. "You taste like the ocean. Salty and fresh."

He opened his mouth and swallowed Alexei's shaft, and Alexei gripped the table and tried to slow his breathing. But it was no use; the orgasm built too fast to be held back, washing over him like the strongest wave, nearly knocking him down with its power.

Luschenko fastened his mouth on Alexei's dick like a vise, swallowing every drop of the boy's cum, reaching around to ride a finger up the boy's sensitive young ass as he gasped and bucked. Then Luschenko pulled back, licked his lips, and said, "Now. I must get back to work on Madame Ostrovsky's portrait. You will prepare my paint."

Alexei nodded dumbly and reached down for his pants. "There is no need for you to dress. It is just the two of us here, after all. You wouldn't want to dirty your clothes, would you?"

"No," Alexei said, shaking his head.

"Good. Then take off your shirt as well. You may fold your clothes and leave them on the chair."

Thus began a pattern. Whenever they were alone in the studio, Alexei would strip and carry out his chores in the nude—scrubbing a spot of spilled paint from the floor, cleaning brushes, packaging canvases for transport to the framer. He began to enjoy the freedom, as well as the chance to flaunt his body to the painter.

He would see the maestro poring over a sketch, and take that opportunity to walk past, then bend over to pick at an imaginary spot from the floor. "You torment me," Luschenko groaned, as Alexei stuck the pink rosebud of his ass nearly in the painter's face. Alexei took great pleasure in this tiny role reversal, though of course he took even more pleasure when Luschenko abandoned his painting to take advantage of his young apprentice.

But the best times were when they were both working at their easels. The maestro began work at first light at the tall windows that faced the ocean. Sometimes he turned toward the east, and sketched the sun rising over the grand sweep of the Bay of Angels. Some days he

The Russian Boy

faced directly south, capturing the movement of the waves as they tossed their heads like impatient horses straining toward an imaginary finish line. Other days he turned the easel so that the sunlight streamed over his shoulder, and he painted Mont Boron, the Port Lympia, and the gooseneck curve of Saint-Jean-Cap-Ferrat.

Alexei positioned himself so he could watch the maestro as well as do his own work. He was amazed at the older man's sure strokes, the way his vision seemed to translate so easily to the canvas. Alexei had to look a dozen times before he felt confident enough even to apply a pencil, charcoal or crayon.

By early December Alexei felt his skill improving, and he arrived each morning eager to get to work. The maestro was almost always at his easel, sketching, and Alexei would position his and begin sketching. One morning, however, he arrived to find Luschenko still in bed. "Are you ill, maestro?" he asked, stepping around the screen into the bedroom area of the studio.

Luschenko flipped back the duvet to expose his naked body, and his erection. "No, just waiting for my pupil. Come here for your next lesson."

Alexei smiled, and dropped to his knees beside the bed. Luschenko turned on his side and scooted to the edge of the bed, so Alexei could take his teacher's dick in his mouth. "No, no," Luschenko said after a moment. "This is not a horse race, where you hope to finish quickly." He pulled out of Alexei's mouth and motioned the boy to his feet.

With practiced hands, he undid Alexei's trousers and pushed them to the ground, then unbuttoned his undershorts and pulled his stiff dick out. Alexei groaned. "Watch the master, and learn," Luschenko said.

He licked gently up and down the length of Alexei's dick, teasing the sensitive head with the tip of his tongue. He grasped the shaft and began stroking it slowly as he licked and sucked the mushroom cap.

With one hand, he reached up and under Alexei's shorts and fondled the underside of his balls. Alexei felt like a match had been lit, sending fire through his loins. The maestro's finger kept working him, stroking the sensitive area between Alexei's ass and balls as he sucked and licked, and Alexei felt shudders rising through his body.

But Luschenko pulled back, and Alexei didn't come, though he was still hard, his mouth was dry, and his groin was roiling. The maestro said nothing, but his index finger found Alexei's asshole and started wiggling, and a minute or two later his mouth was back on his student's dick. The maestro deep-throated him, then pulled back to lick him like he was a lollipop. The tip of the maestro's tongue penetrated the slit at the top of Alexei's dick, and goose bumps rose on Alexei's arms.

He felt the pressure build—but so did Luschenko, and he backed off. Three times he nearly brought Alexei to the point of explosion and backed off. By the fourth time, though, Alexei was begging for release. Luschenko took pity on his young apprentice at this point, and as his insides swirled for the fourth time, the maestro didn't let up, and it felt like every nerve ending in Alexei's body became electrified as his semen exploded down his maestro's throat.

"And that is how you suck a dick," Luschenko said, backing away with pleasure. "I can see you will need much practice."

Alexei could only slump back against the dresser and nod his agreement. The next morning began his lessons on how to give the older man maximum pleasure with his mouth and tongue, licking and kissing the maestro's cock until it was stiff and proud, then sucking it down to the pubic hairs until Luschenko could hold out no longer, and came with a burst of Russian and French expletives.

He was also taught how to pleasure himself most effectively, with the application of his index finger to the sensitive spot just below the head of his dick, and how to bend over and spread his ass cheeks wide so that the maestro could penetrate him with his tongue. Luschenko had promised that there was still much to learn—about painting and sex—and Alexei was eager to learn.

The House in St. Laurent du Var

Nice, Tuesday evening

By the time Rowan left the Bar Les Sables, it was too late to go searching for dead men, or those pretending to be dead, so he walked back along the Promenade des Anglais toward the Hotel Negresco. Evening was falling, and the lights on Mont Boron turned on like a rich woman adding pearls to a necklace one by one. Lanes of traffic streamed past as Rowan strolled along the walkway, looking out over the rocky beach and the restless sea.

The beach was ten feet below, with periodic staircases leading down. To his left, a latticework of pipes stretched over café tables with bright blue awnings. Far down the beach, a plane was taking off from the airport, and he watched its tiny lights mount into the sky and disappear beyond the foothills of the Alps.

There was a chill in the air now that the sun was gone, but it was still a lot warmer than New York in January. He walked down the broad planking, passing a dirty barefoot artist drawing on the pavement in pastels. The work was sloppy and amateurish, and Rowan wasn't surprised that there were only a few small coins in his cup. Just beyond the artist, a girl in a red leotard who looked as if she could be twelve or thirty did gymnastics in the middle of the walkway.

Her body was young and supple but her face was taut and lined. An older man and a small boy, dressed in red jackets with gold brocade, walked through the mix of people around her collecting money.

Rowan skirted the crowd, his attention caught by soft music breaking through above the revving of a motorcycle and the klaxon of a car alarm. He saw two sidewalk musicians ahead, a violinist and a saxophonist, both young men in their twenties. Three girls sat by them, smoking Gauloises and listening. Occasionally the prettiest of the three reached over to turn the pages of the music before them.

It took him a moment to recognize that they were playing a rag by Scott Joplin, adapted for those two instruments. He leaned up against a white slatted chair and stared out at the ocean while the music floated past him.

There was something mystical about being there, about the combination of sea, music and sky. He fished in his pocket for change. He dropped a few coins in the open violin case before one of the musicians, and one of the girls smiled at him. He smiled back, and hunching his shoulders, continued to walk.

A cool breeze blew in off the ocean, and Rowan licked his lips, tasting the salt in the air and thinking of the young man who had kissed him that morning. And then he could not help remembering Brian Wojchowski. He leaned forward against the railing, his hands gripping the cold metal, and let the memories flood back.

Brian was a student in his Art History 101 at St. Michael's, back when Rowan had been a tenured professor, married, with two kids, hiding his sexual interest in other men. Brian was nineteen, over the legal age, but Rowan hadn't considered having anything to do with him until Brian came to his office the next semester to ask a question about an erotic drawing called Angelo Incarnato, or Angel Incarnate, by Leonardo da Vinci.

"Do you think this is evidence that Leonardo was gay?" Brian asked, opening his text to the picture.

Thinking back later, Rowan knew he should have heard the alarm bells—handsome young student, in his office to discuss a sketch of a nude male. But at the time, Rowan had been thrilled at the chance to discuss something he could never cover in class at St. Michael's. Brian was a smart young man, with interesting insights, and Rowan was swept up in his own excitement, both intellectual and sexual.

They talked in his office, then agreed to meet the next afternoon at a coffee shop a few blocks from campus. It was a warm spring day, and Brian wore a pair of skimpy shorts and a tank top, exposing his long, untanned limbs. He moved with grace, flopping into the oversized armchair next to Rowan, his leg grazing Rowan's own as he settled.

They talked for an hour, and then it seemed perfectly natural that Brian would bring up another painting, in a book he had back at his off-campus apartment, just a block from the coffee shop, and insist that Rowan had to come over and see it.

Rowan should have said no right then. He should have walked away from the boy right there, without looking back. But he hadn't, and at that moment he had sown the seeds of his own demise.

A police car sped past on the Promenade des Anglais, lights flashing and the peculiar European style siren sounding, and Rowan remembered his purpose in being in Nice. He had to find *The Russian Boy*. He pushed all other thoughts out of his head, and focused on the street ahead. A cluster of British tourists waited at the traffic light, and Rowan followed them across the road and the tram tracks. He stopped

The Russian Boy

a few blocks short of the hotel at a small café, where he order the prix fixe meal: a green salad with goat cheese, steak frites, and a cup of chocolate mousse.

Back at the hotel, he went over what he knew. The painting had been removed from its frame sometime after the restorer went home for the day on Friday afternoon. On Sunday afternoon, Rene Scarano had overheard a Russian speaking on the phone about the painting to a man he believed was the framer, Pascal Gaultier. He had called the curator at the Musée des Beaux Arts, and in turn Rene Desjardins had notified the police in Paris.

They had sent an officer to the Institute des Artistes to meet with the director and survey the property. They had discovered a broken window on the ground floor of the building, the jimmied lock on the restorer's studio, and the frame that had held *The Russian Boy*, which had been carefully taken apart and left in pieces.

Why not just take the painting, frame and all? Rowan wondered. Why risk damaging a valuable painting by removing it from the frame? Had someone at the Institute smuggled it out under the eyes of the staff?

He sent an email to Ron Kramer, explaining what he had found so far. "The restorer is my best lead, even though he has been dead—or pretending to be dead– for three years," he wrote. "I've been told that he is the only framer in Nice illicit enough to handle something like this. I'm going out to his house tomorrow to see what I can find."

Rowan looked at the clock. It was after eleven, and he was tired. He sent the email, closed the computer, and flipped the light off. Leaning back against the pillows, he stared out at the dark ocean. The lights of a plane passed by, and he followed them across the sky, then closed his eyes and was asleep almost immediately.

Wednesday morning, he checked his email and found a brief message from Ron Kramer. "Client is eager to get the painting back. Get on the stick, pal."

"Yeah, yeah," he said, shutting down the computer. After a quick breakfast in the hotel café, he picked up a cab and sat back as the driver headed west on the Promenade des Anglais, across the river and then inland to St. Laurent du Var. The street looked like many in the small towns of France, a mix of colorless new construction and quaint dilapidation. The small house at the address Rowan had been given looked abandoned, with vines arching over the front door, untrimmed in years, and a broken shutter hanging loosely from one window.

Perhaps Pascal Gaultier really was dead, Rowan thought, getting out of the cab. The small yard was overgrown, and stones had come loose from the wall at the street's edge. He paid the cabbie, and was about to ask the man to wait for him, when the driver's radio crackled. He slammed the car into gear and took off down the street before Rowan could speak.

He shrugged. He would find a café, and call another cab. He was not likely to stay long at this rundown house.

A three-story modern apartment block loomed across the street. Rowan looked up and saw a housewife, on the second-floor balcony, hanging out laundry. She paused to stare at him, but would not return his wave. He shrugged and walked up the narrow path to the house's front door, nearly tripping over a broken stone.

He knocked sharply on the front door. "Monsieur Gaultier?" he called. "Pascal Gaultier?"

There was no answer. Not surprising, if Gaultier had been dead for three years. But Rowan felt he had to try. And he was curious to know how a dead man could still be framing paintings. He stepped carefully through the overgrown yard, stopping to rap at the window. When he got no response, he moved around to the side of the house.

Tomato plants climbed the wall there. Peering closely, Rowan could see someone had been picking the tomatoes. That did not mean Gaultier was alive, however; an opportunistic neighbor could be enjoying the bounty of the framer's yard.

Rowan circled to the back, where a wooden door hung ajar. There was a crumbling stone wall at the rear of the property, and he doubted that anyone from the high-rise could see back there, where he was. He knocked on the open door, calling out again, and the door swung inward.

"Can't beat that for an invitation," he said.

He stepped into the musty interior of a kitchen. The remains of a meal sat on a small table, and the lone chair had been knocked over. Unless dead men had begun eating scrambled eggs, someone very much alive had been in that room within the past few days.

He sniffed the air. A nasty smell rose from the small tiled bathroom next to the kitchen, where someone had used the toilet and neglected to flush. Through an arch he could see a small living room, and another room off to the side he assumed was a bedroom. He stepped through the arch and peered around in the dim light. It was not until he looked down at the ground that he saw the body there. A large, evil-looking roach clambered across the dead man's face, and there was a cluster of ants around his right hand.

"Jesus!" Rowan exclaimed, stepping backward into the kitchen so quickly that he stumbled over the fallen chair and went sprawling.

His first instinct was to flee. Get the hell out of that house in case the murderer was lingering in the bedroom. But that was stupid, he realized. The food on the table had to be at least a few days old. That didn't mean he should linger. But he could at least look at the corpse, and see if it matched the description Scarano had given him of Pascal Gaultier.

He got up from the floor, careful not to leave any fingerprints or disturb the crime scene. Though he was working for Kramer's agency, he had no private eye license of his own, and he didn't want to have to explain what his prints were doing at the scene of a murder.

He stepped carefully back into the living room and peered down at the body. The fat man on the floor was younger than he had been told Gaultier was, with black hair. Rowan had just noticed the soul patch on the man's chin, and was processing that piece of information, when a booming French voice announced, "Stop! Police!"

He looked up and saw a scared-looking police officer standing in the open back door and brandishing a baton. He was barely into his twenties, wearing a navy uniform that was too big on his skinny frame. "Raise your hands," the flic said.

Rowan complied. The young officer radioed for backup, and they stood there in a standoff until more officers arrived. No one bothered to ask him any questions, and when he tried to demand that the flics call Ron Kramer, or even Rene Desjardins, he was silenced.

He was handcuffed and put into a police cruiser, and taken to the Commissariat on the broad Boulevard Georges Pompidou, along the river, where he was left in a small room for several hours. His stomach grumbled and he was irritated more than frightened. If someone would just talk to him, he could clear all this up.

He was sure the man had been dead for a few days, and a simple check of his passport, and the airline's records, would put him in New York at the time of death. But that did nothing to ease the roiling of his stomach.

Finally, an officer came into the room. "You are to come with me," he said in French.

He was put into the rear of another Citroen police cruiser. "Where are we going?" Rowan asked.

"The Service Régional de la Police Judiciaire," the officer said. "In Nice."

"Why? Why hasn't anyone spoken to me yet, or checked out my credentials?"

"I cannot say, Monsieur. Now you will please be quiet."

It wasn't a long trip, to a tall, curving building on the other side of the river Var. Rowan was turned over to another officer, then led to yet another interview room. After a few minutes, a short man in a dark suit came into the room. He was about Rowan's age, with curly hair that came to a point on his forehead.

"M. McNair?" he asked, pronouncing it in the French way, mick-na-eer. He continued in English. "I am Claude Rochambeau. I am an investigative officer with the police judiciare for the department of Alpes-Maritimes." He sat down across from Rowan. "What brought you to St. Laurent du Var this morning?"

Rowan sketched in the basics—the theft of the painting, the NYMFA hiring The Kramer Agency to find it. How Ron Kramer had called him in, because of his art expertise.

"Yes, yes," Rochambeau said, nodding impatiently. "But what does the theft of a painting in Paris have to do with a murder in St. Laurent du Var?"

Rowan explained about meeting Scarano, and the man's belief that the Russian had been speaking to Pascal Gaultier.

"But Gaultier died three years ago," Rochambeau said. "This man did not tell you that?"

"Yes, he told me. But he also told me he was sure the Russian had been speaking to Gaultier on the phone. So I wanted to see for myself."

"You gained access to the house how?"

"The rear door. When I knocked, it came open. So I walked inside."

"You are sure this is the first time you have been in that house?" Rochambeau asked. "You were not there, say, two days ago, to meet with someone?"

Rowan shook his head. "Two days ago I was in New York. You have my passport. Check the customs stamp. My airline ticket is back at the hotel—I can show you my receipt. I didn't arrive in Nice until early yesterday morning."

"And why did you not notify the police of your suspicions?"

Rowan laughed. "A man in a bar told me that he overheard a

The Russian Boy

conversation between an unknown Russian and a man who has been dead for three years, about a painting stolen in Paris. What would you say if I came to you with that story?"

Rochambeau grunted. "You looked at the dead man?"

"Yes."

"Did you recognize him?"

"I think he's the Russian man with the soul patch—the small beard—that Rene Scarano heard speaking in the bar. But that's only a guess. Scarano could tell you more."

"We will bring in this man Scarano," Rochambeau said. "And I will check with your airline."

He walked out before Rowan could ask about lunch while he waited. Another hour passed before Rochambeau returned.

"Do you know the name Yegor Rostnikov?" he asked.

Rowan shook his head. "Is that the dead man?"

"We matched his fingerprints. He is wanted for questioning in several crimes."

"Won't get much out of him now," Rowan said.

"You are staying at the Negresco in Nice?" Rochambeau asked.

"Yes."

"You must stop your investigation now that this is a police matter. Do not leave the area without notifying us." Rochambeau turned to leave. "You are free to go. But we may call you again."

"I can't stop," Rowan said. "My client is expecting results. If I don't find the painting, I don't get paid. And I need the money."

"Your money problems are not my concern," Rochambeau said. "What does worry me is an American who does not even have a private investigator's license bumbling around in a French murder investigation. I will not tolerate that."

Rowan stood up. It was useless to argue with the man. But there was no way he was going to stop looking for *The Russian Boy*. It was his job, and if he gave up and returned to New York he might never get another job from Ron Kramer.

And as well, the painting meant something to him—it had spoken to him at an emotional level, ever since he first saw the postcard of it at that sleazy bookstore in Times Square, and then after he'd seen the painting in person at the NYMFA. He was determined to return it to where it belonged so that it could continue to inspire other men who might be as confused as he had been.

Internet Café

Nice, Wednesday morning

"My poor head," Albin said, when he woke on Wednesday morning. "Too much wine."

Dmitri watched from bed as the Frenchman struggled to prepare for work, then forced himself to get up and kiss Albin goodbye. He promised to be there that evening when Albin returned from work, even though he knew that if Yegor arrived he'd walk out of the apartment and not look back.

With a sigh, Dmitri ran a tepid bath. He dressed and set his easel up again on the balcony. At least if he could paint something, he could try and sell the picture and then make some money. He cursed Taylor's easy ability to paint what tourists wanted—he sold five paintings of Sacré Coeur for every one of Dmitri's.

By noon, he was frustrated and disgusted. He had no inspiration, and all he could think about was *The Russian Boy*, in the locker at the train station.

He remembered an internet café a few blocks away. Perhaps Yegor had sent him an email, he thought. Once he had the idea, he rushed downstairs and over to the café, where he paid a euro for a few minutes online.

There was a message from Taylor from Sunday. "Where are you? Are you in trouble? Please let me help you."

Dmitri felt tears welling up in his eyes. Taylor cared about him. Taylor had tried to convince him not to get involved with Yegor—and he had been right.

He clicked "reply" and began typing. He hardly ever wrote in French, so he had to struggle to get the words and the accents correct. "I am in Nice. Yegor no come to Bar Les Sables like he promise, and I do not know what to do."

He hesitated. "Please no tell police where I am."

The woman at the next table was yelling at someone on her cell phone, and making it hard for him to concentrate. His time ran out, and he had to pay another of his dwindling stock of euros for more time. He went back to the message, and typed, "I am sorry for everything that has happened." He signed the email with the single initial D, and hit send.

He wondered if there would be anything in the press about *The*

The Russian Boy

Russian Boy. He typed his own name into the search box and hit the enter key. He was horrified to see a dozen results spring up, all of them indicating he was a suspect in the theft. He struggled through the report in *Le Monde*, translating the unfamiliar words into Russian. *Oh Christ*, he said under his breath when he read that Interpol had gotten involved. Police like that must have immense resources. They could probably track him to Nice.

What if there was a flic after him right now? He looked around in fright. Then he took a deep breath. Even if they knew he had come to Nice, there was no way anyone could know he had been staying with Albin.

He clicked through to the website for *Nice Matin*, the local paper. The article there was very brief, mentioning only that a painting had been stolen in Paris and was believed to be in Nice. Thank Christ for that, he thought, sitting back.

His hand was shaking on the table. He needed money, and food, and a way to get rid of *The Russian Boy*.

The woman at the next table raised her voice even louder and began pounding her knuckles on the tabletop. He looked in her direction as she stood up. She did not notice that her wallet tumbled out as she grabbed her purse. With her hip, she knocked the newspaper over the wallet.

She stalked toward the ladies' room at back of the café, still arguing with her caller. Dmitri watched her go, then looked around the room. He stood up, and with a quick motion he grabbed the newspaper from the chair, with woman's wallet clutched beneath it. He strode out the door, his heart pounding as he expected to be challenged every moment. And if the flics picked him up, they'd know he had the painting, too. But he had no choice; he needed money, and it was too risky to steal anything from Albin. Plus, the Frenchman had been good to him; Dmitri wasn't going to pay him back by stealing from him.

He got outside without incident, and hurried around the corner, ducking into an alleyway. There was nearly a hundred euros in the wallet, which he picked out. Then he tossed the wallet to the ground and walked in the opposite direction from the internet café. He stopped a few blocks later at a takeout café and bought himself a long Italian sandwich of meat and cheese, along with a big bottle of Orangina.

He took the food back up to Albin's apartment, where he ate at the kitchen table. He felt much better when he had food in his belly and money in his wallet. Then he went back to the balcony, determined to finish a painting.

But he couldn't concentrate. Now that he could look back on what he had done, he realized he should never have left Paris. He should have told Yegor that. Then he could have spoken with the police and deflected suspicion away from himself. Instead he had reached for the easy money, and failed to think through the consequences. And now he was fucked. Could he just call the flics himself, let them know that *The Russian Boy* was in the locker at the train station? Would that let him off the hook?

He doubted it. If he went back to Paris, the flics would pull him in. Though he had been careful, only handling the painting itself with gloves on, his fingerprints were probably somewhere on the carrying case.

Could he shift the blame to Taylor? Pretend that his boyfriend had stolen the carrying case from him, stolen the painting, then fled to Nice? Could he do that?

No, that wouldn't work; Taylor was still back in Paris. And Dmitri didn't think he could do something so evil anyway, not to Taylor, who had done him no harm.

He looked at the clock. Albin would be coming home from work soon. How much longer would he let Dmitri stay with him? Would he ever get suspicious? What if the local paper published a picture of him, and Albin saw it?

He realized he was beginning to become fond of the Frenchman. Yes, Albin wasn't the most handsome man in the world, but he was kind and trusting, and Dmitri had been taking advantage of other people for too long. Perhaps it was that tendency that had brought him to this point. Would his luck change if he adjusted his attitude? He had never wanted to take care of anyone before, not even Taylor.

He and Taylor were both passionate men, and they argued about art and painting technique as much as they had sex. But Dmitri knew in his heart he had never loved the American, just found it convenient to share the apartment with him, and satisfy his urge to fuck without having to work at it.

But there was something about Albin that stirred his heart. Even now, when he looked at a picture of the Frenchman, he smiled. Yes, his dick rose, but his heart skipped a beat as well. He'd never felt that way with Taylor.

He paced around the small living room, still checking the street

The Russian Boy

below every few minutes. Everywhere around him he saw artifacts of Albin's life. Souvenirs from trips to Corsica, Tunisia and Morocco. His diplomas and certificates of achievement in computer courses. Framed photos of him with his brothers and sisters and their children.

He imagined those kids calling the Frenchman *Oncle* Albin, and the generosity their uncle would treat them with. He sat down at his canvas and began sketching Albin, partly from memory and partly from the photos.

As Albin took shape on the canvas, Dmitri was surprised and energized. He rarely painted portraits, preferring landscapes or still lifes. And yet, this picture inspired him more than the street outside, more even than Paris or Sacré Coeur. He was so engrossed in his work that he was startled by the sharp knock on the door. He threw a cloth over the painting and stepped into the living room. If the flics had tracked him, he was determined not to involve Albin.

Jousting

Nice, Wednesday afternoon

Taylor gave up searching for Dmitri early Wednesday afternoon and bought another baguette and a big bottle of water from a convenience store, dismayed to watch his remaining euros diminish. When he finished eating he set up his easel on the Promenade des Anglais, across from the pink-roofed turret of the Hotel Negresco, and began sketching. He was still inspired by his vision from the night before, and he could feel something new and different in his sketching.

He had done a rough sketch in the evening light, then hurried to the train station where he had stored his backpack and easel at a locker. He had rented a bunk bed in a shared room at a cheap hostel. A German student snored loudly in the bunk below him, and Taylor stayed awake for hours, turning thoughts over in his head. Where was Dmitri? He had to be in Nice. And yet Taylor had found no trace of him. Taylor had spent most of his money on the train ticket. He could only afford to stay another night in Nice, or else he'd have nothing left for the return train ticket.

He had brought his sketchpad and folding easel with him on the train, hoping that he'd get a few minutes to do some sketching once he found Dmitri. But now he thought he might be able to sell a drawing on the Promenade des Anglais to supplement his dwindling stock of euros, and within a few minutes he had a group of tourists around him as he drew. Painting outside Sacré Coeur, he had learned to assess crowd. Did the women wear expensive necklaces, the men heavy gold watches? The better dressed the crowd, the more Taylor could charge.

He finished shading the hotel's roof, and then quickly sketched in a couple of palm trees and a sprawling, spike-tipped aloe next to it. "How much?" a sallow American man asked, as Taylor carefully tore the page from his pad.

"Twenty euros," Taylor said, smiling. "Cheap at twice the price."

The man looked at his wife, who said, "It's very pretty. It would look lovely in the guest bathroom, and everyone would know we've been to Nice."

The man opened his wallet and pulled out a twenty-euro note, and Taylor handed the picture to his wife, who beamed.

Taylor sketched and sold three more drawings of the Negresco and the Promenade before he noticed the man he'd kissed the day

The Russian Boy

before at the edge of the crowd. His pulse rate accelerated, his dick began to unfurl, and he struggled not to look the man in the face, feeling unaccountably embarrassed.

When he finished the picture and sold it, he smiled at the rest of the crowd and said, "Sorry, I'm losing the light."

It was true; dusk was falling. Taylor began packing up, waiting for the man to approach him, as he was sure he would.

"You have a real talent," the man said.

"For kissing?" Taylor said, turning to him. He was pleased to see the man blush.

"Well, that too." The man stuck his hand out. "Rowan McNair."

"Taylor Griffin." Taylor shook his hand, feeling the strength in his grip. The fingers were too thick and stubby to hold a brush well. "You're not a painter, are you?"

Rowan shook his head. "I was an art history professor once."

"Sounds like there's a story there."

"Not much of one." Rowan shifted from one foot to the other, then said, "I believe we have a common interest."

"Beyond kissing?" Taylor couldn't help it—he wanted to tease this handsome man, flirt with him. Kiss him again. Maybe even do more than that, if the opportunity arose.

"I believe we're both interested in *The Russian Boy*."

For a moment, Taylor thought he meant Dmitri, then he realized Rowan was talking about the painting. His heart raced again, this time for a different reason. "Do you know where it is?"

"No. Do you?"

Taylor shook his head.

"But you are looking for it, aren't you?"

Taylor wasn't sure how to answer. In a way, he was looking for the painting, because when he found it, he thought he'd find Dmitri. And then maybe he could talk some sense into him, convince him to return the painting to the restorer's studio, forget this crazy scheme that was sure to put Dmitri in danger.

Rowan looked at him, waiting for an answer. "Yes, I guess I am," Taylor said.

"Well, so am I. Perhaps we can join forces."

Taylor looked at him. "What do you mean?"

"Let's talk about it over dinner," Rowan said. "My treat. I hate to eat alone."

At the word dinner, Taylor's stomach grumbled. He had the

money he'd collected for the four drawings in his pocket, but who knew how long he would have to stay in Nice, what other expenses he might run into. "Dinner sounds great." He attached the strap to his easel and slung it over his shoulder, then picked up his backpack, filled with pencils and charcoal and the extra clothes he'd brought with him.

As they walked down the Promenade, he took a sidelong glance. Rowan was just as handsome in the fading evening light as he'd been in the morning sunshine. Short dark hair, going gray at the sideburns. A five o'clock shadow that highlighted his strong chin.

As he often did, Taylor began drawing Rowan's face in his mind. He'd start with his Progresso pencil, a thick graphite stick with a lacquer finish, to sketch in the heart-shaped outline of Rowan's head. Then a thinner stick for the broad strokes of the man's hair. A soft pencil for his eyes, which looked like ebony pools in the harsh streetlight.

He turned to look at Rowan, to analyze the height of his forehead in relation to his cheeks, and realized the man was looking at him, too. "Sorry," he said, blushing. "I do that sometimes. Start to draw someone in my head and then lose track of conversation. Were you asking something?"

"Only if seafood was all right with you," Rowan said, smiling. "I'd love a good bowl of bouillabaisse."

"Fine with me."

They settled on a quaint little hole-in-the-wall place with fantastic smells wafting out the open door. Gas lamps inside metal cages flickered on each table, the tablecloths and napkins were bright yellow Provençal designs, and the servers bustled with cheer, heaving huge platters on the tables.

Rowan and Taylor ordered a massive bowl of steamed mussels to share, accompanied by a bottle of dry, fruity Cotes de Provence rosé. Rowan ordered the bouillabaisse, while Taylor asked for a bowl of tagliatelle in tomato sauce. Pasta was filling, he thought. With luck, he wouldn't have to eat again until the next evening.

The waitress, a friendly young Italian girl named Ilaria, uncorked the bottle at the table and filled both glasses, then left the bottle on ice in a metal stand next to Rowan.

Rowan sipped his wine, then smiled and put the glass back down on the checkered tablecloth. "You freaked out Bruno Desjardins yesterday. He was sure you had *The Russian Boy* and were looking for a fence who could take it off your hands."

The Russian Boy

"He thought I was that stupid? That I'd go to a museum for help in selling a stolen painting?"

"That is what you asked, isn't it? Where someone could go to find a customer with loose moral standards—or words to that effect?"

"Well, yes," Taylor said. "But I wasn't asking for myself."

"Why don't you tell me what you know."

Taylor was glad for the distraction provided as Ilaria delivered the fragrant, steaming bowl of mussels, with two plates and an empty wooden bowl for the shells, along with a fresh-baked baguette. When she left, he said, "Why don't you start. I don't know if I can trust you."

Rowan speared a mussel with his fork, holding the shell in his left hand as he pried the juicy pink-orange oblong from the shell. "You'll kiss me but you won't trust me. Interesting. But I'm paying for dinner. So that means you start."

His face reminded Taylor of a professor chastising a student for a bad paper, or perhaps a plagiarized one. But he had already graduated from college, and he wasn't cowed by this man, handsome as he was, when he knew nothing about him. He folded his arms and leaned back in his chair.

"Go on, eat." Rowan ripped a hunk from the baguette and dipped it in the garlicky broth beneath the butterflied mussels.

Taylor's hunger got the best of him, and he dug in. Neither of them spoke for a few minutes except to make appreciative noises about the food. All the time, though, Taylor's mind was racing. Was Rowan the client Yegor had mentioned? He was most certainly gay, and his clothes, while not new, looked to be of good quality. Rich men were often like that, Taylor had discovered; they only spent their money on what mattered to them.

"Fine, I'll start," Rowan said. "I found a dead body this morning. A Russian."

Taylor gasped. Dmitri? Could he be dead? "Who was it? Where? What happened?"

"All in time," Rowan said. "It's your turn." He sopped up the very last of the liquid with a heel of French bread, and smiled.

"You're a bastard, you know that?"

Rowan drank the rest of his rosé, then refilled his glass and Taylor's. "I'm waiting," he said.

"Fine." Taylor pushed back from the table. He was scared that the dead man Rowan had mentioned could be Dmitri, but he knew he couldn't just give away everything he knew without getting anything in return. "I know who took the painting, and I know why. I just don't know where the thief, or the painting, are now."

Rowan laughed. "I like your style, Taylor. You don't just roll over, do you?"

"Only for the right man," Taylor said, a smile playing on his face. Then he realized Dmitri might be dead, and he sobered quickly. "The body you found—he was young? My age?"

"No. He was fat and middle-aged, with a soul patch. Police said his name was Yegor Rostnikov. "Is he the man who stole the painting?"

Taylor shook his head. Thank god, he thought. Dmitri was still alive. Or at least Taylor hoped he was. "I met him once. But I don't know anything about him."

Rowan poured him another glass of wine. "So it was the young one—the guy your age. Also a Russian?"

"What's your interest in all this?" Taylor asked.

Rowan shifted on the wooden chair. "I freelance for a private investigation agency in New York," he said. "Specializing in art theft. The New York Museum of Fine Arts hired us to look for *The Russian Boy*."

"You're a private eye? I thought you were an art history professor."

"I was, once upon a time. It's hard to lose a tenured professorship, but I managed. Now I write the occasional article, do some editing for an art journal, and when called on, look for stolen paintings, drawings and sculptures."

Ilaria removed the big bowl of empty mussels shells. She asked how they were and Rowan kissed his fingertips. She laughed and turned away.

"Your turn," Rowan said to Taylor.

"Hold on. You lost a tenured professorship? How?"

Rowan's eyes flashed. "Not your business. Now tell me how you're involved in this."

"I got my BFA in painting from Northern Illinois, and one of my professors recommended me for a fellowship at the Institute des Artistes in Paris."

"Good program. The painting was stolen from a restorer affiliated with the Institute – was it in the same building where you go to school?"

Taylor nodded. "One of the professors specializes in art

The Russian Boy

restoration. He had *The Russian Boy* in his studio."

"You saw it?"

"A couple of times. It's amazing."

"Yes, it is."

Ilaria returned with two huge platters, one on each arm. Taylor's stomach grumbled again as the rich tomato scent rose up into his nostrils. He couldn't remember the last time he'd had such a good meal. Too bad this wasn't a date.

That thought stopped him. A date? With Rowan? When the whole purpose of his trip to Nice was to rescue Dmitri—his boyfriend? Then he remembered how Dmitri had walked out on him, and he realized that though he was fond of the Russian boy, what he felt wasn't love. And this, this feeling for Rowan? That was lust, for sure.

"Was he a student, too?" Rowan asked, when Ilaria had gone.

Taylor was confused. Had he said something out loud about Dmitri, about their relationship or their breakup? "What?"

"Did one of your fellow students steal the painting?"

Taylor nodded.

"And you weren't involved at all?"

"I knew he was asked to steal it," he said, looking up at Rowan. "I tried to change his mind, but I couldn't. Then he disappeared and I came here to Nice to look for him."

Taylor hadn't slept well for two nights, and the delicious food made him sleepy. He yawned, and Rowan laughed.

"This is all a big snooze to you?" he asked. "Art theft, dead bodies? You must live a very exciting life if you can yawn at all this."

"I didn't get much sleep on the overnight train Monday night, or last night either, for that matter. Who knew Germans snored so loudly?"

Rowan raised an eyebrow. "You slept with a German? Did you kiss him, too?"

Taylor laughed. "No, just shared a room with him at a hostel. You're the only man I've kissed since I got to Nice." He was starting to feel that he could trust Rowan, that he wasn't alone in this. He only hoped his instincts were right.

Dinner and Conversation

Nice, Wednesday evening

Dmitri's body shook as the door opened. But it was Albin who stepped into the living room, not the flics. "Why you knock?" Dmitri asked.

"Just to warn you," Albin said, as Dmitri skipped across the room and kissed him. "You are still here!"

"You think I will leave?" Dmitri asked, as Albin put down his bag and keys.

Albin nodded. "You are like a beautiful bird, and I did not think you would stay in this cage for so long."

"It's not a cage if I stay here because it please me." Dmitri kissed him again on the lips, then stepped back to survey him, to see how close his memory had come and to judge Albin against the picture, under a cover out on the tiny balcony. Albin was a few inches taller than he was, though that wasn't hard, considering how short Dmitri was. His body was lean and wiry, not too big in any one part.

Albin's hair was too scruffy; he needed a good cut. And he should shave more carefully. But he had a deep-set green eyes, a narrow nose and a wide mouth. With a little care, he would be quite handsome.

Dmitri kissed him a third time, with more passion. Albin wrapped his arms around Dmitri's back and pulled him close. He felt the Frenchman's dick rise as they embraced.

Then Albin pulled back, looking sheepish. "Eh, bien, what will we do for dinner?" he asked. "Italian again, so you can watch for your friend? Only I will not drink as much tonight."

"That is very nice. But tonight is my treat, to thank you." Dmitri had those stolen euros in his pocket; he could put them to good use, taking care of this man who had already been so good to him. They walked downstairs, Albin chattering, and back to the Italian restaurant.

Albin was courtly, offering Dmitri the seat by the window so he could keep an eye out for Yegor, even though Dmitri had begun to believe that his contact would never arrive. There had been some mistake, and Dmitri was left on his own. He had no idea what he would do.

"Tell me about yourself," he said to Albin, as they ate their soup. "I don't know what you do for work."

The Russian Boy

"It is very boring," Albin said. "I work in IT, for a bank. It is nothing like having a talent."

"Sometimes I wish I have no talent," Dmitri said. "If I not have to paint I am still in Odessa, with job and apartment and friends."

The waitress brought their pasta, and they both ate, talking as they did. Dmitri found it so easy to talk to Albin, about his life in Odessa and in Paris. Though Dmitri's French was rough, Albin never pushed him or tried to finish his sentences, as Taylor had. He didn't need to compete with Albin, either, the way he had with Taylor, always wanting to be the best, the most serious artist.

It was quite a relief, he discovered. When the waitress cleared the plates away Albin said, "You have hardly looked outside at all, not like last night. What if your friend has gone into the bar and you did not see?"

Dmitri realized that Albin was right. He had been so busy in conversation that he had forgotten to keep an eye out for Yegor. Though he knew he had to get rid of the painting, for another few minutes he wanted to pretend he was just a guy on a date. He reached out to squeeze Albin's hand. "If he is there, he will wait," he said. "Dessert?"

They ordered chocolate mousse and coffee, and after they finished they looked in at the bar. The bartender confirmed that no one matching Yegor's description had come in. As they walked back to Albin's apartment, the Frenchman said, "What will you do if he does not come?"

"I don't know," Dmitri said. "I cannot go back to Paris."

"Paris is cold and damp in the winter," Albin said. "You don't want to go back there anyway. You should stay here in Nice. I see artists on the Promenade des Anglais. You could paint there and sell your pictures to tourists, just as you did in Paris."

Dmitri considered that idea as they climbed the five flights to Albin's apartment. Would that be enough for him? Would he be able to keep learning and growing as an artist without the pressure of the Institute, the teachers and his fellow students? Perhaps he could sell *The Russian Boy* himself, without Yegor's help. Would the police catch up to him if he no longer had the painting?

By the time they reached Albin's apartment he had resolved not to think any more, at least not then. Once they were inside he turned to Albin, leaned his face up, and kissed him lightly on the lips. Albin grinned broadly, a smile that lit up his face. He wrapped his arms around Dmitri, and Dmitri nestled against Albin's chest.

Then he backed away, took Albin's hand, and led him to the bedroom. In the moonlight, he pulled his T-shirt over his head, kicked off his shoes, and stepped out of his pants. "So handsome," Albin said, with an intake of breath.

"And all for you." Dmitri unbuttoned Albin's cotton work shirt and slipped it off his shoulders. Then he slid his hands beneath Albin's white undershirt, and the Frenchman shivered.

"Not cold, my dear?" Dmitri murmured, his hands roving over Albin's stomach and chest.

"You warm me." Albin leaned down and kissed the top of Dmitri's head, then bent over so that Dmitri could slip the shirt over his head.

Dmitri fumbled with Albin's belt in the dim moonlight, and Albin helped him along, pushing down the pants and kicking off his loafers. His dick was stiff and pressed against his plain white nylon bikini briefs until Dmitri pushed them down.

He led Albin over to the bed, lay down, and patted the place next to him. Albin joined him there, and they kissed. He climbed on top of Albin, discarding his own bikini on the way. He sat on top of Albin's dick, pressing it against his asshole, as his own dick banged against his abdomen. Albin groaned beneath him and reached forward to grasp Dmitri's dick.

He rubbed his ass back and forth over Albin's dick for a few minutes, then slid down so he was resting on the Frenchman, their dicks rubbing against each other. He kissed Albin greedily, sucking on Albin's lips. Was this what love felt like, he wondered. This desire to possess the other completely, a feeling that he could never get enough of the man beneath him?

He had never felt this way with Taylor. Their love making had been rough and furious and fun, like things had been with so many men before him. With Albin, things were different, though he couldn't figure out why.

"I want to have you inside me," he whispered to Albin. "So we are one being."

Albin leaned over to the bedside table and scrabbled in the drawer for a condom, which Dmitri took from him. He opened it and slid it over Albin's stiff dick, then licked the dick up and down to lubricate it. Then he positioned himself over Albin, who looked up at him with eyes glazed with lust.

The Russian Boy

With one quick movement, he slid his ass down over Albin's dick. The momentary pain brought tears to his eyes, but once the dick was impaled in him he felt warmth rising out of that pain.

The Frenchman groaned beneath him, and Dmitri began an up and down motion as Albin panted and then whimpered. Dmitri balanced himself with one hand and put the other on his dick, stroking himself. Albin's cries pushed him harder, though Dmitri himself never made a sound during sex. This was so much better than their first night together, he thought, this connection.

He bounced up and down on the Frenchman and jerked himself fast and hard. Albin squealed and Dmitri felt the rush of his ejaculation, and then he came himself, with a sudden intake of breath and an involuntary exhalation in guttural Russian that surprised both of them.

Honor and Offer

Nice, Wednesday evening

Rowan watched Taylor's face carefully. "You never told me how you knew Yegor Rostnikov."

"I only knew his first name," Taylor said. "And I only saw him once, at a café in Paris. But Dmitri told me all about him."

"Dmitri? Is that who stole the painting?"

Taylor seemed to let loose some of his reserve. "Yes. He's a friend of mine from school."

There was something about the way Taylor spoke that made Rowan think the relationship was more than just a friendship. But he put that idea aside. "Who was this Yegor?" he asked. "A friend of Dmitri's?"

Taylor shook his head. "He started talking to Dmitri one night at a café where we hung out after painting. He knew a lot about Dmitri, which made me suspicious. That he was from Odessa, that he studied at the Institute, and that he had a part-time job there cleaning the studios."

"You were right to be suspicious," Rowan said. "Anyone who knows that much has already done his research. This wasn't a casual meeting."

Taylor ate his pasta and drank another glass of wine, and looking at him, Rowan remembered his own student days, how he had savored everything he ate when he was broke. Somehow, food tasted better when you had to worry about every penny you spent.

When he put his fork down, Taylor said, "Yegor knew that Dmitri was broke, that he had run through his fellowship money and would have to leave Paris if he didn't make some quick cash."

It was an old, established pattern, Rowan thought. Find a mark with access to the goods and figure out his weakness, then exploit it. He ate some of the bouillabaisse, picking out the baby octopus, the only ingredient he couldn't stomach.

"You're not eating that?" Taylor asked.

"Help yourself." He watched as the young man speared the rubbery creature and popped it in his mouth. There was something so sensual about that act. It made him wonder how Taylor's lips would taste after dinner, if Rowan had the chance to kiss him again.

The Russian Boy

He saw Taylor looking at him and realized he'd probably made his intentions too clear. "This Yegor set the hook," he said.

"I tried to stop Dmitri. I said we could get by, that it would be spring by the time his fellowship ran out, and that we'd both sell more paintings at Sacré Coeur. But he was worried he'd have to go back to Odessa, that he'd lose his one chance to succeed in Paris."

"Where is he now?"

"I don't know." Taylor finished the last of his pasta and picked up a piece of bread to soak up the remaining sauce. But looking at the viscous red liquid, he frowned, and then looked back up at Rowan. "What if Dmitri's dead?"

Rowan spooned up the last of the soup in his china bowl then sighed with pleasure and patted his lips with his napkin. "Let's move forward under the assumption that Dmitri is still alive. You're here in Nice because you think Dmitri is here?"

Taylor nodded. "Yegor bought Dmitri a cheap prepaid cell phone. He called Dmitri Friday morning and said that Dmitri should bring *The Russian Boy* to Nice."

"Why Nice?"

"I have no idea. Dmitri knew I didn't approve so he wouldn't tell me anything. He just packed his bag and left the apartment."

"You were living together?"

"Yes. He was my boyfriend."

"If he's not your boyfriend any more, why are you here?"

Taylor sighed. "Dmitri seems tough on the outside, but inside he's still kind of a kid, and he doesn't always think things through. I'm done with him as a boyfriend, but I don't want to see him end up in jail."

Rowan was pleased by the past tense in that statement but tried not to let that show. He pulled his pen and notebook from his jacket. "When did Dmitri leave Paris?"

"I'm not sure. The cheapest way to Nice is the overnight train, but for he could have taken the Metro out to the autoroute and hitchhiked."

"What did you do?"

"I was so pissed off at him for getting caught up in this mess. But then I kept thinking, you know? Like what could happen to him, and that he would need a friend to help him. I had some cash I was saving for paint and I used that for a train ticket." He laughed. "I guess I was kind of naïve myself. I thought I'd come to Nice and find him right away and then we'd go back to Paris."

Ilaria returned and took away their dirty plates, leaving them small cards with a list of desserts. "*Clafoutis*!" Rowan said. "I haven't had that in years."

"What is it?"

"A cherry custard pie." Elizabeth had made that every year when cherries were in season. She was a huge Francophile and loved to cook. Once Rowan was established in his teaching job, she had made coq au vin, moules mariniere, even chateaubriand, along with a host of other dishes. Desserts weren't her specialty, but she had made a killer chocolate mousse along with the clafoutis.

"What looks good to you?" he asked Taylor. The young man's face was flushed, and he was starting to look drunk.

"I don't know. Maybe the Crème Brûlée, or maybe the Tarte Tatin."

"Have them both." He waved Ilaria over and ordered the *mousse au chocolat* and the clafoutis for himself, and both the desserts Taylor wanted, along with two cappuccinos.

When Ilaria had left, Rowan drained the last of his wine and looked back at his notebook. "You arrived yesterday morning? Tuesday? You must have gotten into town a couple of hours before my plane landed."

Taylor nodded. "I went right to the Musée des Beaux Arts. I guess I thought maybe Dmitri had been there."

"But he hadn't been?"

"No. Then I got a list of cheap hotels and hostels from the tourist office and went to every one, showing a picture of Dmitri. No one recognized him."

Rowan wondered, not for the first time, if Dmitri had ever made it to the Riviera. What if the same person who killed Yegor Rostnikov had intercepted Dmitri somewhere, and his body was lying unidentified in a morgue somewhere between Paris and Nice? Or that Dmitri had killed Yegor, and was on the run himself.

"So that was yesterday," he said. "What about today?"

"I hung around the Musée this morning, hoping he'd show up. And then I got hungry and thought I could pick up some cash by painting along the Promenade."

Rowan had gone back to the Negresco after his interview with the Police Judiciare. He'd been staring out his window when he saw a young man at an easel. His curiosity had drawn him outside.

The Russian Boy

"You never thought of going to the police?" he asked.

"I can't," Taylor said. "They'll lock Dmitri up and then send him back to Russia."

"Incarceration or deportation are not unfair punishments for theft."

"But it wasn't Dmitri's fault. That Russian, Yegor, it's his fault."

"And Yegor's dead."

Ilaria brought their cappuccinos. Taylor stirred some sugar into his coffee. Without looking up, he asked, "Where did you find... the body?"

"At the home of a man who creates frames for stolen paintings. A man who's allegedly been dead for three years."

"I don't understand," Taylor said, looking up.

"Join the club. Monday morning, Bruno Desjardins, at the Musée, got a call from a contact of his who had been in a bar, and overhead a Russian—Yegor—talking on a cell phone about the painting. Scarano told me that the Russian had to be talking to a man named Pascal Gaultier, that he was the only framer in Nice who would consider working on a stolen painting."

Rowan took a sip of his cappuccino. It was delicious. "Up till that point, Scarano had thought Gaultier was dead. He gave me the man's name and address, and when I went to his house I found Yegor's body."

"Any sign that Dmitri had been there? Or the painting?"

Rowan shook his head. "Impossible to tell. Did Dmitri have a gun?"

"A gun! No way."

Rosa delivered their desserts with a big smile on her face, and Rowan handed her his credit card. He tasted the clafoutis, and it was every bit as custardy and delicious as he remembered. "You have to try this," he said, lifting a forkful toward Taylor's mouth.

Taylor smiled slyly and opened his lips, and Rowan felt an electric charge through the metal fork as it met the younger man's lips. They traded tastes back and forth, and Rowan felt his face flushing. To steer the conversation back to its purpose, he said, "After we finish, why don't we check some of those hostels and budget hotels again? See if Dmitri has shown up?"

"Can't hurt," Taylor said.

Rowan signed the credit card receipt with a flourish, noting on the back that he had bought dinner for Taylor Griffin, an informant. Ron

Kramer's assistant was a stickler for receipts, and Rowan was glad that she was the one who'd booked him at the Negresco—so that she wouldn't complain about the hotel's prices.

The night was cool and Rowan buttoned up his jacket as Taylor led him through the crowded streets near the train station, stopping at a half-dozen hotels and hostels to show Dmitri's picture.

"This is the place I slept last night," Taylor said, just before midnight. They were in front of a dingy hostel that smelled like burned food and urine. "Let's hope there's a different guy in the bottom bunk tonight," Taylor said. "One who doesn't snore."

Rowan had a feeling that if he let this young man go, he'd never meet him again, and he'd lose the one link he had to the painting and the thief. "That's ridiculous," he said. "There's a sofa in my hotel room in addition to the bed. You can stay with me."

Taylor raised his eyebrows. "Is that a pickup line?"

Rowan felt the heat rise in his groin again and his heart beat faster. It was a ridiculous thought. Taylor was a boy—hardly older than Rowan's son Nick. But he had to ask, "Do you want it to be?"

"Right now, I'd love a comfortable bed in a quiet room," Taylor said.

"I can offer you that."

"Well, then, I accept your offer."

Rowan remembered a bawdy rhyme he'd learned in college. "She offered her honor; he honored her offer. Then all night long he was on her and off her." But there was no chance anything more would happen with Taylor. Taylor needed a bed, and Rowan needed to keep an eye on him. End of story.

Taylor's pack was like a third passenger in the back seat, forcing Rowan and Taylor close to each other. Rowan's leg touched Taylor's, and their hips butted up against each other. Rowan longed to put his arm around Taylor, let the younger man rest his head against his shoulder.

There was something about him that set every nerve in Rowan's body tingling. It wasn't just his youth, or his beauty. He was a handsome man, with dancing eyes, a shock of brown hair that always flopped over his forehead, and clear pale skin that stretched over strong cheekbones.

He had an inner light that glowed, especially when he talked about art. At those times he looked like an El Greco Jesus, full of passion. Rowan looked over at him in the cab, and Taylor grinned. Rowan's

The Russian Boy

heart skipped a beat or two as he drank in that smile.

The cab pulled up at the Negresco and the doorman opened the door. As Rowan paid the fare, Taylor scrambled out, grappling with his backpack. He saw the young man hesitate at the front door, so Rowan took the lead, marching through the lobby with its ornate coffered ceiling and marble fireplace. They took a wrought-iron elevator up to Rowan's floor, and he unlocked the room and stepped back to usher Taylor in.

Seeing the room through Taylor's eyes, Rowan realized how over-the-top it was. The Oriental carpet was faded just enough to seem authentic, not a modern reproduction. The ornately carved sideboard, where Rowan had tossed his suit bag, looked as fine an antique as any in a Madison Avenue shop. A divan that would have been at home in Madame Recamier's 18th century Paris salon was poised against the wall, next to windows overlooking the Bay of Angels.

And the bed. For Christ's sake, the four-poster had a carved wooden valance over it, and a silk bedspread in a black and gray pinstripe. It was a bed for an odalisque in an Ingres painting. At the same time, though, Rowan imagined Taylor sprawled naked on rumpled sheets, smiling at him the way he had in the cab. His dick swelled, pressing against his pants. Through the open door he spied the marble bathroom, with its gold sinks and tub, and in the floor-length mirror he watched Taylor's reaction.

"There must be a lot of money in being a detective," Taylor said finally.

"Nope. The NYMFA is footing the bill for this trip." He noticed that the young man stood there, looking paralyzed. "You probably want to take a shower. You can leave your pack over there."

"Yeah." Taylor left the pack leaning against the wall and went into the bathroom. A moment later, Rowan heard the shower run.

His stiff dick pulsed at the thought of the young man naked, the water running down his gorgeous body, soap lathering at his groin. Was he hard, too, Rowan wondered? He'd noticed a few glances over the course of the evening. Would Taylor say or do something?

He shrugged. They were both tired, and each wanted something from the other—something that had nothing to do with sex. He sat down on the sofa and was startled to discover how rigid and unforgiving it was. Taylor could never sleep there.

The bed it was, then. They'd have to share. He turned down the covers on each side, carefully preserving a space between where their two bodies would lie, and stripped to his boxers. The shower stopped, and Rowan took a moment to pause before an ornate Louis XIV mirror and look at himself.

He was still handsome, he thought, in a fifty-year-old way. He could never compete with the fresh beauty of a twenty-something, but his stomach was firm, his chest dusted with golden hairs (and a few white mixed in), and his dick still worked just fine.

He didn't hear the door open. "Checking out the view?" Taylor asked, smiling.

Taylor looked impossibly young, framed in the bathroom light, only an oversized white towel wrapped around his waist. Droplets of water glistened on his hairless chest, and his brown hair was damp and tousled.

"The sofa's too hard," Rowan said. "You wouldn't get a wink of sleep. We'll have to share the bed."

"Said the big bad wolf to Little Red Riding Hood," Taylor said.

"I don't see any hood on you," Rowan said.

"So you didn't realize that I'm not circumcised?" Taylor asked. "I saw you looking at me closely enough."

Rowan knew that game. He'd played it himself a time or two. Distract the subject with thoughts of sex. But if he had sex with Taylor then, he'd feel he was taking advantage. If they did go to bed, it would be when both were sober, and neither had anything to gain other than pleasure.

"I'm going to bed," he said. "I suggest you do the same."

Taylor pouted. Rowan guessed he didn't get rejected often. Well, here's a life lesson for you, he thought. He slid between the sheets on one side of the bed, and said, "Turn the lights out when you're ready."

He rested his head against the pillow, facing away from Taylor, but did not close his eyes. The lights went out, and he heard the soft noise of Taylor's towel falling to the ground. Christ, was the boy coming to bed naked?

A moment later, Taylor slid in beside Rowan. This is when he'll make his play, he thought, waiting for the boy's hand to reach out to him, caress his shoulder or the curve of his ass. He found himself holding his breath, waiting for it.

But there was nothing. And then, a few moments later, he heard Taylor's slow, rhythmic breathing, just the hint of a snore as breath ruffled his lips.

The Life of an Artist

Nice, December 1912

Alexei's parents, his older brother, Gavril, the heir to the title, and his younger sister, Natasha, all arrived in mid-December to spend a few months at the villa, away from the frigid St. Petersburg winter.

On a Sunday just before the Orthodox Christmas, his parents threw a party at the Villa des Oliviers and invited all those who mattered in the Russian community. The warm glow over the villa's grounds combined with glasses of iced vodka to bring a festive mood to the assembled company.

Late in the afternoon, Alexei stepped outside to watch the sun drop slowly over the foothills of the Alps. He was joined there a moment later by his older brother.

Gavril looked like his father—the same pale blond hair, pointed nose and military bearing. He and Alexei had never been close; even as boys they had rarely played together. Gavril had an army of metal soldiers and often reenacted the battles of the Russo-Japanese war, in which their father had served as a cavalry officer in the Battle of Yalu River.

Alexei preferred playing with a series of small animal toys, for whom he constructed tea parties, complete with a miniature samovar he had found in a storeroom at their country dacha.

The two had little to say to each other, so they stood there awkwardly, staring at the sunset, until Alexei said, "How goes it with your application to the Horse Guards?"

The Horse Guards were the oldest cavalry regiment in the Imperial Russian Guards' Corps, and the most prestigious. Their father had served in the Horse Guards as a young man, as had their grandfather. Even so, Gavril had to submit to a rigorous examination and secret ballot.

"It will be at least another six months before I am notified," Gavril said. "Papa has already purchased me the two black chargers I will require, however." He turned to his brother. "And you? Your painting studies are going well?"

Alexei nodded. "I learn more each day."

"And you are not… bothered… by the man's reputation?"

"What reputation is that?"

Their sister Natasha came to the doorway. "Papa would like you inside. It is time for the unveiling of the painting of Grandmamma."

Natasha looked like her mother, with a mass of dark curls and a simple, plain face. She was a quiet girl who excelled at needlework and the piano. She would be brought out to society soon, with the expectation that she would be matched with a wealthy husband.

In Alexei, the best characteristics of both parents had combined. He had his father's blond hair, but it was thick and wavy like his mother's. The severe cheekbones and thin nose he inherited from his father merged with his mother's broad forehead and full lips. In truth, the whole was much greater than the sum of the parts.

Alexei and Gavril followed Natasha inside, Alexei puzzling over his brother's comments. What kind of reputation did the maestro have, other than one of artistic excellence?

Their parents stood at the front of the salon, along with the Dowager Countess, and the Count motioned his children to join them. An easel with an old tablecloth over it stood to their left; on the other side of the easel was Fyodor Luschenko. The crowd represented a Who's Who of Russian Nice, the ranks of minor royalty combined with those of great wealth.

The Count welcomed the group, and then turned to Luschenko.

"Some portraits," the painter said, "require a greater degree of artistry than others. But with a beautiful subject as the countess, it requires only to recreate what nature has done such a wonderful job with."

The Dowager Countess blushed. Luschenko pulled the tablecloth off the portrait and the audience gasped. He had painted the Dowager Countess in a pensive mood, sitting in a window seat with a floral cover, the green lawns of the villa and the ocean behind her. It was a beautiful image, filled with the watery light that Alexei had admired in the work of Monet and Luschenko.

"It's marvelous!" the Dowager Countess exclaimed. "Fyodor, you are truly an artist!"

She kissed him on both cheeks, then turned to Alexei. "You must learn much from our darling Fyodor."

The family stepped aside so that the crowd could survey the painting, and the Count complimented Luschenko on capturing his mother's very spirit.

Gavril nodded. "It is quite nice." To his brother, he said, "You'll

The Russian Boy

never be that good, though."

"Alexei has a talent," Luschenko said. "It just requires nurturing. Show your parents the sketches you have made."

"Oh, no," Alexei said. "I cannot follow your masterpiece!"

"Come, come," the Count said. "Let me see the results of your apprenticeship."

Alexei reluctantly collected his sketchbook from his room, and laid it out on a table overlooking the ocean. His parents, his brother and sister, and his grandmother crowded around, as the rest of the room oohed and aahed over the portrait of the Dowager Countess.

Luschenko stepped over and flipped the book open to one of Alexei's earliest attempts at the landscape before them. "You can see he has some talent," Luschenko said, turning the page so the family could see it. "The composition is interesting, the way the eye follows the arc of the waves across the page. But his lines are too simple, too tentative."

He flipped forward a few pages. "Here is the same view, a few weeks after he began to apprentice with me. See how much stronger the hand is, already? And the attention to detail here, in the trees?"

"Yes, it is better," the Count said, nodding.

"And now, we see what Alexei is working on today," Luschenko said, flipping to the last page. "Now that he understands lines and composition better, I have allowed him to begin using watercolor. He has a real talent for color, as you see."

The last image was a similar view of the ocean, but Alexei had begun filling in the waves with a combination of indigo, pale blue and white. The picture was not finished yet, but the color sprung up from the page, and looking from it to the view, the Count commented, "How marvelous! Alexei, you have learned so much in just a few months!"

Alexei blushed at his father's praise. It was not unaccustomed; because of his great physical beauty his parents had always favored him and anything he tried, no matter how poorly he performed. But this time, Alexei thought he could see real admiration in the Count's face.

"Of course, he still has much to learn," Luschenko said. "There is only so much I can teach in the few hours a day we are together. The apprentices of old, you understand, lived with their masters and worked many more hours at their art."

"Would you consider allowing Alexei to live with you?" the Count asked. "Of course, I would increase the remittance paid to you, to accommodate your extra expense."

Alexei's heart rushed. He wanted nothing more than to spend every moment with the maestro—eating, painting, sleeping, making love. He held his breath waiting for the maestro's response.

"It would be up to the Dowager Countess," Luschenko said, looking at Alexei's grandmother. "I would not like to steal your companion away from you."

"I hardly see my grandson as it is," she said. "Between his time with you, and his furious drawing and painting till all hours. If you promise to bring him each Sunday for dinner—coming yourself as well, of course—then I think I can spare him."

Out of the corner of his eye, Alexei saw Gavril frown, and wondered again what his brother had meant.

"A most gracious request," Luschenko said, bowing his head slightly. "I would be pleased to honor it."

"It's settled, then," the Count said.

Alexei wanted to jump up and down with glee. He wanted to grab the maestro in his arms for a deep kiss, feel the older man grasp his straining erection, strip off his clothes and make love right there on the lawn. But instead he restrained himself, and said only, "Thank you, father. I will do my best to make you proud of me."

The party broke up soon after and Alexei went up to his bedroom to pack a trunk of his work clothes, his toiletries, and his art supplies. His brother appeared in the doorway as he was finishing. "I understand you have been riding every day," Gavril said. "Will you come for a ride with me before you leave?"

Alexei was surprised, but felt he couldn't ignore his brother's request. One day, their father would die, and Gavril would be the head of the family. If Alexei chose to become an artist, he would have to depend on his brother's good will—and his fortune.

"It would be a pleasure," he said.

They walked to the stables in silence, where the groom had already prepared two horses for them—the pony that Alexei rode regularly, and a black stallion for Gavril. "Your new horse?" Alexei asked.

"One of them. The other remained in St. Petersburg."

Gavril rode uphill and Alexei followed. When they reached to the empty countryside above the city, Gavril spurred his horse forward. Alexei was nowhere near as good a rider as his brother, nor was his horse as strong, but he shook the reins and pressed his feet into the horse's flanks, and soon both brothers were streaking across the

The Russian Boy

hillside. When they reached a promontory with a view of the city, Gavril reined his stallion in, and Alexei stopped beside him.

"You are not a bad rider, little brother," Gavril said.

"Not so little. Remember, I am only two years younger than you are."

"But you are younger, and it is my responsibility to look after you." He turned his horse sideways to look at Alexei. "I am worried about your association with this painter."

"Worried? Why?"

"It is not to be spoken of." Gavril's blond hair shimmered in the last fading rays of the sun.

"Then how am I to know what you are talking about?"

Gavril frowned. "They say... they say he lies with men, as a man should lie with a woman."

Alexei burst into laughter. How foolish of Gavril not to realize Alexei would already know that! But then he looked at his brother's stern face and knew he had to lie. He composed himself and said, "You see me laugh, brother. The maestro has treated me only as a disciple. There has been nothing of what you suggest in his behavior toward me."

Gavril nodded. "Well, I felt I should warn you. If he makes any approach, you simply tell me, and I will deal with it."

Alexei smiled. "Thank you, brother. I appreciate your concern."

"Good. Then we should return for dinner."

He spurred his horse homeward, and Alexei followed. The maestro had been right; people did disapprove of men who slept with men. He resolved he would have to be very careful when others were around.

After dinner, the footman drove Alexei and Luschenko down to the studio, and dragged Alexei's trunk upstairs. When he was gone, Alexei finally indulged himself by taking his master's hand and squeezing it. "I am so happy to be here."

Luschenko leaned across to him and traced the outline of Alexei's lips with his tongue. Alexei's whole body yielded to the touch, pressing his chest against his maestro's. Then the painter stepped back, and yawned. "Too much good wine at dinner," he said. "I am not at my best. Come, we will sleep together for the first time."

By the time Alexei had taken off his good clothes and hung them carefully over a chair, the maestro had already stripped down and gotten under the cotton comforter. Alexei donned a long cotton nightshirt and slid into bed next to him. The maestro pulled him close, with one arm draped protectively over him, and they both fell into sleep.

In the morning, Alexei awoke to Luschenko's hands under his nightshirt. "You are so beautiful," the maestro said, between kisses. "You are my inspiration, my love. As I painted your grandmother's portrait I felt something new evolve in my work--a passion that I had been missing for so long." He took Alexei's right nipple in his mouth, licking and nibbling at it, and Alexei squirmed under the tantalizing preview of what would happen when his dick entered the maestro's mouth in the same way.

"I can see it in the portrait—the strength of my brushwork, the way the light illuminates. It is as if I am pouring my semen into the painting, the way I pour it into you when you embrace me."

The painter licked his way down Alexei's hairless chest, stopping to explore his navel, and all the while Alexei groaned and squirmed and begged to be sucked. "Please, maestro," he said, over and over again, trying to push the maestro's head downward to his dick, which leaked precum and strained with emotion and passion.

"I must experience you completely," Luschenko said, pulling back. "Please fetch me the hand cream that the Princess Mariana gave me for my chapped hands."

Alexei was confused, but he said, "Yes, maestro." He got out of bed, shucked his nightshirt, and found the pot of cream on a low table across from the bed.

To that point, the only way in which Luschenko had penetrated his apprentice had been with his tongue and fingers. Luschenko took the jar of cream from Alexei and said, "Turn your back to me, please, and bend over, holding onto the table."

Alexei had no idea why he was asked to do so, but he did.

"Such a beautiful ass," Luschenko said, rubbing the flat of his palm gently against one cheek, then the other. Then he pried the two apart, and assaulted the crack with his tongue. Alexei's dick sprang to attention and his body shivered at the warm, moist touch.

Luschenko withdrew his tongue, then stood up. Alexei looked to his side and see his maestro's dick sticking out from his body at a forty-five degree angle. "Give me your hand," Luschenko said.

Alexei remained bent over the table, balancing on his right hand, as he extended his left to the maestro, who tipped some hand cream into it. "Rub it on me," he said.

The Russian Boy

Alexei reached for the maestro's hand—but the painter pulled it away. "Not my hand, silly boy. On my dick."

"Oh." Alexei loved the feel of the maestro's warm, stiff dick in his hand, and he rubbed the cream gently up and down its length.

"That's enough." Luschenko stepped behind Alexei again, who shivered to feel more of the cream greasing his ass, as the maestro snaked a finger straight up into him. "If you like that, you'll love what's to come," Luschenko said.

He pried Alexei's ass cheeks apart, and Alexei felt something hard and warm pressing against his channel. He gasped as the maestro's dick penetrated him, then cried out in pain. "Breathe," Luschenko ordered. "Take deep breaths. The pain will pass."

Alexei didn't see how it could. It felt like he was being impaled on a sword as the maestro jammed his dick inside Alexei's ass. He cried and whimpered and begged, but the maestro kept on fucking him.

And then, almost magically, the pain in his guts turned to a fire that warmed him. He stopped crying and focused on the sensations of pleasure that swarmed through him. It felt like he and the maestro were merging into one being and he began to buck back onto the painter.

They set up a ferocious rhythm, Luschenko slamming into Alexei, the table shaking. Luschenko howled and his cum spurted out of his dick and up Alexei's ass, and the boy's dick erupted without ever being touched, spraying white viscous fluid on the table top and on a sketch of a minor Russian noblewoman.

Luschenko was just pulling his dick out when someone knocked on the studio door. "Jesus, she is early!" Luschenko panted. "One moment," he called out in breathless French. "Go, go, clean yourself up," he told Alexei. "We will continue this lesson later."

Alexei's ass ached as he scrambled around the room, picking up his clothes and then scampering behind the screen to clean up and dress. But already he was thinking of the next lesson the maestro could teach him.

Room Service

Nice, Thursday morning

Rowan woke to find Taylor snuggled into his side, the younger man's arm over Rowan's shoulder. Gently, he extricated himself and used the bathroom. When he finished, he used the phone there to order room service for himself and Taylor.

Then he sat at the ornate Louis XVI table by the window and opened his laptop. As he watched Taylor sleep, he opened his email program and retrieved his latest messages.

The first was from Ron Kramer, titled "New Developments in Theft." He clicked it open.

Paris police interviewed the staff at the Institute des Artistes, Kramer wrote. *A student named Dmitri Baranov, who cleaned the studios at night, is missing, and the police are looking for him. Also missing is his roommate, potential accomplice. Pictures of both are attached.*

Rowan glanced up at the message header. There were two attachments; one was called Baranov, the other Griffin. He looked at the first, then the second.

A knock at the door startled him, and he realized it must be room service. He put on a white terrycloth robe, tying the belt, and went to the door, as Taylor stirred on the bed.

The valet was young, barely out of his teens, in a uniform that was slightly too large for him. "Bonjour, M'sieur," he said, holding out a tray with a carafe of coffee, another of hot chocolate, and a plate with a half-dozen chocolate croissants.

Rowan took the tray and placed it on the table next to his laptop, then signed the check for the valet, who closed the door quietly behind him.

"Room service?" Taylor said. "Did I do something last night I've forgotten about?"

"Good morning to you, too." Rowan flipped the laptop closed. "Want to join me?"

Taylor stretched, his biceps rippling. His blond hair was tousled, sticking up on one side like wheat sheaves in a painting by Van Gogh. He looked around him, obviously searching for his clothes, which he'd left in the bathroom the night before. "Um..." Taylor said.

"I've seen naked men before," Rowan said. "Even a few as handsome as you are. You don't need to be bashful."

The Russian Boy

"Well, then."

Taylor flipped the covers back, stood up, and stretched again. His body was gorgeous, Rowan thought. He had long, lean arms and legs, a flat belly, and what looked like a generous dick nestled half-hard in a bush of dark blonde pubic hair. He sauntered past Rowan, into the bathroom.

When he came out, a few minutes later, he was wearing a pair of skimpy briefs in form-fitting black nylon. "You didn't need to dress up on my account," Rowan said.

"Is that coffee?" Taylor said, sniffing, as Rowan filled an oversized cup.

"I'm making café mocha. Half hot chocolate, half coffee, with a generous dollop of heavy cream. You want?"

"You bet."

He sat across from Rowan at the table and accepted his cup with both hands, then drank deeply. "This is nectar," he said, sighing, when he had finished.

"Here, have some ambrosia." Rowan pushed the platter of chocolate croissants toward him, taking one for himself. The pastries were flaky and buttery, filled with rich chocolate that oozed out onto his lips.

"You know how to spoil a guy," Taylor said.

"Oh, honey, I haven't even started to spoil you." Rowan laughed. "Did I actually say that?"

"Oh, you did," Taylor said, rubbing his foot against Rowan's bare leg. "I might just hold you to that."

Rowan's dick swelled beneath the robe, but he pushed aside what he'd like to do with Taylor Griffin.

"Business before pleasure," he said, pulling the laptop toward him. He opened it again, then clicked to open the two attachments. "Recognize him?" he said, turning the computer's screen toward Taylor.

"Dmitri. How'd you get that?"

"Paris police are looking for him." The photo must have come from Dmitri Baranov's passport, because one corner was stamped with Cyrillic characters Rowan recognized as spelling out Ukraine. Dmitri looked like a teenager, with short dark hair, pimply skin and the faintest hint of a mustache.

"Shit." Taylor put down his half-eaten chocolate croissant. "Dumb fuck. I can't believe I let him get himself into this mess."

"There's another picture. I recognized this one." Rowan minimized the photo of Dmitri, leaving the one of Taylor on the screen.

"Mother fucker." Taylor's mouth dropped open.

Taylor's passport photo didn't do him justice—but then, whose did? Especially when it was being sent around in place of a mug shot. "You guys are a pair of complete fuck-ups, you know that?" Rowan said casually. "You didn't consider that the cops would want to interview everyone who had access to the studios?"

"Dmitri was supposed to hand off the picture in Paris," Taylor said, through gritted teeth. "I told him he'd have to talk to the police, but he thought he could bluff them, just pretend to be a dumb Russian."

"Instead he left town."

"It wasn't his idea. The only way he could deliver the painting and get his money was to follow Yegor down here."

"And you? You didn't consider sticking around, telling the police what you knew?"

Taylor looked up at him. "Not for a minute. I wouldn't turn on Dmitri."

"Not even to save your own hide? I don't believe that."

"I cared about him. That kind of thing matters to me."

Rowan sipped his café mocha, then leaned back in his chair. "I couldn't help but notice the past tense there. What happened between you? Someone else?"

"Only Yegor. And not like that. I tried to convince Dmitri this was a stupid idea, but he wouldn't listen."

"And?"

Taylor sighed. "It was somewhere in the middle of the argument. I looked at him, and I realized that I liked Dmitri. We had fun together. But I didn't love him." He looked down at the table. "I didn't even know him."

He looked back up at Rowan. "You can't love someone you don't know, can you?"

"Innocent youth. You can love someone you've never even met, and then meeting him can break your heart."

Taylor picked up his chocolate croissant and took another bite. He chewed, then said, "Are you going to call the police? Are they already on their way—did you call them when I was asleep?"

"No. Calling the police doesn't serve either of us."

The Russian Boy

"What do you mean?"

"If I turn you over to the cops, I lose the only connection I have to the painting. They'll keep you locked up somewhere, hell, maybe even ship you back to the States. I need you here, helping me figure out what Dmitri's next move is going to be, and where the damn painting is."

"What are you going to do if we find him?"

"That depends on Dmitri. If we can get the painting back before the cops implicate him any further in the theft, there's a chance he can play dumb. He could say Yegor threatened him, and that's why he ran. Make it look like Yegor stole the painting himself."

"You could do that?"

"Your ex-boyfriend is out there somewhere with a half-million dollar painting, the guy who hired him is dead, and the cops are closing in. The best thing we can do right now is find him, and find the painting. Then we worry about spinning the story."

"But I don't know where he could be," Taylor said. "How could he just disappear? Unless he's dead."

"Don't think that way. Put yourself in his position. You're all alone in Nice, you're scared, you're short on cash."

"Not hard for me to imagine."

"So what do you do?"

Taylor's eyes widened and a smile played on his lips.

"What?" Rowan asked. "You thought of something."

Taylor looked down at the table.

"Come on, Taylor. We're drowning here. Anything you can think of helps."

When Taylor looked up again, his eyes glistened, but his mouth was set in a hard line. "I'd pick up a guy and go home with him. No need to spend money on a hotel or hostel. No way anyone can track me. And if I'm lucky, he gives me breakfast before he kicks me out on the street."

Rowan leaned his head back and roared with laughter. "Now we're getting somewhere."

"I'm not Dmitri," Taylor said.

Rowan smiled. "I know."

On the Balcony

Nice, Thursday morning

While Rowan used in the bathroom, Taylor woke the laptop and logged into his own email account. He and Dmitri often used email to connect with each other, since neither of them had cell phones. There were computers at the Institute students could use, and they both had an arrangement with the manager of Café SiSi. If they'd sit in the front window of the café, looking decorative, they could have free Internet access.

He scanned through the list of messages. A couple of pieces of spam, a notice from the Institute about registration for the upcoming semester. And then, from the day before, an email from Dmitri. He clicked it open just as Rowan walked out of the bathroom with a towel around his waist.

Taylor looked up from the computer. Rowan was a hell of a handsome man, Taylor thought. His face was just lived-in enough to be interesting, with a few laugh lines around his full, very kissable mouth. His sideburns were shaggy, as if he hadn't trimmed them for a few weeks, and gray predominated. But the rest of his hair was brown, with just a few gray streaks.

Droplets of water glistened off Rowan's beefy pecs as he stood there. His flat stomach disappeared behind the white towel. Taylor felt his dick stiffen. What would Rowan be like in bed, he wondered? Taylor had never slept with an older man, and he thought he might like that very much.

"Anything interesting on line?" Rowan asked, nodding toward the laptop.

"Oh. Yeah. There's a message from Dmitri." He leaned back against the spindly, gilt-covered chair and pointed at the screen.

"Really?" Rowan hurried across the room to stand behind him, and Taylor smelled the fresh scent of his soap and shampoo.

They read the message together. "My god, that's the bar where I met Scarano," Rowan said, pointing at the name. "Dmitri might have even been there when I was there, and I didn't know. Fuck me."

"Maybe later, dude," Taylor said, not even realizing what he'd said until the words had spilled out of his mouth.

"I'll take that under advisement." Rowan pulled off his towel and

The Russian Boy

walked naked back to the bathroom. Taylor couldn't help following his tight ass, noticing the thin trail of fine hairs that ran down his crack. Rowan tossed his towel into the bathroom and turned toward the dresser. "Are you watching me or getting yourself dressed, picture boy? We've got a lead and we've got to get moving."

"*Carpe diem*," Taylor said. "It means seize the day. Something looks good, I look at it."

"I know more Latin than you'll ever forget. If you don't get your act together I'll be seizing something more than your day."

A shiver ran through Taylor's body at the thought of Rowan seizing him. But he pulled a clean T-shirt and shorts from his duffle as the older man got his boxers and slacks on. "You think Dmitri will be hanging around this bar?" Taylor asked.

Rowan buttoned his shirt. "I figure the bar won't be open until at least noon, but I'd like to walk over there and get a feel for the neighborhood. It's our only lead, so we're going to have to hope it pays off."

"What if he's already handed off the painting?" Taylor said.

"To Yegor? He's dead, remember?"

"Oh, yeah. But Dmitri won't know that."

"Points to the boy from Illinois," Rowan said, as they left the hotel room.

"I'm not a boy. I'm twenty-five."

"I'm fifty," Rowan said. "You're a boy to me."

"Ah, but I can be a man to you, too."

Rowan threw a sharp glance at him. "Save that thought for later. Unless you're so tired tonight that you fall asleep again as soon as your head hits the pillow."

Taylor felt his mouth go dry as they stepped into the elevator.

They rode down in silence, then walked out the front door of the Negresco. The sky was a crystalline blue, with just a few cirrus clouds. The air was fresh and crisp. Across from them, a paraglider in a rainbow-colored chute flew just above the ocean.

Rowan hailed a taxi and said, "Cours Saleya," to the driver. When Taylor was seated next to him, he said, "It's the open square where they hold the Marché aux Fleurs. The bar is a block or two away from the market. It'll be a good place for us to start looking."

The traffic on the Promenade des Anglais was stop and go, and Taylor fidgeted in the cab. "We're going to find him," Rowan said quietly. "Don't worry."

Taylor turned to look at him. "You thought that I…" he stopped. "That's not why I'm nervous."

Rowan's eyes met Taylor's, and there was a warmth, and a mischief, between them. "Oh," Rowan said. "Well."

"Yes. Well."

The cab pulled up a moment later, and they could see the colorful striped awnings of the flower market through a tall arch. Rowan paid the cabbie and they stepped out onto the broad sidewalk. The sun was sparkling off the ocean waves, and tourists in shorts and T-shirts were already lining the rocky beach.

Rowan put his arm around Taylor's shoulder. "Let's go find a painting, shall we?"

Taylor felt overwhelmed with sensation as they crossed the street and stepped through the archway to the Marché aux Fleurs. His shoulder tingled where Rowan's hand rested, and the rest of him was assailed by the colors, sounds and smells of the market.

He wanted to pull out his easel and start painting—capturing the profusion of iris, lilies and carnation, the piles of tiny round melons, the rough script of the price signs. A Serge Gainsbourg song he had often heard in Paris was playing from an iPod hooked to speakers at the lavender vendor's stall, and the fragrance combined with the music to be nearly hypnotizing.

The garish colors of the gerbera daisies demanded the brightest colors in his palette, while the pile of ferns wanted the darkest green. "Beautiful," Rowan breathed next to him.

"I want to paint it," Taylor said. "Right now. I can't take it all in otherwise."

"We'll come back. Once we find both of the Russian boys we're looking for."

Taylor sighed. "I guess you're right."

"Do you think the market would have the same effect on Dmitri?"

"We're different," Taylor said. "I love color and light. Dmitri's more interested in texture, in contrast." He looked around for an example. "See that rooftop up there?" He pointed down a narrow street that led off the market. "The way the downspout has stained the tile? Dmitri would paint that."

Rowan followed Taylor's gaze. "Look up there," Rowan said. "There's a guy on a balcony with an easel. Looks like he's got the same idea."

Taylor looked where Rowan was pointing, to a man hunched over

The Russian Boy

a canvas. There was something familiar in the way the man held his brush in his right hand, the loose grip he maintained on the palette with his left.

"Jesus," he said. "It's Dmitri."

Inside the Apartment

Nice, Thursday morning

"What the hell is he doing up there?" Taylor asked

"Looks like painting to me," Rowan said. "But more important, who's in the apartment with him? It can't be Yegor, because he's dead. And it doesn't look like Dmitri's a prisoner, either."

"Maybe I called it," Taylor said. "Dmitri picked up a guy."

"Keep going." Rowan put his hand on the small of Taylor's back and gave him a gentle push. They hurried through the market to the narrow street, four- and five-story buildings hemming them in. Rowan alternated navigating with keeping an eye on Dmitri on the balcony above.

They approached the building, and Taylor opened his mouth to call up to Dmitri, but Rowan clutched his arm. "Let's take this easy," he said softly.

Taylor nodded. The tall wooden door that led into the building was patterned with incised rectangles, and surmounted by a half-round arch. A column of buzzers stood by its side. Rowan peered closely. "No concierge." He tested the handle. It wouldn't turn.

"You're not seeing this," Rowan said to Taylor. He pulled a small leather case from his pocket, and withdrew a thin metal file with a pointed end. He inserted the file in the lock, jiggled it a couple of times, and then the handle turned.

"Cool," Taylor said, as Rowan replaced the pick.

"Just one of my many skills," Rowan said. "Now, on to the fifth floor."

The stairs curved around and around like an Escher drawing, the marble worn from centuries of footsteps. By the fourth floor Rowan was winded, and stopped to catch his breath. Taylor, on the other hand, was full of energy.

"I want you to knock when we get up there," Rowan said. "Call out for Dmitri. See if he'll open the door for you. Then I'll come in behind you."

"What if he's not alone?"

"I'll stay back until we see what's up. If I need to, I'll call in the gendarmes."

Taylor was scared, but he didn't want Rowan to think he was a coward. "OK." He climbed the last curving set of stairs, and took a

The Russian Boy

moment to orient himself, figuring out which apartment had a balcony that faced the street. Then he knocked.

There was no answer.

He rapped again, and called out in French, "Dmitri. It's me. Taylor."

He waited, his ears focused for any sound from inside the apartment, and then he heard footsteps, and the sound of a body pressed against the door. An eye peered through the fisheye lens, and then the door popped open.

"Taylor!" Dmitri said, embracing him. "But how did you find me?"

He tried to kiss Taylor, but Taylor backed away, motioning Rowan to come up beside him. "I have someone with me. This is Rowan."

"Can we go inside?" Rowan asked.

Dmitri looked from Rowan to Taylor, and back again. Then he shrugged and retreated into the apartment.

Taylor followed Dmitri into a small living room, and Dmitri sat down on a battered old couch covered with a bright yellow Provençal throw like the tablecloths in the restaurant where Taylor and Rowan had eaten the night before. Taylor followed him, sitting at one side of a small kitchen table.

Rowan closed the door behind him, then sat across from Dmitri. "Rowan's a private detective from New York," Taylor said. "The NYMFA hired him to find *The Russian Boy*."

"And you led him to me!" Dmitri said angrily.

"Yes, because you're an idiot, and you're in trouble. Yegor is dead, you know."

Dmitri's mouth dropped open. "Dead? But how? And how do you know?"

Rowan took over, picking the French words carefully. He explained how he'd been hired, that he had spoken with Bruno Desjardins at the museum and been sent to the bar to meet Rene Scarano.

"Old man I meet in bar tell me about you," Dmitri said. "You are in bar asking about Yegor."

Rowan nodded. "A man I spoke to gave me the name of a man who frames stolen paintings, but who is supposed to have been dead for three years."

From the confusion on Dmitri's face, Taylor thought Rowan had confused his tenses. "People say this man is dead, but he may not be," he explained.

Dmitri still looked confused. "But you say Yegor is dead?"

Rowan nodded. "I got to the house, and discovered a dead body. The police came, and took me for questioning. They told me the dead man's name was Yegor Rostnikov."

"You can describe him?" Dmitri asked.

"Heavyset, dark hair, a soul patch here." He used the English words because he had no idea what the French term was, and fingered his chin for emphasis.

Dmitri sat back on the sofa as if all the air had been punched out of him. "What am I to do?" he asked.

"Simple," Rowan said. "Turn the painting over to me. I'll take it back to Paris and return it to the restorer so he can finish his work."

"But the police?" Dmitri asked.

"If I can get the painting back, the police don't have to be concerned," Rowan said.

Taylor had a feeling that wasn't true, but he wasn't going to say anything. Somehow, with just a single kiss, he had transferred his allegiance from Dmitri to Rowan. He didn't want the Russian hurt—but he realized he was on Rowan's side, and had been since that moment outside the museum.

Rowan looked around the rumpled living room. "Now tell me, where is it? Is it here, in this apartment?"

Dmitri was about to speak when they all heard the sound of a key in the apartment door. Taylor looked up as a worn-looking Frenchman in his thirties walked in, saying, "I am home for lunch, my little one," then stopped to stare at all of them.

The Russian Boy

A Trip to the Station

Nice, Thursday morning

Dmitri stayed on the sofa. He had no idea what to do next. Fortunately the older American helped him out.

Rowan stood up and extended his hand to the Frenchman. "My apologies, M'sieur," he said. "We are acquaintances of your friend here. I am Rowan McNair, from New York, and this is Taylor Griffin, from Illinois."

The man shook Rowan's hand, but looked back at Dmitri, who nodded and stood up shakily.

"What is going on?" the man asked.

"This is my friend Albin," Dmitri said to Taylor and Rowan. "He let me stay with him, while I wait for Yegor."

"Dmitri has something that does not belong to him," Rowan said to Albin. "As soon as he gives it to me, so I can return it to its rightful owner, we'll leave you alone."

"It's almost over, Dmitri," Taylor said. "Just give Rowan the painting and we can go back to Paris and be safe."

"But what I do for money if I give painting up now? And what will police do?" He looked at Rowan. "Is there reward for returning painting?"

Rowan laughed. "Not for the thief, my friend. It should be reward enough that you don't end up like Yegor."

Dmitri looked around him. Albin was confused, Taylor angry. He didn't know Rowan and he didn't trust him. What could he do to turn the situation to his advantage? None of the three men looked like they were ready for seduction.

He remembered a time when he was six, back in Odessa. He had stolen a candy bar from the local store, and the owner caught him. He had begun to cry then, and the man took pity on him and let him go with a stern warning.

It was worth a try. He dredged up a memory of a small dog he'd had when he was a boy, who had been run over, and how he felt seeing the dog's mangled body in the street. He began to cry as he let the true danger of his situation wash over him.

Albin immediately crossed the room to him and took him in his arms. "Do not cry, my little one."

Taylor looked at Rowan and said, "You don't have to be mean to him."

Dmitri resisted the impulse to smile at how easily these men could be manipulated.

Rowan, however, was not moved. He turned to Albin. "Let's not forget how things stand. Dmitri stole a painting worth half a million dollars from a studio at the school where he studies in Paris. The man who hired him to steal the painting is dead, and Dmitri's in danger until he gives me the painting to return."

"This is true?" Albin asked Dmitri.

Dmitri nodded.

Albin removed his arms from Dmitri's shoulders and stepped away. "I should never have gone down to meet you. You have brought danger into my house. You, who look like such an innocent boy! I must learn to follow my head, not my dick."

"I'm sorry, Albin," Dmitri said in a small voice. "I do not mean to hurt you or put you in danger." His tears did not seem so fake to him anymore, as he looked at Albin's face.

Albin stood there with his arms crossed. Dmitri looked from him to Rowan, who said, "The painting, Dmitri?"

Dmitri did not see any other options. "All right. But painting is not here. I take it out of frame and carry in cardboard tube. I leave tube in locker at train station." He pulled a key from his pocket. "Number forty-three."

Rowan walked over and took the key from him. "You're coming with us. I'm not letting you out of my sight until I get that painting."

"M'sieur," Albin began.

Dmitri interrupted him. Perhaps honesty was the best way to go. "No, he's right, Albin. I have to go with him. I'm not bad person. I just make mistake. I hope you forgive me."

"Will you come back?" Albin asked. "Once this is all resolved, and it is safe?"

Dmitri allowed himself a smile. He remembered their love making the night before, and how he had come to feel for the Frenchman over the last few days. "Yes, I will like that."

"Eh, bien, you should go," Albin said. "I will get some lunch on my way back to the office. But you will be here when I return?"

Dmitri kissed his cheek and hugged him. "Yes, I will."

Rowan led the way back downstairs, followed by Taylor, Dmitri and Albin. In the lobby, Albin hugged Dmitri again, kissing him on the lips and squeezing his hand. Then he led Taylor and Rowan to a taxi

The Russian Boy

stop on the Promenade, where they hailed a cab to the train station.

Rowan sat in the front, giving Taylor and Dmitri the privacy of the back seat, but neither of them spoke. Dmitri was aware of the distance between them, the way Taylor was so careful not to touch him.

The cab pulled up at the front of the station. "The lockers are this way," Dmitri said, taking the lead. They moved through crowds of tourists and backpackers lined up for tickets or waiting for trains, coming to a bank of lockers against one wall.

Rowan looked at the key. "Forty-three," he said, walking down the line.

Ahead of them, the broken door of a locker hung off its hinge ahead of him, and when they reached it, the number was clear. Forty-three. "*Merde*," Dmitri said. "I swear, I left painting here."

"I believe you," Rowan said grimly. "But unfortunately someone else knew the painting was here as well. You didn't tell anyone?"

Dmitri shook his head.

"Did you notice anyone following you—on the train, or here in the station?"

"No," Dmitri said, in a small voice. He felt cold and wrapped his arms around himself, even though it was hot and humid in the station.

"What do we do now?" Taylor asked.

Rowan looked around. "This place is too crowded and noisy. We need some peace and quiet to brainstorm a plan. I think Albin had the right idea. Let's get some lunch."

They took a cab back to the Negresco. "We're going to need privacy to brainstorm," Rowan said. He pointed to the café next door to the hotel. The tables were way too close together. "Let's get something and take it up to my room."

They ordered sandwiches and Orangina sodas, and then Rowan led the way to his room. "*Mon dieu*, this is beautiful," Dmitri said as he walked in. He turned to Taylor. "I think you have landed much better than I have, Taylor."

Taylor looked uncomfortable, and Dmitri wondered if Taylor and Rowan had slept together yet. There was only one big bed in the room, and that was Taylor's duffle bag by the wall.

As Rowan and Taylor began to eat, Dmitri looked from one of them to the other. He knew Taylor, knew those sly little glances he was shooting at the older man. Taylor had once done the same thing with him—looked at him whenever they were in a situation together, made eye contact.

But today that contact was all to Rowan.

For his part, Dmitri could see that Rowan was a handsome man. Too old for Dmitri's taste; he had to be at least fifty, though his body was in good shape. But Taylor had always admired older men, flirted with those Americans touring the continent with their wives and families.

Was he jealous? He examined his mind as he ate his sandwich. No, he decided, not at all. He liked Taylor, but the American had always been a means to an end—someone to share an apartment with, someone to have some fun with. They'd never been in love—merely lust, and convenience.

But could he use that to his advantage? Seduce Taylor once again, perhaps even Rowan with him, to twist them to his own purposes? But what were his purposes, anyway? Could he use them to help him find the picture, and then the eventual buyer, and still cash in, without Yegor as intermediary?

Passion and Art

Nice, January 1913

Once he moved in with Luschenko, Alexei was astonished to learn that the painter did not observe the Nativity Fast, as the Dubernin family did, in preparation for the Russian Orthodox Christmas in early January. "But we cannot have lamb for dinner!" he protested, the first night he ate with the painter in a tiny restaurant a few blocks from the studio in Vieux Nice. "At the villa we do not eat red meat, eggs, milk, oil or wine. The Patriarch tells us that fasting with humility and repentance draws us closer to God by denying the body worldly pleasure."

Luschenko laughed. "Does this mean you will not be sucking my cock until Christmas? Because surely that is a worldly pleasure as well."

Alexei blushed. "It's not the same!"

"My boy, if you wish to become a true artist, you must forget these archaic teachings. The true artist suffers through his soul, not through depriving his stomach. And your Patriarch would remove you from my bed if he knew what we did there."

Though he could not help hesitating, Alexei ate from the lamb platter the waitress delivered. Throughout the fast he ate whatever the maestro ordered for them, except on Sundays, when he and Luschenko joined the rest of the Dubernins at the villa for Sunday dinner. The cook, Tatiana, had come with the Dowager Countess from St. Petersburg, and she was skilled at creating wonderful meals that adhered to the letter of the religious law. Because fish, wine and oil were allowed on Saturdays and Sundays, she prepared gorgeous platters of *rouget*, a Mediterranean rockfish, roasted in oil with fresh herbs and lemons from the villa gardens.

Luschenko charmed the family with his wit and his knowledge of the Russian community, but he was careful to couch his gossip in initials or pseudonyms. It was never good to get a reputation as a man who couldn't keep his mouth shut. He counseled Alexei to do the same, especially when it came to the nature of their relationship.

"Your parents must never find out what we do together," he said one evening when he and Alexei were out walking along the Promenade des Anglais, enjoying the decorations, even as he pronounced them gaudy. "You understand that, don't you?"

"I don't see why," Alexei said. "Look at Diaghilev and Nijinsky.

Everyone knows they are lovers, and no one minds. They are artists, and you're always telling me artists live outside the bourgeois world."

"Yes, but Diaghilev does not rely on his parents for support. And there is the difference in our ages, as well."

"You know that is no matter to me."

"But your parents would not approve. Your father the Count and I are almost the same age."

"No!" Alexei said. "You must be wrong. My father is nearly fifty years old!"

"And how old do you think I am?" Luschenko stopped in front of the Hotel Negresco, and its electric lights shone on his face.

Alexei had never thought about how old the maestro was. After his first impression of the man, he'd focused solely on specific things—his sense of humor, his smile, his dick. "I guess I don't know. I thought you were thirty or so."

Luschenko laughed. "You flatter me, my little one." He put his arm around Alexei's shoulders and pulled him close. "But do you understand now, the need for secrecy?"

Alexei nodded, and the maestro went on to criticize the décor as they strolled back to the studio. But Alexei could not stop thinking about the fact that his lover was the same age as his father. He tried to imagine kissing his father the way he kissed the maestro, and the idea repulsed him. He had never seen the Count naked, nor wanted to. He could appreciate that his father was a handsome man, despite his age. But love him? He would leave that to his mother. And even that idea made him queasy.

Alexei returned to the villa for a few days to celebrate the Russian Orthodox Christmas, observed in early January on the old Julian calendar. The Dubernins fasted on Christmas Eve, until the first star appeared in the sky. Then Luschenko arrived to join them for the Holy Supper, and the family sat around the large table in the formal dining room, covered with an embroidered white linen cloth which represented the Christ Child's swaddling clothes.

A tall white candle symbolizing Christ as the light of the world stood in the center of the table. Beside it was a large round loaf of Lenten bread, the *pagach*, which represented Christ as the bread of life. At the far end, the downstairs maid had placed a small pile of hay, to remind them of the manger where Jesus was born.

"Christ is Born!" the Count said, from his place at the head of the table.

The Russian Boy

Alexei and his family replied, "Glorify Him!"

Fyodor Luschenko sat next to him, and as the Count recited the Lord's Prayer, Alexei felt Luschenko's leg pressing against his own. Immediately his dick rose, making it hard to follow his father's prayers for health and happiness in the new year.

He looked over at Luschenko as the maid placed a shallow dish of honey in front of the Dowager Countess. But the maestro would not meet his gaze, staring at the Dowager Countess as she stood and said, "In the Name of the Father and of the Son and of the Holy Spirit, may we all have sweetness and many good things in life and in the new year."

She broke off a piece of the bread, dipping it first in honey, to represent the sweetness of life, then in chopped garlic, as a reminder of its bitterness. Luschenko rubbed his leg against Alexei's, and Alexei's heart raced. He was afraid he would shoot off right there, staining his pants and embarrassing himself. But he could not get the maestro to look at him.

The Dowager Countess passed the bread to her son, who followed her suit. When the entire family had broken bread together, the maid brought a large porcelain bowl of *kutia*, a traditional porridge with wheat berries, honey and poppy seeds, symbolizing hope, immortality, happiness and peace in the new year.

Luschenko pulled his leg away as the Countess began serving everyone at the table from the bowl so that they could all share together in its benefits. Alexei caught his breath and tried to slow his pulse. He ate his *kutia* quickly, not looking at anyone else.

When the family had all finished, the maid began bringing in the platters of food. Luschenko grumbled about the lack of meat on the table, and Alexei tried to shush him. "You must not say anything, maestro!"

Luschenko responded by rubbing his leg against Alexei's again as they worked their way through the meal. There were bottles of local red wine, a mushroom soup, platters of baked rouget, and slow-cooked kidney beans seasoned with shredded potatoes and garlic, salt and pepper to taste, and *bobal'ki*, small poppy seed and honey biscuits.

The maestro seemed to be an expert at tormenting Alexei, pressing against him under the table until Alexei felt he was about to shoot, then backing away to continue the meal innocently.

For dessert there were nuts, apricots, oranges, figs and dates. "Not even a proper cake," Luschenko muttered under his breath. "We will have to have our dessert back at the studio." His grin was so wolfish that Alexei had to look away.

After dinner, the family retired to the living room to open presents beside the *yolka*, a fir tree decorated with garlands of fruits and greenery. The first gifts went to the servants, mostly clothing and other household items. The Count had bought his wife a pearl necklace and his mother a diamond brooch. Alexei and his brother received velvet waistcoats, his sister a beautiful white dress embroidered with tiny seed pearls.

His parents had bought him art supplies, and in turn he had sketched a series of views from the villa, one for each of his parents, his grandmother, his brother and sister. The best gifts, though, were acknowledged to come from the maestro; he had sketched each family member, then had the portraits matted and framed. Even Alexei's brother was impressed with his, which made him look masculine and martial, despite his skinny frame and wispy blonde mustache.

After dinner, Luschenko declined to accompany the Dubernins to mass at the new cathedral on Boulevard du Tsarevich, erected in memory of the tsar's late son, who had died after a riding accident on the Riviera. Alexei fidgeted as the service droned on, no longer as intoxicated as he had been in the past with the incense, the music, and the stately rituals. Even the beautiful icons of the saints did not move him as they had in the past.

He was an artist, he thought to himself. He had to set aside these old-fashioned, bourgeois affectations and look to the future instead of the past, to his own inner talent instead of to some amorphous undocumented God who did not control him or his destiny.

Late on Christmas day, his father drove him back down to Luschenko's studio in his brand new Lancia Epsilon motor car. "I am pleased you are happy, Alexei," his father said. "Perhaps someday you will find favor with the Tsar, and paint the royal family. That would bring great honor to all of us."

"I'll try, Papa," Alexei said. But as he spoke, he remembered how unhappy his parents would be if they knew the true nature of his relationship with the maestro.

His father patted his shoulder, then pushed him gently toward the door of the car. "Now you must continue your studies."

Alexei gathered his gifts, then waved goodbye as his father motored away. By the time he reached the top-floor studio, the maestro was waiting for him.

The Russian Boy

"I have missed you, my little one," he said, hugging Alexei and kissing his cheek. "My bed has been cold without you."

Luschenko began unbuttoning Alexei's shirt, sliding his hands over the boy's smooth chest and sighing with pleasure. They kissed, their lips roving over each other's mouth, cheeks and chin as Alexei sighed and arched his back.

"You are such a beautiful boy," Luschenko said, unbuttoning Alexei's pants and dropping them to the floor. "I find it hard sometimes to remember that you are mine."

"You are my maestro," Alexei said, standing naked in the moonlight streaming in through the studio windows. He turned his back to the maestro and bent down. "Will you take me?"

"No, I wish you to penetrate me," the maestro said, taking him around the waist and turning him around. "But you must be gentle. I have not had such an experience since I was much younger."

Alexei's mouth went dry. Such an intimate invitation! He felt blessed and gratified, and filled with lust at the same time. He knew the transports of rapture he had experienced as the maestro fucked him, and he was thrilled to think that he could provide some small semblance of such pleasure to the man who had given him so much.

"The cream," Luschenko panted. "From the bureau."

Alexei rushed to retrieve the tub of emollient. The maestro was on his knees, naked, his hands grasping the headboard. Alexei leaned his head down and experimentally flicked his tongue at his maestro's puckered asshole. He had never tasted anything like it—a musty earthy flavor, like wild mushrooms. He loved it.

As he had felt the maestro do to him, he pulled apart the older man's ass cheeks and leaned his face in, licking his way up the crack between the cheeks. Then he pulled together the sides of his tongue, making a narrow missile, and penetrated the ass before him.

His maestro shivered and moaned. Alexei's dick was harder than he had ever felt it, as if it was made of iron, and the tip was covered with viscous precum. He pulled back from his maestro's ass and smeared a handful of the cream up and down his dick. The sensation was incredible and he was afraid he would erupt even before he entered his target.

But he calmed himself by imagining the implacable ocean, and considering just which shades of blue he would have to use to capture it. "Please," his maestro begged. "Do not toy with me. I am a desperate man."

Alexei positioned his dick at the entrance to the older man's ass, and pressed slightly. It was a wonderful sensation, as the head of his dick slipped a few centimeters in. The maestro panted beneath him, pressing his ass back toward Alexei, and with a push, Alexei entered him. The maestro cried out in pain, but Alexei could not hold back. He pushed deep, then pulled back and plunged in again.

He could hear the maestro weeping but it didn't matter. He pressed on, an animal in heat, desperate for the sensation of his dick penetrating the older man's ass. And the maestro seemed to be enjoying it, too; he stopped weeping and began pressing back, and Alexei upped his tempo.

All too quickly, he felt the electricity surge through his body, and he floated, caught on the wave of passion as his dick erupted into his maestro's ass. He wanted nothing more than to stay that way forever—but his maestro pulled back from him, and dropped to the bed, panting. After a moment, he turned over, exposing his own stiff dick to Alexei, who leaned down and took his maestro in his mouth.

Just a few quick sucks and the older man was erupting himself, his pleasure spewing out of him and into his apprentice's throat.

"My god," Luschenko breathed. "And to think you will be sharing my bed every night. What passion we will achieve together! What art!"

Over the next few days, Alexei and Luschenko returned to the rhythm of the studio. Luschenko painted in the morning while the light was strongest, and Alexei did his own work in between fetching paints and canvases for his maestro. In the afternoon, prominent Russians came to sit for portraits, and Luschenko sketched them, to fill in with paint later.

In the evenings, they dined at one of the small restaurants within a few blocks of the studio, and at night they made love.

One evening they traveled up to the Villa des Oliviers for dinner, and the Count announced that he was so delighted with the portrait of his mother that he would like Luschenko to paint one of his wife and himself.

"But I must ask you to come up here to paint," he said. "I am busy preparing for the Rallye de Monte Carlo at the end of this month."

He sat at the head of the dinner table, his wife at his side and his mother at the far end. Alexei and Luschenko faced Gavril and Natasha.

"You have heard of it, I am sure," the Count said.

"Only in passing," Luschenko said.

The Russian Boy

"Prince Albert I began the rally the year before, to show off the beauty of Monaco and encourage the tourists who come to Nice to venture a few miles to the east. He wishes to demonstrate that the January climate is just as beautiful in his tiny principality."

"I have been there a few times," Luschenko said. "To play roulette at the Casino and see shows in the theater there. It is a marvelous building."

"The roads there are marvelous for driving," the Count said. "Every day I take the Lancia out for a drive, sometimes following the oceanfront curves of the *Corniche Inferieure*. Gavril and Natasha have already been out with me. Alexei, you must come one day."

"I must go to Cannes tomorrow to sketch a portrait," Luschenko said. "Perhaps Alexei could join you then."

"Excellent!" the Count said. "Alexei, I will pick you up tomorrow morning."

The next morning was the kind of bright, crisp day when Alexei would have preferred to be at his easel, but instead he put his paints aside and joined his father in the Lancia.

"This road, the Grande Corniche, was constructed by Napoléon on the site of the old Route Aurèlienne," the Count said as they drove.

Soaring high above the ocean, it provided thrilling views of the ocean and the coast. The Count kept up a narration as they drove, pointing out the sights, though Alexei would have preferred him to concentrate on driving as the road curved and twisted back on itself, and occasionally they passed other cars coming toward them.

"I have a special treat for you," the Count said, as he swung the open car up a narrow, twisting road, coming out at a magnificent ruin perched on the edge of the cliff. "La Trophée des Alpes. Built by Caesar Augustus to celebrate his victory over the Gauls. It marks the gateway between France and Italy."

"It's just a ruin," Alexei said, looking at the few remaining limestone columns.

"But it reminds us of the glory of Rome," the Count said. "Our word tsar comes from the Roman Caesar." He lowered his voice. "If our illustrious tsar does not wake up, he may be following in the footsteps of those ancient Caesars. And we will all be in very great trouble."

Alexei did not concern himself much with the politics of his homeland. He knew that his family owned a great deal of land, farmed by serfs loyal to the Dubernins, and this money paid for the grand house in St. Petersburg, the villa in Nice, his own schooling and that of his siblings, and all the other pleasures of life. But he had no idea what his father meant about a sleeping tsar.

"What kind of trouble?" he asked.

The Count looked around, but they were quite alone there, at the top of the promontory overlooking the spread of ocean from Villefranche to Monaco. "There are revolutionaries," he said. "Men who seek to destroy Russia, to topple the tsar and ruin everything that our people have built for centuries."

Alexei shivered. "Are we in danger, Papa?"

The Count smiled and wrapped his arm around his son's shoulders. "Not at all, my boy. Mother Russia will always protect us."

Another Station

Nice, Thursday afternoon

Rowan had just bitten into his sandwich when he noticed the message light blinking on the hotel phone.

Washing the sandwich down with a mouthful of Orangina, he dialed in for his message, listened, then hung up.

"Who was it?" Taylor asked. "Someone who has the painting?"

Rowan shook his head. "Claude Rochambeau. The investigator from the police judiciare I spoke to yesterday. He wants me to come back in for some more questions about Yegor Rostnikov."

Dmitri dropped his sandwich and bolted for the door of the hotel room, but Taylor tackled him and took him down to the elegant Oriental rug. Rowan jumped up, and grabbed Dmitri's hand, pulling him up.

"Thanks," Rowan said to Taylor, who stood up and straightened his shirt.

As he did, Rowan got a glimpse of smooth, tanned stomach, and he swallowed hard. "Why did you run?" Taylor asked Dmitri.

"He take me to police," Dmitri said, looking down at the carpet.

"No, I'm not," Rowan said. "At least not yet. You don't have the painting—I believe you. That means someone else does. And I'm going to need your help to figure out who that could be."

He looked at his watch. "I should get over to the police station. Rochambeau left that message this morning. I don't want him to send an officer over here to pick me up." He looked at Dmitri. "Can I trust you to stay here?"

"I'll keep an eye on him," Taylor said.

Rowan raised his eyebrow.

"I told you, Rowan, Dmitri and I are finished," Taylor said in English, walking back to the table. He sat down and picked up his sandwich. "But he's in this jam and I think you're the one to get him out of it."

Rowan wasn't so much afraid that Dmitri would run away as he was that he and Taylor would kiss and make up, and then have wild monkey sex while they waited for Rowan to return from his police interrogation. But he couldn't say that. It wasn't rational, and if the two of them wanted to get back together, it was their right, even though it would kill any chance that he would get to kiss Taylor's full lips again—not to mention do anything more than that.

He sighed heavily. "Fine. Don't leave until I get back. If I'm not back by dinner, at least leave me a note so I know where to find you." He opened his wallet and peeled off a handful of euro notes and handed them to Taylor. "In case you need anything."

Taylor took the bills, then stood up again. He and Rowan were just about the same height, and their lips fit together as if they'd been made for each other, as Taylor leaned in and kissed him.

Rowan's heart rate accelerated. He wrapped his arms around Taylor and pulled him close. He closed his eyes and focused everything on the kiss, inhaling Taylor's warm breath and relaxing in his arms. But then he knew he had to pull back.

"That's a promise," Taylor said. "An IOU. I expect you back here to cash it in."

"Will do," Rowan said, smiling. He gave Taylor a two-fingered salute and turned for the door.

In the cab on the way to the *Police Judiciare* offices on the Rue de Roquebilliere, he realized that he had not told Ron Kramer yet about the police involvement in the case. He opened his cell phone and dialed the agency's number.

"You find the painting yet?" Ron asked, when he got on the line.

"Not quite yet. But I'm working some leads."

"More dead guys?"

Rowan was startled. For a moment he thought Ron already knew about Yegor Rostnikov. Then he realized Ron was thinking of Pascal Gaultier, who he had come to believe wasn't dead at all.

"In a manner of speaking." Rowan explained about going to the house in St. Laurent du Var and finding the body of the dead Russian.

"The police don't consider you a suspect?"

"Nope. I wasn't even in France when the man was killed. But there must be some news. I'm on my way to see the police right now."

"Keep me in the loop," Ron said.

The cab pulled up in front of the police headquarters, and Rowan ended the call. He paid the cabbie and realized that his wallet was starting to fill up with receipts rather than cash, and he made a mental note to shift that balance.

He waited in the lobby for a few minutes, until an officer arrived to take him to another interview room, where he waited nearly an hour for Claude Rochambeau to arrive. He determined to shut out all thoughts of Taylor and Dmitri back at the hotel and what they might

The Russian Boy

be doing.

Instead he focused on who could have stolen the painting from the locker at the train station. It was doubtful that it was a random theft; anyone watching the lockers would have seen a scruffy student place a cardboard tube in the locker. Your common thief would be more likely to assume it was a poster from some Paris museum than a valuable painting.

So that meant someone had been watching Dmitri at the station, someone who knew what he was carrying. Had that person followed him from Paris? Or had Yegor revealed to his killer that he was expecting Dmitri on the overnight train? If the killer had staked out the station, waiting for Dmitri, he would have seen the young Russian place the tube in the locker.

Rowan kept turning the permutations over in his head until the door opened and Rochambeau walked in. "Tell me again how you knew Yegor Rostnikov," he said, without an introduction or greeting. He sat down at the table across from Rowan and placed a manila folder before him.

"I told you, I didn't know him." Rowan repeated the story he had told many times the day before—going to the Bar Les Sables at the suggestion of Bruno Desjardins, meeting Rene Scarano, then going to the house in St. Laurent du Var. "I didn't even know the man's name until you told me."

Rochambeau remained impassive through Rowan's story. Then he opened the manila folder. "You were once a college professor. In America, like in France, that is a very good job, no?"

"It is."

"A job for life, they say." Rochambeau tapped a finger against the papers in the folder. "So why did you leave?"

"It was a personal decision."

"Nothing, perhaps, to do with drugs?"

Rowan was startled. "No, nothing like that."

"Then what?"

"I said, it's a personal matter. Not relevant to your investigation."

"I will decide what is relevant to my investigation," Rochambeau said. "If you decline to tell me, I will hold you here until I am able to receive the information I seek from the United States."

"There's nothing to find," Rowan said. "I was never even accused of a crime."

"Then why, M'sieur McNair? Why give up such a prestigious

position for an existence such as you have now? I see your wife divorced you after you left your job. I believe you were selling drugs to your students, and you were fired."

"That's just ridiculous," Rowan said.

Rochambeau stared at him implacably, and Rowan gave up. "I had an affair with a student," he said, looking the inspector in the eye. He would not be embarrassed by what he had done; he was long past that. "A young man. He was over eighteen, and he was not my student at the time, but the administration did not approve. I was brought before a disciplinary board, and the young man testified against me. He was angry that I had broken off with him, because I wanted to try again with my wife. So he said things that weren't true, and I lost my job."

Rowan glared at the inspector. "My wife divorced me and took my children from me. I will never be able to teach again, because of the stain on my record. So I struggle, and I try not to be bitter or resent Elizabeth, and stay in touch with my children. But I have never sold drugs and I have no idea why you think that—or my past troubles—should be relevant to this investigation."

Rowan took a deep breath and stared at the detective. Rochambeau did not say anything, just looked down at the pages in front of him. When he raised his head, he said, "Yegor Rostnikov was an employee of a Russian named Nikolai Demidov. It is our belief that Rostnikov was killed during a drug deal. Which brings me back to your connection to him."

Rowan's brain kicked back into gear. "Drug dealers have money," he said. "This man, Demidov-- do you know if he had any interest in art?"

"You think Demidov is behind the theft of the painting you seek?"

"It makes sense." Rowan leaned forward. "*The Russian Boy* is a valuable painting, and it could be an important part of a collection of Russian art. A drug dealer would have the money to buy it, and the ability to keep it hidden."

Rochambeau wrote a note on the page in front of him. "It is a possibility." He closed the folder. "You will stay at the Negresco?"

"Until I find the painting."

Rochambeau stood. "If you find any information that would be important to my case, you will tell me." It was a statement, not a question, and Rowan nodded. "Then you are free to go."

There was a bank across the street from the offices of the *police*

The Russian Boy

judiciare, and Rowan stopped there to replenish his supply of cash. There were no cabs in sight when he came back out to the street, so he made sure the setting sun was to his left, and began to walk toward the ocean.

It made sense, he thought. Yegor arranged for Dmitri to steal the painting, planning to deliver it to his drug-lord boss. Suppose he waited for Dmitri to arrive at the train station, and saw the boy leave the painting in the locker. Why bother to pay him, then, when a simple break-in could leave the kid out in the cold?

Rowan crossed a busy street with a flood of homeward-bound office workers, and considered. Yegor contacted the framer, Gaultier, and arranged to meet at his home in St. Laurent du Var. Someone else from the drug trade followed him there and killed him.

But where was the painting? It wasn't at Gaultier's house. Did Gaultier, the man supposed to be dead for three years, have it? Did the killer take it with him?

There was only one lead—the name of the Russian drug lord. But how could Rowan find out anything about him?

He was finally able to hail a cab back to the Negresco, and he got there as the sun was setting over Mont Boron, the low mountain that towered over the port. He went up to his room and found Dmitri and Taylor about to leave. "I left you a note," Taylor said, pointing to the table. "Just like I promised. We were going to get something to eat."

"We'll go together," Rowan said. "But I need to look for some information first."

As his laptop booted up, Rowan told them what he'd learned from Rochambeau. "You really are an idiot," Taylor said to Dmitri in French. "I told you that Yegor was bad news."

"I had no way of knowing he was a drug dealer."

"Because you weren't thinking," Taylor said.

"Guys, please, don't argue," Rowan said. "It's all behind us. Let's figure out where we go from here."

He did a quick internet search for Nikolai Demidov. There wasn't much to find; the Russian had maintained a low profile. The few articles mentioned him only as a shadowy figure in the drug underground.

Several of the articles were in Cyrillic, and Rowan had to call Dmitri over to read and translate. "There!" Dmitri said in English, as he was reading the last article. "It say Demidov have home on French Riviera." He stumbled over the words and had a heavy accent, but

Rowan understood him, and it was easier than having to talk in French all the time.

"Where?" Rowan asked.

"That is all it say," Dmitri said.

"Not much help," Rowan said, sitting back. "It's a big coast."

"Maybe Albin help," Dmitri said. "He tell me he work with computers much, that he very good to find information."

"You know his phone number?" Rowan asked.

Dmitri shook his head.

"Well, then," Rowan said. "Suppose we make a trip back to Vieux Nice. We can have dinner after we speak to Albin."

Rather than jimmy the lock on the front door of Albin's building, Rowan let Dmitri press the buzzer for the top-floor apartment. "*Oui?*" Albin's voice came through the speaker.

Dmitri returned to French. "It's me. Can I come up?"

The buzzer sounded, and they pushed the door open, then began mounting the stairs. By the time they reached the third floor, Albin had come down to meet Dmitri. "Oh," he said. "You have brought back your friends."

"We need your help, Albin," Dmitri said. "May we explain?"

Albin sighed, a deep, Gallic exhalation that Rowan recognized well. "Come with me." He turned back up the stairs.

They sat in the living room of the apartment, and between Rowan, Taylor and Dmitri they explained the situation to Albin. The Frenchman looked completely confused, and Rowan empathized with him.

"Your problem is that you're jumping all over the place," Taylor said to Rowan. "I think you should go back to the last time Dmitri saw the painting." He turned to Dmitri. "Someone had to have been following you. Who knew you were coming to Nice?"

"Only Yegor, and you. And anyone Yegor told."

"I was still in Paris when you got to Nice, so I think we can safely agree that I don't have the painting."

"Which means Yegor meant to double-cross you," Rowan said.

Dmitri didn't understand that term, and Albin had to explain it to him. "Bastard," Dmitri said. "I am glad he is dead."

"Did you tell him you were taking the overnight train?" he asked Dmitri.

"He told me to take it. He even said he would give me the money for the train when he saw me."

Rowan nodded. "Yegor was on the phone at the Bar les Sables on Sunday, arranging to meet Pascal Gaultier at his house once he had the painting. I'll bet he was in the train station on Monday morning when the train arrived, and that he watched you put the painting in the locker. He probably had it in his hands before you made it to the bar."

"But if he is in the train station, why not come to me, and I give him the painting?"

"Twenty thousand euros, dumb ass," Taylor said. "Why give you the money if he could just steal the painting from you?"

Rowan ignored the comment and continued. "When Yegor had the painting, he went to Gaultier's house in St. Laurent du Var, where someone killed him. Since I didn't find the painting at Gaultier's house, it seems logical to assume that Yegor's killer has it now."

"Gaultier?" Taylor asked.

"Or someone he told about the meeting, and the painting."

Taylor leaned forward. "Then where is Gaultier?"

"I don't know. The only lead I had on Gaultier was his home address, and even if he was living there, he's sure not going back now."

Dmitri turned to Albin. "You can search for him with your computer?"

"I can try. But it may take some time." Albin led the four of them into a small room off the bedroom, where there was a bank of computers and laptops on an ancient wooden table.

The room was too small for all of them, so Dmitri and Taylor stayed in the hall as Albin sat down at the table and began typing. He went from computer to computer, starting programs, inputting information.

"While you're at it, can you look for anything on Nikolai Demidov as well?" Rowan asked.

Albin nodded and kept typing. After about ten minutes he said, "*Eh, bien,* now we wait. You have had dinner?"

Blue Chambray

Nice, Thursday evening

Taylor looked around the table and wondered at how much his life had changed in the past seven days. A week before, he had been a student at the Institute, living with his boyfriend Dmitri in a tiny attic studio. It was cold and grim in Paris and he had lost some of his inspiration to paint.

Now he was in Nice, which was gorgeous and a whole lot warmer than Paris, and he had a feeling that the light on the Cote D'Azur could revolutionize his painting technique.

Albin had taken them to a French café a few blocks from the apartment, deep in the heart of the old city. The interior looked like a cave, the walls covered with white plaster and curving up to the ceiling. The waiters wore long white aprons and changed the silverware with each course. It was by far the fanciest place Taylor had ever eaten.

The food was wonderful, too. They shared a big platter of garlicky escargots in their shell, then had their own crocks of onion soup, covered with so much melted cheese that it crept down the sides of the earthenware in patterns that reminded Taylor of icicles.

Rowan ordered them a big bottle of red wine, and they laughed and told jokes until they had been served their entrees. Dmitri had followed Albin's lead, ordering the roast duck; Rowan and Taylor each ate steak frites. For a while Taylor forgot all about the stolen painting and the dead Russian.

Rowan yawned when he finished his meal and patted his stomach. "Too much rich food." He ordered café au lait for all of them. "We'll need our wits about us when we get back to Albin's."

By the time they returned up the five flights to Albin's apartment, his computer search had yielded a few pieces of information. "Start with Demidov, please," Rowan said.

Taylor had trouble following it all, between the complicated corporate material and the arcane French, but it looked to him like Demidov owned a network of corporations, registered in both France and Russia. They all traced back to a company called Znatok. "Means art lover, connoisseur," Dmitri said.

"Bingo," Rowan said. "He's our man, then."

Znatok owned a piece of property on the Chemin des Douaniers, in St. Jean Cap Ferrat. Albin pulled up online maps to show them both

The Russian Boy

street and satellite views. Zooming in on the satellite view they could see a wall surrounding the waterfront property. "It's a very wealthy place," Albin said. On another computer, he had brought up photographs of Demidov. "I recognize him. He goes to a club I like sometimes."

"A gay club?" Dmitri asked.

"Yes. They have very good dance music."

"You do not fuck with him, do you?" Dmitri demanded, his hands on his waist. Taylor was interested to see how quickly Dmitri had transferred his affections to the Frenchman—but then, their relationship had been on the rocks anyway.

Albin laughed. "Not with him, no. He likes beautiful young boys. Like you. He would never even speak to me."

"We don't know that he has the painting," Rowan said.

"But Yegor work for him," Dmitri said.

"And someone killed Yegor. Would Demidov have done that? Or someone else?"

"Perhaps it was this man Gaultier." Albin pointed to one screen. "Here are the records from before he died. This is the address in St. Laurent du Var, no?"

Rowan looked at the screen. "Yes, that's it."

"Let me enter that in my database." He typed it in. "Good. He is one of our clients." He looked up. "Did Dmitri tell you where I work?"

"You say you work with computers," Dmitri said. "That is all I know."

"I work for a company which provides Internet access to individuals and businesses up and down the Cote d'Azur. France is the second-largest ADSL market in Europe, you know." Albin smiled proudly. "This client had an email address attached to this house in St. Laurent du Var. Now we do a cross reference, and see if that email is still being used." He peered at the screen. "Yes. But the client lives at a different address now."

He read it out, and Rowan wrote it down. "Where is this?"

"I don't recognize it." Albin pulled up a different screen with a mapping program. "Ah, it is a tiny street off the road to St. Paul de Vence. I will print you directions."

Rowan looked at his watch. "It's too late to do anything tonight. I'll go there tomorrow morning."

Taylor noted that use of the personal pronoun I—not we. But he didn't say anything.

Rowan looked at Dmitri. "Can I trust you to stay here tonight?"

Dmitri pulled himself up to his full height—five foot six, and put his hands on his hips once more. "I am not leaving Albin."

"Fine," Rowan said. "Do you have a cell phone?"

"This one Yegor gave me." Dmitri pulled it out of his pocket.

Rowan copied down the number. "I'll call you tomorrow morning." To Taylor he said, "Are you coming with me?"

Taylor felt almost as insulted as Dmitri had looked. Of course he was going with Rowan. How stupid could this man be? But he decided to play it cool instead. "If that's what you want."

Rowan glanced at him sharply. "Yes. Well, then, let's get a cab."

They walked downstairs and out to the Promenade in silence. Even though it was after eleven, the street still pulsed with traffic, and Rowan was able to catch the attention of an empty cab. Taylor made sure to keep a formal space between them for the quick ride to the Negresco.

Rowan paid the driver and they took the elevator up to the room. "I can sleep on the sofa," Taylor said, as they walked in. "It won't bother me."

"What's the matter?" Rowan said, turning to him. "You haven't said a word since we left Albin's apartment."

"If you don't know then it's useless to even talk about it." Taylor took one of the pillows from the bed and placed it on the sofa.

"Taylor. Stop." Rowan put his hand on Taylor's arm, and the warmth coursed along Taylor's skin.

Taylor looked at him. "You had to ask if I was coming back here with you?" He felt his lower lip quivering.

Rowan smiled, and his whole face lit up. "You don't mean you..."

Taylor leaned over and kissed him. Rowan's cheek was rough with gray and black stubble, and Taylor loved the feel of it beneath his lips. "This is what I mean."

As they kissed, Rowan wrapped his arms around Taylor and pulled him close. He could feel Rowan's heart beating through his chest. He closed his eyes and sighed.

"This is crazy, you know," Rowan said, against Taylor's cheek. "I'm old enough to be your father."

Taylor leaned back. "Did you ever sleep with a woman in Chicago?"

Rowan laughed. "Nope."

"Then you're not my father. So feel free to go on kissing me."

The Russian Boy

Taylor leaned forward once more and began nuzzling Rowan's neck, unbuttoning the older man's chambray shirt. What a beautiful shade of blue, Taylor thought, as the shirt folded away. He could use that shade for the blue of the sky over the hills beyond the city.

Rowan groaned beneath him as Taylor ran his fingertips through Rowan's chest hair, the same mix of gray and black as in his stubble. Then he used both hands to tweak Rowan's nipples, and Rowan shivered.

Rowan shucked his shirt, then unbuttoned his khakis and stepped out of them, kicking off his deck shoes. Taylor released Rowan's nipples long enough to pull off his own T-shirt and jeans, leaving him in a pair of white cotton briefs, Rowan in boxers decorated with Van Gogh's Room at Arles. "You have good taste," Taylor said, looking down. "That's one of my favorite paintings."

"I'm glad you like it," Rowan said, smiling.

"I can see I'll have to explore your wardrobe at length. But for now there's something I'd rather see." He tugged the boxers down, and Rowan's stiff dick sprung out. "Another work of art."

He dropped to his knees on the plush carpeting and licked his tongue up and down the length of Rowan's dick. Rowan trembled and his dick pulsed as Taylor swallowed it. He grabbed the sweet globes of Rowan's ass, covered with a light dusting of hair, and began bobbing up and down on his dick.

"Oh god, oh god," Rowan moaned, grasping Taylor's head.

Taylor backed away. "You're not getting off so easily." He stood up and kissed Rowan again, feeling the older man's slick, stiff dick pressing against his own through the pouch of his briefs.

He loved the feeling of Rowan's fingers against his own smooth back, the way Rowan traced the planes of his shoulders like a blind man exploring. Taylor's own dick was so stiff it hurt, and he skinned down his briefs and kicked them away. He was still wearing his sneakers and white athletic socks, and there was something very sexy and almost transgressive about being naked yet still wearing those.

Unbidden, a memory jumped into his head, of his high school gym teacher, Mr. Gaetano. He had no idea how old the man was; as a teenager he thought everyone over thirty was ancient. Mr. G was hairy like Rowan, though more muscular. Taylor had entertained fantasies, never carried out, of being alone in the locker room with Mr. G.

He hadn't known what that meant, back then. When he jacked off to a mental image of Mr. G in his form-fitting T-shirt and tight white shorts, he never got farther than being naked in the man's presence before he shot off.

Now he knew just what he wanted to do with a naked man, especially one as handsome and sexy as Rowan. He pressed his body against Rowan's, their dicks bumping against each other. He nibbled on the side of Rowan's neck. Then he sucked the skin into his mouth, feeling Rowan squirm and moan beneath him.

He held that pose for thirty seconds or so, then backed away, rewarded by the sight of a bright red circle.

"You gave me a hickey!" Rowan said in surprise, as Taylor turned the older man's face toward the mirror.

"Yup. That's my mark. You're mine, and don't you forget it."

Rowan laughed. "You're crazy. Fortunately I find crazy very attractive, at least on you."

Taylor wrapped his arms around Rowan again and began rubbing his smooth body against Rowan's hairy one. Quickly both of them were panting as the pressure on their dicks increased. Taylor upped the pace, rubbing his body against Rowan's in a frenzy.

Rowan clamped his mouth on Taylor's, kissing him with a lip lock that made them both breathe out of their noses. Taylor felt light-headed, filled with a wave of euphoria that was half sexual and half lack of air.

Rowan pulled away, gasping for breath, as his body shook with the power of his orgasm. Taylor followed almost immediately, his cum squirting out against Rowan's stomach and getting absorbed by the hair there. Rowan's body sagged, and Taylor grabbed him and pulled him close again.

Out of the corner of his eye he saw Rowan's blue chambray shirt on the floor, and the color grabbed him again. Tomorrow, he thought. Tomorrow he would paint that color into the sky.

Motorcycle Rides

Nice, Thursday night

Rowan was having trouble getting his breath back. It had been a long time since he'd tried that trick, restricting air flow to enhance the power of an orgasm. He had wanted so much to show Taylor that he still had some sex left in him. But had he succeeded only in showing how old he was.

"I have never had sex like that before," Taylor said into Rowan's shoulder, holding him tight. "That was awesome."

"Glad you liked it," Rowan panted.

Taylor pushed him down to the bed and then sprawled next to him. They were both asleep in moments.

Rowan woke in the middle of the night with an urgent need to pee. He stumbled to the bathroom and relieved himself, then cleaned up the dried cum from his chest and groin with a wet washcloth. When he went back into the bedroom Taylor was still asleep on his back.

With a fresh cloth, Rowan cleaned up the sleeping Adonis, then pulled back the covers and shoveled Taylor in. He mumbled something but didn't wake. Then Rowan slipped into the bed next to him and went back to sleep.

He woke just after eight, Taylor still asleep next to him. He ordered them room service, jumped in the shower, and was dressed when the waiter arrived with the platter of chocolate croissants, hot chocolate and café au lait.

Taylor woke up as Rowan was laying the food out on the small round table by the window. "Did we... last night?"

"Yup." Rowan felt himself grinning.

"Wow. So it wasn't a dream."

"I thought it was pretty dreamy myself," Rowan said.

Taylor laughed. "You're a goof." He threw off the covers and stood up, and Rowan was once again amazed that this gorgeous, naked boy had been in his arms the night before. Taylor's body was long and lean, with hardly an ounce of body fat. He had a scruff of dark blond hair under arm and a thatch of pubic hair, but the rest of his skin was smooth, spotted with only an occasional freckle.

"You're gorgeous, you know that?" Rowan said.

"Get out of here." Taylor stood up. "Don't take that literally, though."

Rowan laughed as Taylor went into the bathroom. The young man's ass was a vision to behold, the kind that must have inspired Michelangelo to create the David. Taylor wasn't muscular, but he moved with a limber grace, like a young colt just released to pasture.

He came out of the shower a few minutes later, a big white towel wrapped around his midsection, and Rowan thought he was even handsomer with something left to the imagination.

"What's your plan for the day?" Rowan asked.

Taylor picked up a chocolate croissant. "Aren't we going out to see this Pascal Gaultier?"

"I appreciate the offer, but I'd rather do this myself. I don't know how dangerous this guy is. He may be the one who killed Yegor Rostnikov."

"And you think you're going out there alone?"

"I'm not putting you at risk." Rowan put down his coffee cup. "And besides, I rented a motorcycle this morning and I only have one helmet."

"You ride?"

"Don't look at me that way. I've been riding motorcycles since before you were born."

Taylor pouted. "I can ride behind you."

"Or you could take your easel out and do some painting," Rowan said. "And when I get back I'll tell you everything I found out."

He could see Taylor was torn. Finally Taylor said, "Can I take your shirt?"

"Excuse me?"

"Your shirt." Taylor leaned over and picked up the blue chambray Rowan had worn the day before. "I want to match the color."

Rowan laughed. "Sure."

He had left his leathers back in New York, not expecting to ride on this trip, but made do with a pair of jeans, a long-sleeved T-shirt and a jacket. "Here's my cell number," Rowan said, scribbling it on a piece of hotel stationery. He pulled out a wad of Euros and left a pile with the paper. "Get yourself a prepaid cell so we can keep in touch. Call me when you have it."

He leaned over and kissed Taylor, who was still sitting at the table. "I'll be back later."

He showed the operator of the motorcycle rental his class M New York driver's license and endured a short lecture about driving laws in France. Then he was on his way up the Boulevard du Marechal Juin,

The Russian Boy

connecting to the D336, the Avenue des Alpes. He stopped at a traffic circle outside the city to check his directions and then continued, the four-lane road eventually giving way to a two-lane that wound through the picturesque countryside.

It was a gorgeous day to be out on the bike, and he was able to put aside thoughts of his destination and just enjoy the ride. Outside La Colle-sur-Loup he pulled up again to check his directions once more, and then found the tiny street he was looking for a few minutes later.

He passed a small farmhouse surrounded by an overgrown yard, then drove a short distance and hid the bike in a stand of trees. Then he walked back down the deserted road to the farmhouse.

There was a power line and a satellite dish on the roof. A battered Citroën sat in the driveway and the front window was open. Rowan prowled around the property, seeing an skinny, white-haired man through the window.

He didn't have a gun, or a knife, or any weapon other than his wits. He thought about trying to sneak in the window and take the man by surprise. But realistically, though the man was old, Rowan himself was fifty and no longer as limber as he once was. He decided to brazen it out instead. He walked up to the front door and knocked.

"Who is it?" a voice asked from behind the door.

"M. Gaultier? Pascal Gaultier?"

"Who wants to know?"

"I'm here about the painting. *The Russian Boy*."

The door opened, the old man pointing a pistol at Rowan's stomach. "Who are you?"

Rowan stepped back. The gun looked old and rusty, but he still held his hands in the air. "My name is Rowan McNair. I'm a detective hired by the New York Museum of Fine Arts to recover the painting."

"Why should I believe you?"

"I'll give you my card." Slowly he put his hand in his pocket and pulled out his card holder, then withdrew a card from The Kramer Agency. He handed it to the old man, who took it and peered at it.

Then he looked up. "You had better come in."

Rowan followed him into a front room that smelled of sawdust and resin. He wore an old paint-splattered undershirt and worn jeans, and he was slim and walked without any hint of arthritis

There was a half-made frame on the long oak table. "Are you Pascal Gaultier?" Rowan asked as the man motioned him to a seat in an overstuffed armchair.

"Yes."

"Do you have the painting?"

The old man sunk into a chair opposite Rowan's. "No, not any more. It was stolen."

"From the museum."

"Yes, there was that. But I mean there was a second theft. The Russian brought it to my house, but it was stolen from him before he could give it to me."

"You didn't kill Yegor Rostnikov, then?"

"No, not at all." The old man looked offended. "I am a framer, not a killer."

Yes, but you have a gun, Rowan thought, but didn't say it. "Then who killed him? And where is the painting?"

"I don't know."

The old man wouldn't meet Rowan's eye. "I don't think that's true," Rowan said. "I think you know who killed Rostnikov, and you know where the painting is."

"How did you find me?" Gaultier said.

"Your email address. Very sloppy to connect it to your old house and your new one. I'm surprised the police haven't found you yet."

"You have not told the flics where I am?"

"No. And I won't, if you tell me what I want to know."

"I only want to be left alone," Gaultier said. "I am an old man."

"You're an old criminal and I know Inspector Rochambeau from the Police Judiciare would like to talk to you, and put you in a room a lot smaller than this one, with bars on the window."

He didn't like bullying an old man, but he didn't have any choice. He watched as Gaultier's shoulders sagged.

"Let's start with the house in St. Laurent du Var. You still go there?"

"To meet clients. I don't want them to know I am here."

"Rostnikov got your name from someone and you arranged to meet him there?"

Gaultier nodded. "Monday morning. I was early, so I made myself some scrambled eggs while I waited. Then the Russian came. But the eggs were bad, and I had to go to the bathroom." He shook his head. "It's terrible to get old. Your bowels don't work like they once did."

Rowan nodded. "And then?"

"And then I heard an argument. The Russian, and another man. I didn't want to be a part of any problem. So I left, through the

The Russian Boy

window."

Rowan remembered back to the cottage, the unflushed toilet and the open window. He imagined the skinny old man hoisting himself out the window. "So you didn't see who Rostnikov was arguing with? Recognize his voice?"

Gaultier shook his head, but Rowan had a feeling he knew more than he was saying.

He remembered the woman on the balcony opposite, the one he was sure had reported his visit to the house to the cops. "Who is that woman?"

"Woman?"

"The one across the way. The one who keeps an eye on your house for you."

Gaultier sighed. "My niece. I pay her a little money every month, and she takes the vegetables from the garden as well."

"She saw the man, didn't she?"

"Keep her out of this."

"I will. If you tell me what she saw."

"You are a very troublesome man, Mr. McNair."

Rowan noticed the old man's long, slim fingers, freckled with dark spots, the veins close to the surface. He could easily imagine that Gaultier had been a very talented craftsman once, and probably still was.

"So I've been told." He leaned forward. "The man who killed Rostnikov, who stole *The Russian Boy*. You must know who he is, because how else did he know Rostnikov would be at your house with the painting?"

"He is a mec, this man, a common criminal. Very dangerous."

"People who kill others do tend to be dangerous. What's his name? Where can I find him?"

"He works at a garage off the Provençale highway. His name is Henri Scarano."

"Scarano? A relative of Rene Scarano?"

Gaultier nodded. "His son."

Rowan sat back in his chair. That made sense. Scarano was the man at the bar who had figured out Rostnikov was speaking to Gaultier on the phone. But why would Scarano have told both his son, and the curator at the museum, about the phone conversation?

"You have the address of this garage?"

Gaultier shook his head. "I have never been there. But his father will know where to find him."

Rowan stood up. "If your information turns out to be correct I won't mention this conversation to the flics. But if it doesn't, I'll be back, and I'll have Inspector Rochambeau with me."

"You do not need to threaten me, monsieur." Gaultier stood up. "If you will excuse me I have a frame to finish."

Rowan didn't bother to ask about the painting being framed, or where it had come from. He didn't want to know.

His cell phone rang as he walked up the hill to retrieve his bike from the woods. He didn't recognize the number. "Hello?"

"It's Taylor. I got the cell phone and I'm heading out to paint."

"Good. It's a beautiful day for it."

"Did you find Gaultier?"

"Yes. But there's another twist. I'll tell you when I see you."

"All right." There was a long pause, and Rowan thought the connection had been broken. "I… I had a good time last night," Taylor said.

Rowan smiled. Taylor seemed to have that effect on him; he was sure he'd smiled a lot more since meeting Taylor than he had for a long time before. "Me too. Paint well. I'll see you later."

He rode back down into Nice, thinking about Gaultier's information. It made sense that the woman across the way would have recognized the mec and described him to her uncle. She had certainly noticed Rowan going into the house and called the cops.

It was slow going navigating the streets of Vieux Nice even with the motorbike. Rowan couldn't imagine driving a car there. The sun was high in the cloudless sky so there was little shade. He was sweating profusely by the time he reached the Bar Les Sables. He chained the bike to a street sign, snapped the lock, and hoped it would be there when he returned.

Scarano was not at the bar. Rowan ordered a pastis and an extra glass of ice water from the same bald, mustachioed bartender who had been there on Tuesday. He downed the water quickly as the pastis mixed. When he had recovered some of his cool, he asked the bartender, "I'm looking for a man I spoke with the other day. Rene Scarano. I understand he's often here."

The bartender shook his head. "Not today. Today is a sad day."

"Why?" Rowan took a sip of his pastis, tasting the licorice.

"It is his son's funeral," the bartender said.

Rowan put his glass down with a thud on the polished wooden

The Russian Boy

bar. "His son Henri?"

The bartender nodded. "You know him?"

"I know of him."

"A bad sort. Rene, of course, he is no angel. But Henri is another story entirely."

"Really?"

The bar was almost empty, and the bartender was in a chatty mood. He leaned forward and said, "He killed a man, you know."

Did the bartender know about Yegor Rostnikov? How? Rowan said, "No, I didn't know that."

"In a bar fight," the bartender said. "Not here. Another bar, out near the garage where he works. He went to prison, but only for two years. He made some bad friends there, and when he was released he began stealing and dealing in drugs."

Rowan shook his head. "It's difficult having children. I have two myself."

"I have three," the bartender said. "They are all still small, so I have hope for them."

"This funeral. You know where it is? I would like to pay my respects."

"The Cimetière de Caucade, off the Avenue Henri Matisse." The bartender looked up at the clock, which had just reached noon. "The service was called for eleven-thirty so they may still be there."

Rowan left a generous tip and hurried out to the motorbike. It was still there, the seat warm from the sun. He opened up his map and found the Avenue Henri Matisse, just this side of the Var river, near the airport. He navigated back to the Promenade des Anglais and careened down the highway until he switched to the Voie Pierre Mathis, another highway which led him directly to the cemetery.

He pulled up just inside the gate and looked around at the cypress trees, winged angels on tombs, and marble mausoleums. In the back corner of the cemetery, he spotted a group of cars and headed toward it. He held back in the shade of a mausoleum until the mourners were leaving. He spotted Scarano shaking hands with the other mourners, small and wizened, wearing a shabby dark suit.

When the last person had left, Scarano made his way alone toward another grave. Rowan gave Scarano a few minutes at the second grave, which he realized must have belonged to Rene's wife, Henri's mother. When Scarano straightened up to leave, he saw Rowan standing to the side.

"Ah, the detective," he said. "Are you here to tell me who killed my son? Because I already know."

"You do?"

Scarano nodded. "He was a fool, my son. I can say that, now that he is dead. He had great strength, great cunning, and great courage. But he was a fool."

Rowan fell into step with Scarano as they walked toward the remaining car in the cemetery, a bright yellow Fiat Panda. "He thought he could outsmart a very dangerous man. I told him not to, but you know children. They never listen to their fathers."

"I have a boy and a girl. You can't tell them anything."

"So you know." Scarano stopped. "Have you heard yet of a man named Nikolai Demidov?"

"Yes. He's the one who arranged for the painting to be stolen, isn't he?"

Scarano pulled out a packet of Gauloises and offered one to Rowan, who shook his head. Scarano put one in his mouth and lit it, then put the pack away. "It's my fault. I told Henri about the painting, how I had connected the fat Russian at the Bar Les Sables to Gaultier. I didn't know then that Rostnikov worked for Demidov, or I would have said nothing."

He took a deep drag from his cigarette and looked out toward the airport, where a jet was taking off. "Henri heard from a friend that Demidov was here in Nice, to receive a painting. He connected the dots, and thought he would steal the painting from Gaultier and ask for a reward."

He took another drag from his cigarette and began coughing. Rowan watched the jet climb into the sky, then disappear. When Scarano finished coughing, he said, "That was his big mistake. Biggest, you know, in a life of many."

"So he killed Rostnikov?"

"He didn't tell me, but he must have."

Scarano took another deep drag from his cigarette. "Henri told me he had arranged to meet Demidov and exchange the painting for the cash. I told him he was a fool, but he wouldn't listen. Demidov killed him and took the painting."

"You saw it happen?"

Scarano shook his head. "I don't have to have seen it to know what went on."

"Did you tell the police?"

Scarano coughed again. "The flics! You think they will listen to me?"

"But you know Demidov has the painting? Interpol is looking for it. They would listen."

"I don't know for certain," Scarano admitted. "But it is the only thing that makes sense." He looked around him, and then ground out his cigarette beside a tomb engraved with a weeping woman. "If anything makes sense today."

Odalisque Reclining

Nice, February 1913

Early one morning in February, Alexei was reclining in bed, eating an apple while Luschenko was down the hall in the toilet.

When Luschenko returned, he stood in the doorway for a moment staring.

Alexei looked up. "What is it, maestro? Is something wrong?"

"I must paint you. I have resisted for as long as I can. I am only human, after all."

Alexei sat up in the bed and turned his head toward the wall. "Shall I sit like this? The way you posed Olga Stichnayeva?"

Then he turned back to face his maestro and crossed his arms in front of him, frowning. "Or the way you sketched my father for his Christmas gift?"

"No, no, my love," Luschenko said. "I wish to paint you the way I most like to see you, naked in bed, waiting for me to make love to you."

"Maestro, you can't. You told me yourself. We must be very careful."

"It will not be a panting for the public to see. It will be just for you and me." He turned and walked into the public part of the studio. "Come, I will pose you," he called behind him.

Alexei grabbed his linen undershorts and scampered behind Luschenko. "No, no, you must be nude." Luschenko grabbed the undershorts and motioned Alexei to the long divan upholstered in red velvet. "Please, lie down."

Alexei did so, but Luschenko wasn't happy. "No, that is not the pose at all." He turned to his pile of art books, pulling out one which featured images of Delacroix. The books were among his most treasured possessions, and Alexei sat up to watch him page through it. "Here," Luschenko said at last, opening the book to a picture entitled "Odalisque Reclining on a Divan."

A plump female nude lay in a lascivious pose, her right arm dangling, her right leg curved under the left. "Maestro!" Alexei said. "I cannot pose like that!"

"Yes, you must." He arranged Alexei's head against the divan, adjusting his arms and legs. It took him a great deal of time, and Alexei wondered when they would ever get to the morning's work. A portrait

The Russian Boy

subject was due in the studio, and there were paints and canvases to prepare, not to mention breakfast for himself and the maestro.

Alexei realized he had not been able to get to the bathroom yet, and felt an uncomfortable urge to urinate, one that stiffened his dick so that it was almost painful. "Yes, that is perfect," the maestro said finally, stepping back. "Now I must sketch."

"Maestro," Alexei said.

"Silence!" Luschenko picked up his sketch pad and began drawing. Alexei's arms and legs became numb from their enforced position, but he dared not speak. "The expression," Luschenko said a few minutes later. "You must not look like you are in pain!"

"But maestro!" Alexei tried to look happy, then seductive, but all he could focus on was his need to urinate and the numbness in his arms and legs.

Luschenko went back to the sketch pad. Finally he said, "It is enough for today. Tomorrow we try again."

Alexei jumped up, grabbed his undershorts and scampered down the hall to the toilet cubicle. When he returned to the studio, the maestro had already closed the sketchbook and put it away, and they had to hurry to prepare for their first sitting.

Over the next week, Luschenko experimented with his sketches, trying different positions, backgrounds, and lighting. He settled on positioning the divan by the back wall, where the afternoon light streamed in through the windows and glistened on Alexei's shoulder and thigh. Only then did he show Alexei the study for the painting.

"Maestro," Alexei said, catching his breath. The sketch was still rough, but he could tell it was magnificent nonetheless.

"It is good, no?" the maestro said. "But the painting will be even better!"

That afternoon Alexei was surprised when Gavril walked in the studio door, just as an elderly Russian woman was finishing her sitting. "Good afternoon, brother." He looked distastefully at the way Alexei was dressed, in rough cotton overalls and a simple shirt. "I did not realize you were working as a common servant."

"I'm not a servant, I'm the maestro's apprentice," Alexei said. "Why are you here? Is someone ill?"

"I cannot come to see my younger brother sometime?" Gavril was wearing leather riding boots, jodhpurs and a smart jacket with brass buttons. "It was such a lovely day for a ride, and Shadow needs his exercise."

"I have work to do," Alexei said.

"I am finished for the day," Luschenko said, rising from his easel. "Alexei, you should go out and enjoy the afternoon with your brother. I will clean up here."

"Oh, no, maestro, that is my job."

"Go, my boy. Enjoy yourself."

Alexei frowned. "I must change my clothes."

Gavril tried to follow him behind the screen but Alexei stopped him. "This is the maestro's private area. You can wait where you are."

Gavril tried to peer around the screen, but Alexei blocked him, afraid that his brother would comment on the appearance of the bed sheets, and how clear it was that two people had slept there the night before.

"Come, my young count," Fyodor called. "Let me show you the work I have done on the portrait of your parents that your father commissioned."

Reluctantly, Gavril turned around. Alexei quickly shucked his painting clothes and put on a pair of slacks and a silk shirt that were more befitting the younger son of a wealthy Russian family. Then he walked out to the studio.

"There is an excellent café just down the block," Luschenko said to Gavril. "You should take your brother there."

"What a good idea," Gavril said. "Come, Alexei, let us go."

They walked down the narrow stairs in single file, neither of them speaking. Alexei noticed as if for the first time the smells of the staircase, the burnt onions and cleaning fluids, with a faint undertone of piss from the toilet cubicles, and he was embarrassed.

"Why are you here, Gavril?" he asked, when they were standing on the sunlit street.

"I came to check on you. I told you, I have heard disturbing things about this painter. I wanted to make sure you were all right."

Alexei frowned. Gavril had never been such a caring brother. There had to be something else going on. But Gavril was too sly to tip his hand quickly.

"Where is this café the painter suggested?" Gavril asked.

"Down the street. Follow me."

They passed where Gavril had left his black horse, Shadow, in a dim alleyway, with a young boy to look after him. "He is a beautiful horse," Alexei said. "How many hands?"

The Russian Boy

They talked about the horse as they walked to the café, and then about their parents, and Natasha, as both of them ordered glasses of tea and a round flatbread studded with olives and anchovies to share.

"There is a party Saturday evening," Gavril said. "At the home of the Stichnayevas. There will be many pretty young girls there. You should come. There is one in particular I have been spending time with, Viktoriya Andreyevna. She has a sister just your age."

"I am too busy," Alexei said. "I work for the maestro in the morning, and in the afternoon I paint. I cannot go to a party."

"Cannot? Or will not? You must find yourself a girl soon, Alexei. Or people will begin to talk."

"Talk about what? I will find a woman and marry when I am ready."

"You will be coming home with us next month, won't you?" Gavril asked. "Will you drive with Father in his motor car?"

"I would like to stay here with the maestro," Alexei said. "My apprenticeship can't stop just because the rest of you want to go back to St. Petersburg."

"You are not a tradesman, Alexei. You are the son of a count. You must uphold the standards of our family."

Alexei stood up. "I am an artist, brother. And I will uphold my own standards." He smiled tightly at Gavril. "Enjoy your ride back up the hill."

Then he strode out of the café.

The Quality of Light

Nice, Friday morning

Taylor set up his easel on the Promenade des Anglais again, this time a quarter mile from the Negresco, closer to the old city. He had only brought his sketchbook and the portable easel with him from Paris, so after buying the cell phone he had used some of the cash he had made two days before and bought a good canvas and some paint at an art supply store.

He was determined to capture the quality of light over the old city, starting with the chambray blue of the sky. He began with a wash of light blue, but it was too pale, so he began layering in some darker blue. He was so absorbed that he didn't notice Dmitri behind him until the Russian said, "That is different," in his heavily accented French.

Taylor looked up. "You think?"

"Absolutely," Dmitri said. "See how you are so free with your brush stroke? That's not how you paint in Paris."

Dmitri pulled a chair next to Taylor and set up his own portable easel.

"How did you know I would be here?" Taylor asked.

"You say last night you sell drawings of Negresco. I think I share in your success."

Dmitri opened the sketchbook to a new page, and began to draw. "You like him, don't you," he said. "The American."

"Rowan?" Taylor looked up at Mont Boron, looming over the port. Was this the same view that had inspired Matisse, he wondered. "Yes, I guess I do."

"You fuck him?"

Taylor looked over at Dmitri, who was working on a study of the Negresco. "Why do you care?"

"I like you, Taylor. I'm glad you're happy."

Taylor dipped his brush in cadmium green and dotted it against the canvas. "He knows what he's doing," Taylor said. "Last night? Amazing."

Dmitri giggled. "Albin not so much. But he's very sweet."

They painted there until the sun was too high in the sky and all the colors were washed out. Taylor looked at his unfinished canvas and tried to see it the way that Dmitri had. Yes, the brush strokes were bolder than he normally made. So were the colors. In Paris, particularly

The Russian Boy

in the winter, he had favored grays and pale greens, with occasional touches of pink and light purple.

This painting, though, spilled over with brilliant orange, yellow, blue, green and red. It was as though he'd discovered the boldness of primary colors for the first time. It was still representative art; that's where Taylor's heart was. He had little patience for the mental masturbation of abstract art—he wanted his paintings to show something, say something.

They treated themselves to sandwiches at a beachfront bar. The weather was gorgeous, with a crisp breeze setting the umbrellas flapping. Despite the chill in the air, cute guys in tiny bikinis sprawled over the rocky shore. There were girls there, too, but neither he nor Dmitri paid them much attention.

Even surrounded by so many good looking guys of his own age, Taylor found himself thinking of Rowan. The sensual curve of his chin, the security of his thickset body. His unexpected skills, like picking the lock at Albin's building the first time they went there. His ability to ride a motorcycle.

He thought about what it would be like to ride behind Rowan on the curving mountain roads, lined with red anemones, blue iris, and the yellow of wild jasmine. Fields of lavender stretching before them, dark green cypress trees like sentinels. Then his phone rang.

"Rowan? Did you find the painting?"

"It's been an interesting day," Rowan said. "Where are you now?"

"Dmitri and I are by the beach." He looked up to the street and named a few buildings.

"Stay there. I'm at a cemetery just west of you. I'll be there soon."

"Cemetery?" Taylor asked, but Rowan had already hung up.

"A cemetery?" Dmitri asked. "For burying Yegor?"

"He didn't say. But he doesn't have the painting."

They sat on a wrought iron bench in the shade of a towering palm with one dangling brown frond. Rowan roared up on his motorcycle, coming to a smooth stop in the bicycle lane in front of them.

He pulled off his helmet and Taylor was struck with a wave of lust. Rowan's face was a bit red, his salt and pepper hair tousled. He looked like an advertising model, and immediately Taylor thought of painting him that way. He wanted to jump up and kiss Rowan but he felt shy and instead just said, "Hey."

"Hey yourself," Rowan replied in English.

In French, Dmitri asked, "You go to funeral for Yegor?"

Rowan looked confused for a moment. Then he said, "No, not Yegor. Another man. Henri Scarano. I think he was the man who killed Yegor."

Taylor was confused and he could tell Dmitri was, too. "Slow down," he said. "I thought you went to see Pascal Gaultier."

Still sitting on the motorcycle, Rowan explained about his visit to Gaultier, his trip to the Bar les Sables, and Henri Scarano's funeral.

"So Demidov has the painting now?" Taylor asked.

"Rene Scarano thinks so. But we have no proof."

"We should go out to his house," Taylor said. "Look in the window. See if we can see the painting."

"He won't have it in the front window," Rowan said. "It probably isn't even framed yet."

"But you have the address Albin found?"

"Yes."

Taylor stood up. "I'm taking my stuff over to the hotel, and then we'll go for a ride. You can show me how good you are."

Rowan laughed. "I thought I did that last night."

Taylor blushed as Dmitri guffawed.

They made plans to meet up with Dmitri at Albin's after Albin returned home from work. While Rowan rode off to get a second helmet, Taylor carried his easel and the new painting back to the room at the Negresco. He set it up to dry and was back downstairs when Rowan arrived.

Riding behind Rowan was just as thrilling as Taylor had expected. Rowan darted expertly through the traffic on the Promenade des Anglais and the Quai des Etats Unis, past the entrance to the old city, and Taylor got a quick glance of the flower market of the Cours Saleya, the profusion of fruits, vegetables and blossoms spilling out under the striped umbrellas.

They rode alongside the port then circled around the base of Mont Boron on the Boulevard Princesse Grace de Monaco. They stayed on the main road, avoiding the town of Villefranche. The views were spectacular, the bay sparkling blue and green in the early afternoon sunlight. They branched off down along the Cap, and every few feet Taylor wanted to signal Rowan to stop so he could drink in the scenery and memorialize the landscape for painting.

He felt overwhelmed with sensation—the feel of Rowan's legs between his, his hands on Rowan's hips. The cool air buzzing past, the glare of sunlight, the rich sparkle of the water.

The Russian Boy

Rowan pulled to a stop when they reached the Chemin du Roy, which curved around the west side of the Cap. He parked the bike and Taylor slid off the back and stretched his legs. "Beautiful here, isn't it?" Rowan said, pulling off his helmet.

Taylor nodded, his eyes on the view of Mont Boron across the bay. Rowan opened his jacket and retrieved the address Albin had found. It was near the end of the point.

They hooked the helmets on the back of the bike and drove slowly down the curving road, past one million-dollar residence after another. "You ever dream of living some place like this?" Taylor asked Rowan, when they had stopped near a mailbox with the address Albin had found.

"That would be an impossible dream," Rowan said. "Mostly I just hope I can pay my rent and still have enough money left over for food and museum admissions."

"But you're staying at the Negresco. Taking us all out to dinner."

"All on the client. I barely have two cents to rub together myself." He looked at Taylor, who was trying to get his blond hair back in place after the motorcycle ride. "That bother you?"

Taylor looked up at him and laughed. "Dmitri and I eat a lot of rice and vegetables in Paris. We've been sharing this studio apartment that's so tiny we have to crawl over each other to get from the bed to the toilet. Money doesn't matter to me. But it would be amazing to live in such a beautiful place."

Rowan nodded. "Let's see what it looks like."

They stowed the motorcycle behind a stand of oaks and walked carefully up the dirt road that led to the house. As soon as they rounded a bend, however, they came up against a ten-foot wrought-iron fence and an imposing pair of gates.

"Shit," Taylor said.

"Don't give up yet," Rowan said. "We still may be able to get a view of the house. Which way do you want to try, right or left?"

Taylor looked both ways. To the left, the fence was visible for a long way, surrounded by scrub. To the right, though, it disappeared into a copse of olive trees. "Right," he said.

They moved slowly, picking their way between the gnarled olives. The fence had been built years before, and some of the trees had already grown into it. Deep in the heart of the grove, Taylor stopped. "I can climb that." He pointed at a tree with a thick branch arching over the top of the fence.

Rowan looked dubious. "I don't know. There could be alarms or cameras. And how would you get back up once you're on the other side?"

"You'd have to stay on the branch and pull me up."

The more Taylor surveyed the tree and the fence, the more doable it appeared. "I'm going to give it a try." Back home in Illinois he'd loved to climb trees, but he hadn't done any climbing in years. He found a knobbly corner he could use as a foothold, and stepped up into it.

"Hold on," Rowan said, but Taylor ignored him and kept climbing. It was fun, and he remembered how much he'd enjoyed doing this as a kid. He made it to the branch that leaned out over the fence and stopped to analyze.

"I can see the house from here," he said. "Not much, just the roof and what looks like the garage."

"We aren't going to get any closer. Let's go back to Albin's and see if we can get any aerial views through the computer."

"Don't be a wimp." Taylor scooted out over the branch, across the top of the fence, and then sat there with his legs dangling. The branch drooped with his weight, and it was only about six or seven feet down.

"Taylor," Rowan said, with an edge in his voice. "This man is a drug dealer and he either killed Henri Scarano or had someone else do it for him. This isn't a playground."

"I'll be back," Taylor said, in a poor Schwarzenegger imitation, and he swung around and dropped down to the soft, mossy ground.

No alarms went off, no lights or sirens. He looked through the fence at Rowan and grinned. "Back in a flash."

"Don't do anything stupid," Rowan said.

Taylor picked his way through more trees on the inside of the fence until he had the house in his sights. It was two stories tall, covered in white stucco, with a sloping barrel tile roof of orange clay. The driveway ended in a two-car garage; the main entrance was to its left, up a pair of short steps to a tall wooden door with an arched fanlight over it.

He circled around to the right, and was surprised by a shard of bright sunlight. The tree cover ended alongside the house, and the house opened up to a broad patio with sliding glass doors. What looked like the master bedroom was on the second floor, with a big wrought iron balcony.

The Russian Boy

The air was silent except for the crash of the waves below and a bird calling in the woods. Then he heard a loud mechanical noise and hurried back around to the front of the house, staying in the cover of the woods. The garage door was opening, and a Mercedes convertible with the top down was backing out.

He hoped that Rowan had camouflaged the motorcycle well enough. The driver was a dark-haired man in his mid-forties, accompanied by a much taller bald bodybuilder type with a tattoo on the back of his skull. The driver used a remote to close the garage door, then executed a deft U-turn and drove back down the driveway to the street.

There was no other car in the garage. Taylor waited until he heard the wrought iron gates opening, then closing again. He decided to thread his way back through the trees to where he had left Rowan. He was picking his way through the underbrush when he heard Rowan's voice. "Looking for me?"

Rowan was a few feet away. "How did you get in the fence?"

"Scrambled in as the gates were closing. I was worried you'd do something stupid like try to break into the house."

Taylor frowned, but he had to admit the idea had occurred to him.

"Did you see any other cars in the garage when the Mercedes pulled out?" Rowan asked.

"Nope."

"That's a good sign. Let's go up and see what the house looks like."

Taylor led him back through the olive grove, and this time they walked right up and looked in the big glass doors. "That's a Kandinsky, isn't it?" Taylor said, pointing at a zigzag of lines, circles and other geometric shapes.

"You bet," Rowan said. "And that art nouveau woman? I'll bet that's Leon Bakst. And that oil in the corner, the woman in the three-quarter pose? Feodor Bruni."

Taylor peered in through the window. "Jesus Christ. Is that a Chagall?"

Rowan leaned up next to him. "Looks like Demidov is quite the collector," he said. "But does he have *The Russian Boy* in there?"

Taylor wasn't sure if what he felt was due to having Rowan so close or his amazement at the art before him. "I'll bet there's even more up there," he said, pointing at the balcony above them. A circular stair led up to it from the ground. "Want me to climb up there?"

"Not now. Let's do some more recon on the outside."

They walked all around the house, Rowan pointing out the alarm system. "Can you disable it?" Taylor asked. "Just cut the wires?"

"Any good system triggers an alarm when you sever the connection. We could try to knock out the phone line and the power line, but even so I wouldn't be surprised if the alarm company sent someone out to look, or the cops showed up."

Taylor paused just before they went back into the cover of the trees. "It's so gorgeous here. Look at the quality of the light."

"It is, isn't it?" Rowan stood there next to Taylor for a moment, took Taylor's hand in his and squeezed. "Now come on, let's find our way out of this place."

By reorganizing some fallen logs artfully, they were able to gain some height beneath the overhanging olive branch. Taylor hoisted Rowan up, and Rowan lay flat on the branch and reached down to Taylor, who was able to use the fence to walk up and eventually swing himself on to the tree.

By the time they made it back to the motorcycle, they were both tired and sweaty. "I think we need a restorative drink before we go much further," Rowan said. "What do you say we find a café in St. Jean?"

They crossed the island to the port, where they commandeered a table with a view of the boats bobbing in the water. Rowan ordered a pastis, and Taylor said, "I've never had one of those. Are they good?"

"You'll have to try for yourself." Rowan ordered a second for Taylor and then showed him how to mix the cloudy liquid.

Taylor made a face. "It's an acquired taste," Rowan said, laughing. He ordered Taylor a mimosa, and added Taylor's drink to his own.

"Where do we go from here?" Taylor asked. The mimosa was a lot more to his liking.

"Not sure. We still need to establish that Demidov has the painting."

Taylor remembered something Albin had said, about seeing Demidov in a gay club with cute young guys. "I may have an idea about that," he said.

No Commitments

Nice, Friday afternoon

Dmitri didn't like the idea at all. "What if this man is not like me? Or if he doesn't want to take me to his house?"

"It's the only chance we have," Taylor said.

Dmitri glared at him. Was this Taylor's way of getting back at him, trying to turn him into a prostitute? He could see from Albin's face that the Frenchman didn't like the idea any more than he did.

"Taylor's right," Rowan said. "It's the only way we have of getting close to Demidov and figuring out if he has the picture or not."

"Why we don't tell the police Demidov has painting and they arrest him?" Dmitri said.

"Because we have no proof," Rowan said. "All we have is a collection of ideas. We think Henri Scarano killed Yegor, but Gaultier didn't actually see him do it. Rene Scarano thinks that Demidov killed his son, but he has no proof."

"Police can find evidence if you tell what you know."

"The problem is that I don't really know anything. We saw some good Russian paintings at Demidov's house. But we don't know that any of them are stolen. There's nothing to tell the police."

Dmitri looked from Rowan to Taylor to Albin. Albin sighed and said, "It is our only plan, little one. I will go with you to the club tonight, if you want."

"Will you?"

"Of course."

Just before eleven o'clock, the four of them left for the Club Bar, a multilevel night spot in an old warehouse just off the Port Lympia. It was already busy, with a line of men standing in the street waiting to get in.

Dmitri put his arm in Albin's as they came to the door. Rowan paid the cover charge for all of them, and they walked in. Dmitri thought the lights were too bright, the music too loud. Rowan led them in a circle around the bar. When they had gone perhaps two thirds of the way around, Albin tugged Dmitri's arm and pointed. "That's him."

"That's the man I saw leaving the villa in Cap Ferrat," Taylor said. "And that tall bald guy with him was in the passenger seat."

"Not his boyfriend," Dmitri said, evaluating the situation. "Bodyguard, maybe."

"How do we do this?" Rowan asked. "Dmitri, do you want to go over and talk to him?"

Dmitri shook his head. "I must make him come to me." He took Taylor's hand. "Come, we will dance."

He saw the hangdog look on Albin's face. "I'm sorry, my sweet. It is best that Taylor dance with me to get Demidov's attention."

"Have fun," Rowan said. "But not too much fun."

They squeezed their way out to the dance floor. Dmitri realized he had never been dancing with Taylor before; in Paris they had always been too busy or too tired or too poor to go out. He was reminded again that he liked the way Taylor moved his long, lean body.

Dmitri had danced a lot as a teenager in Odessa; it was what he and his friends did for fun. His friend Olga had an MP3 player with a pair of tinny speakers, and she would download bootleg music and they would all dance around her parents' apartment. He closed his eyes and remembered that feeling of freedom, and let his body move in time to the music.

"He's watching us," Taylor said into Dmitri's ear. "I'm going to dance with Rowan. You stay here."

Dmitri continued to dance by himself, gyrating his hips and swaying his arms, as Taylor walked to the edge of the dance floor, tugging on Rowan's arm. Reluctantly, Rowan walked back with him and they began to dance. Dmitri noted that the older man wasn't bad, though his movements were slower and more sensual, while Taylor was wilder and moved faster.

They made a nice couple, Dmitri thought. When he looked up, Demidov was there next to him. "May I join you?" he asked in French.

"Please," Dmitri responded, in Russian, and he saw Demidov smile.

Demidov was a handsome man, he thought, as they moved together. Perhaps forty years old, but very trim, without a bit of gray in his wavy black hair. His five o'clock shadow only served to strengthen his chin.

He reached out for Dmitri's hand, took it, and swung him around. Dmitri felt light and free, even as he was conscious that Albin was watching him.

They danced for half an hour, until Demidov took his hand and led him to a table where a bottle of Cristal champagne chilled in an ice bucket. "How does such a handsome young Russian like you come to be on the Riviera?" Demidov asked.

"I came here to paint." Dmitri tasted the champagne—the best he had ever had.

"A painter!" Demidov's eyes lit up. "I am an art lover myself."

"I'll bet you are quite a good lover." Dmitri raised an eyebrow and curled part of his lip into a lascivious grin.

Demidov roared with laughter. "You know what you want, don't you, my boy?"

Dmitri pressed his leg against Demidov's. "You could say that."

"Who are your favorite artists?" Demidov asked.

Dmitri thought back to Taylor's report of the art at the villa, but all he could remember was Chagall. "My very favorite? Marc Chagall. I have seen many of his pictures in museums in Russia."

"Have you ever seen one up close?" Demidov said. "In a private collection?"

Dmitri shook his head. "That is one of my dreams."

"Perhaps I can make your dream come true," Demidov said, reaching a hand over to Dmitri's thigh.

They danced again, then returned to the table, where Demidov plied Dmitri with questions. "You have family back in Russia?" he asked.

Dmitri shrugged. "My mother. But I have not spoken with her in two years."

Demidov shook his head. "Sad. But you have friends and family here in France?"

Dmitri took a sip of champagne and wondered why Demidov was asking. "I am poor; I spend most of my time painting or doing things to earn money. That doesn't leave much time for making friends."

"What about the man you were dancing with earlier?" Demidov nodded toward the dance floor, where Rowan and Taylor were laughing and swinging each other around.

"Another painter, just passing through. You know how these Americans are. They have money to burn. We were both working in front of the Negresco today and he invited me to come out."

"Looks like he has abandoned you."

"We had no commitment," Dmitri said. "We never even exchanged last names."

Demidov smiled. "I hope you and I will have more together than that."

Out of the corner of his eye, Dmitri saw Rowan trying to get his attention. The American nodded toward the men's room.

"You will excuse me for a moment?" Dmitri said. "I think I have had too much to drink."

"You must promise to return." Demidov lifted his champagne glass.

"Of course. And I always keep my promises." Dmitri leaned over and kissed Demidov on his rough cheek.

Rowan was waiting just inside the men's room door. "We're going to call this off," he said. "It's too dangerous."

"Not at all," Dmitri said, crossing the room to the urinal. "He's very sweet."

"He's a criminal," Rowan said.

Dmitri began to pee. "I know how to handle men," he said. "And you said this was our only chance to see if Demidov has the painting. I need to get it back or I will go to jail."

"I'm telling you, it's too dangerous. We'll figure something else out."

Dmitri finished peeing, shook the last few drops from his dick, and zipped up. "I am doing this. Tell Albin I will be back to him soon." He washed his hands as Rowan tried to argue more, but Dmitri wouldn't listen. If there was anything he knew how to do besides paint, it was how to handle men using sex.

A Great Liar

Nice, Friday night

After he returned from the men's room, Rowan leaned against the wall, watching Dmitri flirt with Nikolai Demidov. The little Russian was just too cocky, too stupid. He couldn't see the danger that Rowan did. But what could he do? Send Taylor after Dmitri, trying to pry him away from Demidov?

As if he knew Rowan was thinking of him, Taylor left Albin by the bar and walked over to where Rowan stood. "It looks like your plan is working," he said.

"With luck, Demidov will take Dmitri back to his home in Cap Ferrat, where Dmitri can see if Demidov has the painting."

Taylor smiled. "Looking at the two of them, I don't see that luck has anything to do with it. They're going to fuck before the night is out."

"There's nothing to smile about at this point, Taylor. Dmitri could be in real trouble. I don't like the way Demidov looks at him."

"Dmitri can take care of himself."

"Is he really that tough, though?" Rowan asked. "He's making it seem like this is no big deal at all."

"He hasn't told me much about his life in Russia, but it seems like he's been using sex to get what he wants for a long time. I wouldn't be surprised if Dmitri walked out of Demidov's house with his watch, his wallet and the painting."

"I hope not," Rowan said. "If Dmitri screws with him, things could get very dangerous."

"He doesn't look that bad," Taylor said.

Rowan shook his head. "The police think he's involved in drug smuggling."

"Your generation has such uptight morals about drugs," Taylor said, and Rowan felt the words *your generation* like a knife in his heart. "Everybody I know does drugs of some kind when they can afford them. They free your mind to create."

Rowan frowned. That argument was best saved for another time. "We need to start thinking about what happens if we do establish that Demidov has the painting."

"We go to the police and tell them," Taylor said. "Right?"

"It's not that easy. How do we explain that Dmitri is here on the

Riviera, and that he just happened to go home with the man who has the painting?"

"Oh." Taylor thought for a moment. "Suppose Dmitri was cleaning the studios on Friday night and saw Yegor Rostnikov steal the painting."

"Good start. But why would Dmitri have followed Rostnikov to the Riviera?"

"Yegor offered to pay Dmitri to steal the painting," Taylor said. "But what if Dmitri said all he did was give Yegor information about the Institute—where the painting was, for example."

"That makes Dmitri an accomplice," Rowan said. "But it may be our only option. We could say that Yegor never paid Dmitri, and Dmitri followed him here to get his money."

Taylor got excited. "Dmitri's a great liar. He could say that he saw Yegor give the painting to Demidov, and he decided to go after Demidov because he looked richer."

Rowan looked up. "They're on the move," he said, nodding toward the table where Dmitri and Demidov were standing. Rowan sent Taylor to get Albin, and he followed the Russians outside.

The big bodyguard walked down the street, presumably to retrieve the Mercedes, and Rowan stayed in the shadows, watching the body language between Demidov and Dmitri. If Dmitri tried to back out, Rowan wanted to be able to come right to his aid.

But Dmitri showed no interest in leaving. He leaned against Demidov, laughing and flirting. Taylor and Albin arrived as the bodyguard pulled the convertible up, the top already down, then climbed into the back seat.

Demidov slid into the driver's seat, with Dmitri next to him. "I'm going after them on the bike," Rowan said. "Just to be sure we know where they're going."

"I'll come with you," Taylor said.

Rowan's first instinct was to say no, but he realized it was a good idea to have a second man along, in case Demidov didn't go back to the house in Cap Ferrat, or in case Dmitri turned out to be in real danger.

"OK. Albin, you go back home, and keep your phone on."

Albin didn't look happy, but he nodded.

By the time Rowan and Taylor were loaded on the bike, the Mercedes was gone, but they caught up on the Boulevard du Princess Grace, and then kept a solid distance behind. When the Mercedes

The Russian Boy

turned onto the Avenue Jean Cocteau, Rowan took a gamble and remained on the Boulevard du General de Gaulle. He hoped that by coming at the house from the Chemin du Phare, the other direction, he would defuse any suspicion.

They passed the entrance to Demidov's house just as the gates were closing behind the Mercedes. Rowan pulled the motorcycle up just beyond the house and cut the engine. "What do we do now?" Taylor asked, pulling off his helmet.

"We wait."

They both dismounted, and Rowan set the kickstand for the bike.

"Will Demidov take Dmitri back to the club when they're finished?" Taylor asked.

Rowan shrugged. "Don't know. If I were him, I'd have the bodyguard do it."

"You're worried about Dmitri, aren't you?" Taylor ran his hands through his short blond hair, which had been plastered down by the helmet, and that made Rowan self-conscious about his own hair.

"Demidov's a dangerous man," he said. "I can tell just by looking at him."

Taylor took Rowan's hand and squeezed it. "I have a good feeling about all this. It's going to work out just fine."

Rowan squeezed back. "From your mouth to God's ears," he said.

Chagall and Others

Nice, Friday night

After speaking to Rowan in the men's room, Dmitri returned to Demidov's table, where the Russian was talking on his cell phone. He hung up quickly, and they flirted more, moving closer together as they kissed and Demidov stroked Dmitri's thigh.

They left the club shortly after two in the morning. Demidov drove the Mercedes convertible with Dmitri next to him and the bodyguard, Boris, in the back seat. Boris was impassive, but Dmitri didn't like having him there. He hoped that the big bald man would disappear once they returned to the villa.

It was intoxicating, driving in the convertible under the dark sky, with the lights of the city sparkling just across the bay. The trees arched over the road as they neared the villa, making it seem like they were entering a dark tunnel. Dmitri shivered with anticipation. He knew he would have to have sex with this man, but it didn't bother him. He'd had sex with many worse men, for less result. Rowan was a silly old man; he didn't know everything Dmitri had done, and the troubles he'd gotten himself out of in the past.

The only thing that worried him was how Albin would react. He didn't want to do anything to hurt the man who had been so kind to him. But this was something he had to do; he recognized what a foolish act he had committed in stealing the painting, and the only way he could see out of his situation was to do help recover it.

As they waited for the big iron gates to open, Demidov stroked Dmitri's thigh again, reaching up to where his dick was already hard, and Dmitri looked across at him and licked his lips. Demidov smiled wolfishly and pulled into the drive, the gates closing behind him.

The bodyguard disappeared as soon as they got out of the car. Demidov led Dmitri up to the front door. Once inside, he pressed a series of numbers into the alarm keypad, and Dmitri struggled to memorize them, but when Demidov turned and kissed him the numbers flew completely out of his head.

Demidov was four or five inches taller than Dmitri. He nestled his head against the older man's chest and wrapped his arms around him.

"I must show you my Chagall," Demidov said, pulling back and taking Dmitri's hand. He led him into the living room, where a painting of a man in a dark suit, flying horizontally over a townscape, had pride

The Russian Boy

of place above the fireplace.

Dmitri sucked in his breath and walked forward, pulled by the power of the painting. "It's ... it's... I can't say," he said.

"Beautiful. Amazing. Powerful," Demidov said.

"Yes." Dmitri walked up close to the picture, but it was mounted too high for him. He stared up at it worshipfully.

A moment later, Demidov was behind him with a short stepladder. "Go on, climb."

Dmitri stepped up. He was able to get so close to the painting he could see the individual brush strokes. The work pulled him in, and he could imagine Chagall applying the paint in thick swipes.

He turned to Demidov. "Thank you."

Demidov smiled, grasped him by the waist, and lifted him to the ground, then pulled him down on to the modern Scandinavian style sofa. They leaned against the big throw pillows and kissed again, in the shadow of the magnificent painting. Demidov unbuttoned Dmitri's shirt and ran his hands over Dmitri's smooth chest, murmuring in Russian.

Demidov was a handsome man, but Dmitri had lost his earlier erection and was having trouble becoming aroused. He kept thinking of Albin, worrying about what he would think of Dmitri's actions. Demidov pinched his nipples, digging his fingernails into the sensitive flesh, and Dmitri squirmed beneath the larger man. "That hurts," he said.

"Ah, but pain is the portal to pleasure." Demidov leaned down and sucked first one nipple, then the other, and Dmitri had to admit that the sucking felt even better once his nipples were tender.

"Come, my little one," Demidov said, standing up. "Let me show you my bedroom."

Dmitri grabbed his shirt and followed Demidov up to the second floor and into a sumptuous master bedroom. A huge king-sized bed dominated the room, with wooden posts, a brocade spread, and tasseled pillows. There was a long, low wooden bureau to one side, and the other wall was taken up with a large closet. Through the doors, which were partly ajar, Dmitri could see rows of suits and shirts all neatly spaced.

Dmitri crossed the room to stand by the sliding glass doors to the balcony. Demidov's lawn stretched down to a stand of trees; beyond it was the coastal road, and beyond that the dark expanse of the bay. In the distance, Dmitri could see the lights of Nice sparkling against the night. "It is beautiful, no?" Demidov said, coming up behind him. "Like you."

Demidov reached around Dmitri and began running his hands up and down Dmitri's bare torso. The bigger man's hands were smooth and his breath was hot on Dmitri's neck. He finally felt his erection rising as Demidov's stiff dick pressed against his ass.

Demidov turned him around and guided him toward the bed. "Take off your pants," he said. "I want to see you naked."

Self-consciously, Dmitri kicked off his sneakers and unbuckled and dropped his pants. He bent over to remove his socks and when he stood up Demidov was appraising him. He felt like a piece of meat at a butcher shop, and he unconsciously put his hands over his groin.

"No, no, you must show off." Demidov opened his arms and hands broadly, in a gesture he nodded Dmitri should follow.

He did, feeling embarrassed. Demidov motioned him to turn around, and he did.

"Beautiful," Demidov said. "Just beautiful. A work of art."

Dmitri turned back to Demidov, feeling totally exposed as his dick bobbed in front of him. Demidov was still fully clothed, in an Italian suit of dark cloth, with a bright white shirt that contrasted his dark beard. The shirt was open at the neck, and Dmitri saw a ruff of curly black hair spilling out.

He decided to turn the tables. He stepped closer to Demidov and tried to take off the older man's jacket.

Demidov grabbed his wrist. "I make the rules in my house."

Dmitri looked beyond him at the long, low wooden bureau. A cardboard tube rested on its top, and Dmitri recognized it was the one he had brought with him from Paris. The red plastic cap had a nick in it.

He felt the pressure of Demidov's hand on his wrist. "You're hurting me again," he said.

"This is only the beginning." With a practiced move, Demidov swung Dmitri around and snapped a pair of handcuffs on his wrists.

"What are you doing?" Dmitri looked down at his hands cuffed before him.

"On the bed, my little one." Demidov pushed him down. Unable to use his hands to break his fall, he slammed his head against the pillow. The cuffs cut into his wrists and against his chest.

He turned his head and saw Demidov remove his jacket and walk across the room to the closet. The big man hung the jacket carefully on

The Russian Boy

a hanger, then removed his loafers, one by one, putting wooden shoe trees into each one and then sliding them into slots in a wooden rack at the bottom of the closet.

Dmitri said nothing, just watched the big man and wondered what he had in store. Demidov slipped off his slacks and hung them, with equal precision, in the closet. Then he unbuttoned his shirt and shucked it, tossing it into a laundry hamper by the closet door.

He turned back to Dmitri. He wore a pair of white boxer briefs and a white T-shirt in what looked like silk stretched across his broad stomach. As Dmitri watched, Demidov pulled the center of the briefs down so that the waistband cupped his dick and balls. The dick was half-hard and thick, nestled in a bush of unruly pubic hair.

Dmitri put his head back into the pillow, knowing what was about to come. He heard Demidov spit, felt the saliva land in his ass crack. Demidov got behind him and pried apart his ass cheeks. Then without warning he slammed his dick into Dmitri's ass.

Dmitri howled in pain and struggled beneath the bigger man. "No, please," he begged. He had never been fucked like that, without lube or a condom or any kind of preparation, and the pain was nearly unbearable. He began to cry as Demidov slammed into his ass again and again, never even giving him a minute to accept the presence of the big dick inside him.

His own dick was stiff and rubbed against the brocade bedspread as Demidov slammed into him, muttering a string of Russian invective that impugned Dmitri, his mother, and every man he had ever fucked or sucked. His wrists chafed against the handcuffs and his ass ached.

The pillow was wet with Dmitri's tears by the time Demidov gave one final slam into Dmitri's ass and Dmitri felt the hot flow of semen coat the inside of his ass. He gulped a deep breath as Demidov backed away from him.

He turned his head to see Demidov pick up the phone and press a single digit.

"He is ready for you." Demidov hung up the phone, then went into the bathroom and closed the door.

A few minutes later, the big bald bodyguard came into the room. He jerked Dmitri's head up from the pillow and snapped a collar around his neck, with a leash attached. Then he grabbed him under the arms and hoisted him up to stand on the carpet, his cuffed hands before him.

"What is going on?" Dmitri asked.

"Silence!" Boris jerked on the leash and Dmitri shut his mouth.

Boris picked up Dmitri's clothes, tugged on the leash, and began walking out of the bedroom. Dmitri had no choice but to follow him, casting one glance back at the cardboard tube on the bureau.

Boris led him down to the first level, then down a hallway to a small room next to the garage. Dmitri stared inside in horror as Boris flipped the light on. There was a sling in one corner, over a narrow cot. The floor was bare concrete, with a drain in the middle. A short green hose was attached to a spigot. There were a series of hooks in the wall at different heights.

Boris pushed him into the room, and lifted Dmitri's hands up so that the cuffs could link into hooks at about waist high. Then he bent down and slid Dmitri's bare feet into a pair of rubber sandals that had been nailed to the floor, sealing them in with strips of leather.

"What are you going to do to me?" Dmitri asked.

Boris laughed. "You'll see." He walked to the door of the small room, turned out the light switch, and then closed the door behind him.

Return to the Police
Nice, Friday night

Rowan sat against a tree, where he had a view of the gate, and motioned Taylor down next to him. Taylor yawned as he slumped to the ground.

"Why don't you take a nap," Rowan said. "If anything happens I'll wake you."

"Are you sure?"

Rowan looked at his watch. It was almost three-thirty. It seemed to him like Dmitri had been in the house a long time—but maybe Demidov was the type to cuddle and ask his tricks to stay the night. If so, it could be a long time before Dmitri was delivered back to Nice. "If we need to stay here all night, you can spell me after a couple of hours."

"All right." Taylor gathered some brush to serve as a pillow, pulled off his jacket and covered himself with it, then curled up. Rowan smiled at the way he slipped so quickly into sleep. He wished he could feel so confident about what was going on.

After a while, Rowan pulled out his cell phone and checked the time. An hour had passed with no sign of Dmitri leaving the house. Rowan got curious, and worried. What if something had gone wrong, and Dmitri had gotten hurt? Should he call the cops?

And say what? That his friend had left a gay club with a trick—who just happened to be a notorious drug dealer? Whoever answered the phone would probably laugh at him. And he was sure the desk officer wouldn't put him in touch with Claude Rochambeau at that hour.

He left Taylor and prowled around the fence, using a pocket flashlight as a guide. He found the olive tree Taylor had climbed the day before and tested the lowest foothold.

"What the hell," he muttered to himself. He hoisted himself up into the tree, feeling his 50-year-old bones protesting, and then crawled out to the branch that hung over the fence. There was no movement from the house.

With a groan, he swung himself over the branch and dropped to the ground, landing on the makeshift platform he and Taylor had built earlier in the day. He felt a sharp pain run up his right leg as he landed. He walked toward the house, trying not to favor the leg, but it was hard not to.

As he rounded the back of the house, he saw a light wink out in the master bedroom. If he read Demidov correctly, Dmitri was not in that room with him. But then where was he? Had Demidov shuffled him off to a guest room? Was the bodyguard about to drive him back to Nice?

He found a place in the shadows where he could see the garage, and though he kept expecting the door to open, it didn't. After ten minutes, he walked around to it, trying to determine if the Mercedes was still inside. As he stood there, listening, he thought he heard the muffled sound of sobbing. Could that be Dmitri?

He traced the noise, which was coming through a drain that led from just beyond the garage. He got down on the ground and pressed his ear against the grating set in the wall. The sobbing, accompanied by hiccups, was definitely coming from just inside.

"Dmitri?" he whispered.

The sobbing stopped. "Taylor?"

"No, it's Rowan," he said in French. "Are you all right?"

There was a fresh burst of sobbing. "No. I am on the wall."

"What do you mean?" Rowan was worried, but at least the boy was alone, and able to talk, and it didn't sound like he had been seriously hurt.

"I don't know the word in French." Dmitri said something in Russian, but that didn't help Rowan.

"Can you describe?"

Dmitri stumbled through a series of words and descriptions. Finally Rowan understood. "There's a chain attaching your arms and legs to the wall?"

"Yes, that's it. A chain."

Rowan shivered. That was an unexpected complication. He had been hoping Taylor was right, that Dmitri could handle himself in any sexual situation. But things must have gone seriously wrong. Had Dmitri challenged Demidov about the painting? Let slip some detail like Yegor's murder? "What happened?"

"He was so terrible to me," Dmitri said, in broken French. "He fuck me so hard. Then horrible Boris put chain around my neck and lead me down here. I have handcuffs and feet tied down."

"I'm so sorry," Rowan said. "You hold on, and we will get you out." His brain zoomed ahead. Should he call Rochambeau? It was still an hour or more before sunrise, and he doubted he could be persuasive enough to get the inspector on the phone in the middle of the night. If

The Russian Boy

Dmitri was chained up, that implied that Demidov had something more in store for him. If he had meant to kill Dmitri he would have done it right away. He hoped that meant they had time to figure out what to do.

"You can release me now?" Dmitri asked.

"Soon. I'm going now, but I'll be back. I'll have to call the police."

"No," Dmitri moaned. "Don't leave me."

"I have to go." Rowan knew he'd have to have something to attract Rochambeau's attention. "Did you see *The Russian Boy* inside?"

Dmitri sniffled. "Not painting, but I see the tube I bring to Nice. On bureau in Demidov's bedroom."

Rowan felt terrible, but he knew the best thing he could do for Dmitri was get help. "I will be back for you, Dmitri."

His leg still hurt, but not as much. He figured it wasn't even a sprain, just a bruise. He used his flashlight to find his way back to the olive tree. As he approached, he saw Taylor sprawled on the branch, waiting for him. "I thought you might be over here," Taylor said. "When I woke up and you were gone. Without a note. Is Dmitri in there?"

"Things have gone seriously sour," Rowan said. He related what Dmitri had told him. "I need to call the police, but I don't think I can reach Rochambeau at least until sunrise."

"You just left Dmitri there? You didn't even try to break him out? What about your lock picks?"

"Taylor. I've been telling you all night that this guy Demidov is a dangerous drug dealer. I can't just pick his front door lock and walk in there."

He came up to the tree. "Right now, we need to get out of here and do some thinking." He surveyed the tree. "How did you do this? You want to grab my arms and I'll walk up the fence like you did?"

"No offense," Taylor said, swinging around and dropping to the ground. "But I think we're better off the way we were earlier."

He dropped to the ground. "I'm glad you're all right," he said, kissing Rowan on the lips.

Taylor's face was cold and Rowan shivered. Sending Dmitri to check out Demidov's house had seemed like a good idea earlier that day. Rowan blamed himself for not seeing all the potential problems. Taylor and Dmitri were just kids. He was supposed to be the adult, the professional. Instead he'd been as naïve as they were.

Taylor sensed him shivering and wrapped his arms around Rowan.

"You're right. We'd better get out of here." He pulled away, then bent down and cupped his hands. "Up you go."

They repeated their process of earlier in the day, though it was a lot harder to manage in the dark, without a hand free for the flashlight. With some difficulty Rowan hoisted himself onto the branch. He took a minute to catch his breath, as Taylor stretched below him.

Rowan rested his body along the length of the branch, his arms hanging down and his cheek pressed against the bark. Taylor jumped up and grabbed his hands. The pressure pulled Rowan hard against the branch and knocked the breath out of him.

Taylor tried to swing his legs to the fence. He missed, and let go of Rowan's hands to drop to the ground again. Rowan tried to shake the pain out of his arms. It was a good thing he'd been religious about his gym workouts, he thought. Though there was no training for something like this.

"Just a practice run," Taylor said. "I'll get it this time."

Rowan reached down and grabbed Taylor's hands. "Too sweaty," he said, letting them go. "You'll slip right away from me. Dry them off."

"Picky, picky." Taylor wiped his hands on his jeans and reached up again. He took a running leap, and his feet darted up the fence. For a moment he was suspended there, Rowan hanging onto his arms, his legs wrapped around the tree trunk. Then he swung around. "See, piece of cake," he said, but Rowan noticed he was breathing hard.

Rowan himself was wiped out by the effort. He struggled to get back down the tree, slipping on the last foothold and landing hard again on his right leg. He cursed under his breath and grabbed it.

"What's the matter?" Taylor asked.

Rowan stood up. "Just landed funny. I'll be all right."

Taylor leaned down and put his hands on Rowan's leg. "Feels stiff. Let me give you a quick massage."

Rowan wondered if massage was code for something else. "Don't have time."

"We won't make any progress if you're limping. Drop your pants and sit on the ground."

After that second fall, Rowan's leg hurt like a bastard, despite what he had said to Taylor. He unbuttoned his khakis and let them drop to the ground, kicked off his loafers, then stepped out of the pants. The night air was cold against his boxers and he shivered.

Taylor bent down and folded the pants to make a place for Rowan to sit. Using the tree for support, Rowan lowered himself to a sitting position and stretched his right leg out.

Taylor sat on the ground next to him and pulled Rowan's leg into his lap. He began slowly rubbing the leg up and down, gently easing the pressure. Then he pressed the ball of his thumb against the leg and pressed harder. Rowan yelped.

"You're so tight," Taylor said. "I wish I had some massage oil."

"Yeah, and I wish I had some flannel boxers on. This ground is cold."

"Is your equipment all shriveled up?" Taylor said, in a mocking tone. "Poor baby."

"I'll show you my equipment when we get out of here." Rowan pressed his hands against the ground and tried to get up.

"Five more minutes." Taylor kept rubbing and pressing, kneading the muscles in Rowan's leg. Then he sat back and let Rowan's leg go back to the ground, and stood up. He put his hands under Rowan's arms and pulled. "Try and stand up."

Rowan stood. His leg felt a thousand percent better. "You've got magic hands."

"Your back gets ruined leaning over an easel all day," Taylor said, as Rowan pulled his pants back on. "Dmitri and I used to rub each other's back."

Rowan pushed that image right out of his mind. "Let's go."

As they walked back to the motorcycle, Taylor said, "I don't like leaving Dmitri here. What if he gets scared?"

"I need to tell the cops that he's there," Rowan said. "They can go in there and get him. We can't. And you can't stay on the grounds when the sun comes up. We don't know what kind of security they have here—they may have cameras everywhere."

"Then I'll stay here outside the fence and watch the house. What do I do if they try to take Dmitri somewhere else?"

"Call me. Hopefully by then I'll be with the police and they can go after the car."

Rowan rode the motorcycle back to Nice as the sun began to rise. He was very worried about Dmitri. Was he chained up to be a sex toy for Demidov? Or was there something even more dangerous in store for him?

By the time he arrived at the offices of the Service Régional de la Police Judiciaire it was almost seven. He parked the bike and walked inside the building. "I would like to speak with Inspector Claude

Rochambeau," he told the officer on duty.

"It is Saturday," the officer said.

"Yes?"

"Inspector Rochambeau is off duty."

"Can you call him, please? Tell him my name is Rowan McNair and I have more information on the case he is investigating."

The officer pushed a pad and pen toward Rowan. "You may leave him a note. He will receive it when he returns to work on Monday."

"I found the man who stole the painting Interpol is looking for," Rowan said, struggling to keep his tone even. "He is being held hostage in a house in St. Jean Cap Ferrat. By Monday he may be gone, or dead. When Inspector Rochambeau reports to Interpol that you have destroyed their case with your refusal, I am sure they will find a new position for you."

The officer glared at him. "Write your name and the case information."

Rowan did so, and pushed the paper back to the officer. "Wait over there." He pointed to a row of hard plastic chairs. The officer picked up a phone but Rowan couldn't hear what he said.

He called Taylor's cell while he waited. "Anything happening out there?"

"Nope. Where are you?"

"The police. I'm waiting for the inspector."

"Did you call Albin? He's going to freak."

"Exactly why I haven't called him."

"Be careful," Taylor said.

Rowan waited. He called Ron Kramer's cell but got his voice mail, and he left a message. "I know where the painting is, and I'm at the police station now to arrange to get it back. More info when I have it."

The clock ticked past eight, and then nine. Each time he stood up to go over to the officer on duty, the man glared at him, and Rowan sat back down. Just before ten, Rochambeau entered the waiting room from a side door.

"M. McNair," he said. "You have more information on the death of Yegor Rostnikov?"

Rowan had forgotten that was why he had originally come to the police. "Yes, I do."

"Eh, bien. Come with me."

Rochambeau led him to another interview room. Rowan sat in a hard metal chair at a table with a scratched wooden veneer.

Rochambeau remained standing.

From his previous encounters with the police, in France and the United States, Rowan knew the best thing to do was start from the beginning, rather than rushing into the need to rescue Dmitri.

He told the Inspector about tracking Pascal Gaultier, and Gaultier's identification of Henri Scarano as Rostnikov's killer.

"Excuse me, monsieur," Rochambeau said. "In one day you found a man the police have wanted to speak with for three years?"

"It's not like you were looking for him day and night," Rowan said.

"His address?"

Rowan gave it to him. "You know that Henri Scarano was killed as well, don't you?"

"I am aware of every murder that takes place in my department." Rochambeau crossed his arms over his chest. "I suppose you are going to tell me you know who killed him?" Rochambeau pulled a Gauloise from a pack in his pocket and lit it. He did not offer one to Rowan, who would have declined anyway.

Rowan figured there weren't any restrictions on smoking in public buildings in France. "Nikolai Demidov," he said. "Or his bodyguard. I don't know which one actually pulled the trigger."

At Demidov's name, Rochambeau pulled the cigarette from his mouth. "What do you know of Nikolai Demidov?"

"I know he owns a house in St. Jean Cap Ferrat, and he has a young Russian painter named Dmitri Baranov chained up inside."

Rowan realized he'd jumped ahead too far. "Dmitri stole *The Russian Boy*, the painting I've been looking for, from the Institute des Artistes in Paris. He brought it to Nice to hand off to the man who hired him to steal it. Yegor Rostnikov."

"Yes, yes," Rochambeau said impatiently. "Rostnikov worked for Demidov."

"I believe that Henri Scarano killed Rostnikov so that he could steal the painting, and hold it for ransom from Demidov. But Demidov killed him and took the painting."

Rochambeau sucked on his cigarette, then tapped the end into a chipped porcelain ashtray advertising Cinzano. "You know this?"

"I believe it," Rowan repeated. "Dmitri wants to recover the painting in the hope that the court will be more lenient with him. He and I thought that Demidov would be at the Club Bar last night, so we went there to look for him."

"Are you quite so much a fool?" Rochambeau said, leaning forward and putting his hands on the table. The cigarette dangled from his lips. "You went looking for a dangerous criminal like Nikolai Demidov?"

Rowan realized even more clearly what an idiot he had been, and how his actions had imperiled poor Dmitri. "We wanted to know if Demidov had the painting at his home. So Dmitri …" He stopped. He had no idea how to explain in French what had happened. "Dmitri danced with Demidov, and then Demidov took him back to his house in St. Jean Cap Ferrat."

Rochambeau stood up again. "This was last night?"

"Yes. I followed them, and when Dmitri did not leave the house I went looking for him."

"You have been on the grounds of this house?"

Jesus, Rowan thought. Was Rochambeau going to charge him with trespassing? "Yes."

"You just walked up and knocked at the iron gate?"

Rowan noted that Rochambeau seemed familiar with Demidov's house. "Not exactly."

Rochambeau stubbed out his cigarette. He pulled the pack from his pocket, then shook his head and put it back. "How exactly?"

"There is an olive tree with a branch that hangs over the fence."

Rochambeau laughed. "You continue to surprise me, M. McNair. You can climb fences at your age?"

"I managed."

"So you went up to the house. What did you find?"

"I heard someone crying, and I followed the sound. Through a drain pipe I was able to talk to Dmitri, who told me that he had been chained to the wall. He also told me that the stolen painting, *The Russian Boy*, is in the house."

There. He had told the whole story. "We need to rescue him as soon as possible."

"I'm afraid there are problems," Rochambeau said. "And your friend Dmitri's are the least of them."

Hosing Around

Nice, early Saturday morning

Every time Dmitri nodded off in the darkened room, he would lose his balance and begin to fall, and the handcuffs locked to the wall would tug against his weight, and the pain would wake him. There was no window in the dark room, but he could tell when the sun began to rise as light filtered through the drain grate.

Soon after that, Boris came in and turned on the light. He was naked except for a white cotton jockstrap. Dmitri could not help noticing how well-built the man was, the way his muscles were so clearly delineated. He thought Boris would have made a wonderful model for a life drawing class, if you ignored the ugliness of his bald head.

"Aren't you a pretty one?" he said in Russian, tickling his finger under Dmitri's chin. "I will enjoy you."

Dmitri turned his head away from the big bald man.

"Not nice." Boris smacked his broad hand against Dmitri's naked ass. "Boys who are not nice get punished."

Dmitri stiffened his body and closed his eyes, preparing for a beating. But it did not happen. Opening his eyes, he saw Boris picking up a wooden block and positioning it next to Dmitri.

"Are you going to behave?" Boris asked.

"Why am I here? Why don't you let me go?"

"You will be going soon. But before you go, I will have some fun with you. If you behave, you will survive with a minimum of pain. But if you don't..."

Dmitri realized that he was probably going to be fucked again. He had been with men before who had taken pleasure from hurting him, back in Odessa. He had learned that the easiest way was to submit. "I will be good."

"Excellent." Boris leaned down and unstrapped Dmitri's feet, then undid the lock holding the handcuffs to the wall. He put his hands around Dmitri's waist and lifted him up onto the block of wood. His big hands were rough against Dmitri's smooth skin, and he couldn't help shivering with anticipation at the man's touch.

Boris positioned Dmitri's feet on the block, then hooked his cuffs back to the wall so that Dmitri's palms were flat against it. Then he got onto his knees behind Dmitri and spit into the boy's ass.

Dmitri's feet weren't constrained; he could have kicked back at Boris, maybe even succeeding in connecting with his chin or his chest. But there was no escape with his wrists chained to the wall. So he did nothing.

"The boss, he does not have my finesse," Boris said, licking his tongue down Dmitri's crack. "He takes a man without any preparation at all."

Dmitri nodded, feeling his dick begin to swell as Boris licked and tongued his ass.

"Trust me, I know," Boris said. "My ass has taken quite a beating."

"Why do you stay with him, then?" Perhaps a bit of flattery would help. "You are a handsome man, very strong. You could be with someone else."

"The boss is not my lover," Boris said, prying Dmitri's ass apart so he could stick his tongue farther in. "I am his employee, and he pays me very well. If he must fuck me sometimes, when there is no one else available, I accept that as part of my job."

He ran his thumbs down the globes of Dmitri's ass, and Dmitri shivered at the roughness. "And there are other benefits. Sweet boys like you."

He continued to tongue-fuck Dmitri until his ass was leaking juice and his dick was rock hard. Then the big man stood up and positioned his dick at Dmitri's ass. Unlike his boss, though, Boris's entry was slow and sensual. He placed his hands on Dmitri's hips and slid his dick, inch by inch, into Dmitri's prepared chute.

Dmitri knew he shouldn't be enjoying this. He was this man's captive; his clothes and his dignity had been stripped away from him. But he couldn't help himself. Boris was a master cocksman and Dmitri had rarely been fucked so well. The big man spoke soothingly to him, kissed his shoulders, rubbed his thumbs over Dmitri's hips. It was enough to reduce him to a pool of quivering jelly.

"Yes, you like that. Boris takes good care of you, yes?"

Dmitri longed to reach down and touch his own dick, but with his hands chained to the wall all he could do was contract and release his muscles and hope that Boris would be kind enough to jerk him off when he was finished.

He felt Boris's tempo increase, as the big Russian began slamming into Dmitri's ass again and again. The man's voice climbed, then dissolved into guttural groans. With one massive thrust he ejaculated up Dmitri's ass, then sagged against him. "Very good," he said into

The Russian Boy

Dmitri's neck.

He stepped back, and out of the corner of his eye Dmitri could see him stuffing his softening dick back into the jock strap. "But you are messy," Boris said. "You must get cleaned up."

He reached over for the coiled green hose, and turned on the spigot. He turned the spray wide, and began rinsing Dmitri up and down. Then he twisted the nozzle so that the spray became a jet, and aimed the water up Dmitri's ass.

The sensation was exquisite, the pulsing water shooting up his ass and massaging his prostate. He was so hard his dick ached, and he squirmed under the onslaught of water.

"And now the front," Boris said, bringing the hose around to shoot directly onto Dmitri's dick.

He whimpered and moaned at the tiny pinpricks of water shooting against his sensitive dick. He began panting and tried to wiggle his dick away from the water, but Boris was relentless. Then his orgasm began to build, boiling up from his guts and surging through his dick with exquisite pressure. With a moan that was half a cry, his dick erupted in a combination of pain and pleasure unlike any he had known before.

Boris turned the nozzle to spray again and rinsed Dmitri's body, washing away the pearly cum from his pubic hair. Then he shut the water off and said, "You will dry now." He turned and walked out, leaving Dmitri still chained to the wall, soaking wet. At least his feet were no longer strapped down so he could move his legs. He shuffled the box closer to the wall, so that he could lean against it for support. And then, finally, he was able to doze off.

Intercepted Communication

Nice, Saturday morning

Rochambeau left Rowan without explaining what he meant. Rowan used that time to call Taylor. "Anything?"

"No. Are you still with the police?"

"Yes. There's something else going on, but Rochambeau wouldn't tell me what."

"Aren't they going to rescue Dmitri?"

"I'm not leaving here until I know," Rowan said.

Another hour passed. Rowan's stomach grumbled. It was almost eleven, and he hadn't had breakfast, not even a cup of coffee. Taylor was out in St. Jean Cap Ferrat, probably starving, too.

Rowan broke down and called Albin. "What is happening?" the Frenchman said. "I have been so worried."

"Dmitri's still at Demidov's house," Rowan said, not mentioning the chains. "Taylor's waiting outside, and I'm stuck here at the police station. Can you pick up some breakfast and take it out to Taylor?"

He heard Albin suck in a breath. "I will go now."

"Be careful, Albin. These people are dangerous."

It took another hour before Rochambeau returned. This time he sat down across from Rowan. "Here is our situation," he said. "For some time we have been hearing rumors of young people disappearing. For the most part these young men and women are from the former Soviet Union. Whoever is preying on them chooses people without family or friends, so that it is difficult to trace them. And because many of them are here illegally, to work in hotels or fields, there are no records."

Rowan nodded but said nothing.

"Recently we intercepted a message regarding a movement of people from the Côte D'Azur to North Africa. You understand, most of the time such movement goes in the other direction, so it was unusual."

"You think these missing people are being sent to Africa?"

Rochambeau shrugged. "There, or the Middle East. There is still a market for sex slaves there."

Rowan sat back against his chair. "You think Demidov is involved in this ... white slavery?"

"An interesting term," Rochambeau said. "For someone from a

country with a history of black slavery."

"Indeed. But Demidov? I thought you told me he was a drug dealer."

"Criminals often do not specialize." Rochambeau pushed a topographical map across the table to Rowan. "These are the coordinates where the boat will arrive to pick up these people." He pointed to a small inlet on the gooseneck of Cap Ferrat. "And here is Demidov's house. You will notice that his property is one of the very few homes between the Chemin des Douaniers and the sea."

"So you think this boat is docking behind Demidov's house to pick people up for transport?" Rowan asked.

Rochambeau nodded. "Such a place is very difficult for the police to monitor as there is no vantage point. It is a perfect location to accept deliveries of drugs—or to make shipments out as well."

"I didn't get the sense that there was anyone else in the house besides Demidov, Dmitri and the bodyguard," Rowan said. "But I could be wrong."

"We have taken heat-sensitive surveys," Rochambeau said. "You are correct, that the missing people are not being held at the house. But we believe they will arrive there soon."

"When?"

"The rendezvous was called for tonight. So you understand, we cannot mount an investigation at this time. We do not know where these other people are, but we hope they will arrive at Demidov's house sometime today."

Rowan's cell phone rang. He looked at the display and recognized the number of the prepaid cell phone Taylor had bought. "This is my associate," he said to Rochambeau, who nodded.

"Taylor?"

"There are police here, Rowan. They're holding me and Albin." Taylor's voice was strained.

"May I?" Rochambeau held his hand out for the phone. "I am inspector Claude Rochambeau of the Service Régional de la Police Judiciaire. May I speak with the officer with you?"

He spoke rapidly in French, then handed the phone back to Rowan. "They are my men," he said. "I will have someone bring your associates here."

"We would rather stay in St. Jean," Rowan said.

"Not at the house."

Rowan nodded. "Fine. But in the town?"

"That is acceptable."

Rowan took the phone back. "Taylor, have Albin drive you to the café where we went yesterday. I'll meet you there."

Taylor agreed, and Rowan hung up. "Assuming I'm free to go?" Rowan asked.

"Yes." Rochambeau pulled out his wallet and extracted a card. He wrote his cell phone number on the back and handed it to Rowan. "And your number?"

Rowan recited it to him, and Rochambeau wrote it down. "You promise me you will do nothing to compromise this investigation?"

"I have two responsibilities," Rowan said. "I want Dmitri safe, and I want *The Russian Boy* returned to the museum."

"I believe our interests can work together."

"Then I will not interfere."

"The young man who is being held at Demidov's house—Dmitri—do you think they plan to include him with this transport?"

"It's impossible to say, M'sieur."

That was not reassuring to Rowan as he rode back to St. Jean. What if Demidov had Dmitri killed before these other people arrived that night? But why keep him chained up, otherwise?

He worried that this whole enterprise was one big wild goose chase. He was being paid to retrieve the painting, and he didn't even know for sure that Demidov had it. All he had was Scarano's belief that Demidov had killed his son, and Dmitri seeing the cardboard tube in Demidov's bedroom. What if the painting was somewhere else? Suppose the police came in and Demidov was arrested, or even killed. Would they ever find *The Russian Boy*?

And what about Dmitri? Suppose the police were wrong about the coordinates, or the plans, and Dmitri was shipped to Africa or Asia as a sex slave, along with the other young people Demidov had assembled?

By the time he pulled up at the café overlooking the port of St. Jean, his head and his stomach both ached. He ordered two cappuccinos, and gulped the first one while he explained what had happened at the police station, and waited for his food.

"But Dmitri," Albin said, when Rowan had finished. "Why must he stay at the house until this police raid?"

"They don't want to scare Demidov and screw up this other operation." Rowan felt his head starting to clear.

"And we just sit and wait?" Albin asked.

The Russian Boy

The waiter brought a pissaladiere, a French pizza covered with onions, olives, garlic and anchovies rather than tomato sauce and cheese. Rowan dug in greedily. "You guys want any?" he asked, between mouthfuls.

"Albin brought food," Taylor said. "But you didn't answer his question. We just sit around and wait for the police to get their act together?"

"As far as I can tell, the police have their act together already. They're expecting a group of people to be brought to the villa tonight, to be put onto a boat to Africa to be sex slaves. As soon as they show up, the police will swoop in and rescue them, and Dmitri."

Albin laughed bitterly. "You trust the flics too much."

"We have to. But we don't have to wait here." He continued to eat while he talked. "We can stake out a new position, close enough to the villa to watch, but far enough away so the police won't see us."

"We could climb that hill across from the villa," Taylor said.

"We'll have to find a way to approach from the other side of the Chemin des Douaniers. We can't just pull up in front of the villa and start climbing."

He looked at Albin. "You have a laptop with you?"

"In my car."

"The café has a wireless network," Rowan said, nodding toward a sign. "Why don't you see if you can find us any topographic maps of the area?"

Albin's command of English didn't extend to the word topographic, so Rowan had to explain. When he did, Albin got up and walked toward his car.

"How are you holding up?" Taylor asked.

Rowan stifled a yawn. "I'm good, now that I've got some food and caffeine in me. How about you?"

"Dmitri and I used to paint outside Sacré Coeur for hours in the cold, day after day. This is a walk in the park."

Rowan noted that reference to Taylor's life with Dmitri, and wondered again how this situation was going to end. Would the two young painters both go back to Paris?

Albin returned with his laptop and started searching for maps. Rowan finished his pizza and ordered himself a *coupe liegoise*, a bowl of vanilla ice cream, chocolate sauce, and toasted almonds, served with shortbread finger biscuits. "You should get one, too," he said to Albin and Taylor. "We'll need the sugar to keep going."

clxxi

Albin demurred but Taylor said, "Sounds delicious."

While they ate their ice cream, Albin found them a route through the woods alongside the waterfront Chemin de la Carriere that would bring them out above the villa.

"Nothing is going to happen until after dark," Rowan said. "I need to go back into Nice and buy some supplies." He pulled his small notebook out of his pocket and began making a list. "Albin, you want to be my purchasing agent? See if you can find a place in Nice where I can buy this stuff."

They agreed that Taylor would ride with Rowan, and Albin would follow them. They spent the rest of the afternoon traveling around Nice, buying GPS devices, night-vision goggles and other equipment. They stopped for a quick dinner at a café by the Port Lympia, in the old part of the city. Behind them, the tell-tales from a dozen sailboats clanked in the light breeze, interrupted by the occasional boat motor or shouted cry.

Albin had little appetite. "I am worried for Dmitri. He will be so frightened."

"Dmitri's a survivor." Taylor reached over and squeezed Albin's hand. "He's tough and smart and he works hard for what he wants."

Rowan agreed with Albin. Dmitri had sounded terrified, and Demidov was a very bad man to be involved with. And once again he wondered if, despite Taylor's assurances, he and Dmitri would get back together. For one thing, they shared an apartment in Paris. It wouldn't be easy for either of them to just walk out. And he'd be going back to New York, back to the simple existence he had created for himself.

At least he hoped he'd be going back with the $5,000 that his son needed for his art course. That was one good thing that could come out of all this. And if Dmitri got out alive, that would be another.

The Russian Boy

clxxiii

Rescue Operations

Nice, Saturday night

Rowan paid for dinner and then hopped on the motorcycle, with Taylor behind him. They followed Albin's car back to the parking grounds of the big, blocky Hotel du Cap, where they parked, and set out through the streets and woods to the waterfront.

It was dark and spooky in the woods, and in the distance they could hear the sounds of surf crashing against the shore on the south and west sides of the point. He knew from the satellite views he had seen that the cove below Demidov's house was much more protected.

Rowan hadn't been much of an outdoorsman as a kid or adult, and he didn't like the way the trees moved restlessly, creaked and cast shadows. But he sucked it up. Albin had traced a route based on coordinates, and Rowan plugged them into the GPS device and led the way. Since they didn't know how far the police had penetrated into the forest, they moved slowly and carefully, stopping at every unfamiliar noise or movement of a small creature.

At a clearing overlooking the port, Rowan stopped to consider the coordinates, Albin and Taylor behind him. There was a rustling to his right, and he turned toward the sound. A moment later, something big and dark erupted from the underbrush and rushed toward them, growling. His heart rate zoomed and instinctively he stepped in front of Taylor to protect him.

The dog wasn't interested in them, and rushed past. But it took a long time before his heart rate returned to normal. If Taylor noticed Rowan's protective move, he didn't say anything. But Rowan could tell all three of them were equally jittery. In addition to the wild creatures, there could be police, and Demidov's henchmen, anywhere around them.

By eight o'clock they were in position on a ridge overlooking the villa and its grounds. They didn't have a clear view; there were too many trees in the way. But they could see the wrought-iron gates. "Where are the flics?" Albin asked in a low voice.

"If we could see them, then Demidov could, too," Rowan said. "We just have to hope they're still there."

Taylor took the first watch, leaving Albin and Rowan to sit back against trees and rest. Rowan closed his eyes and was surprised to realize he had dozed off, when Taylor shook his shoulder.

The Russian Boy

"Something's happening," he said.

The three of them clustered at the top of the hill as Taylor pointed out a white van at the gate to the villa. As the gates opened, police in riot gear swarmed out of the trees, barking orders and waving guns.

"We go now?" Albin asked.

"Are you crazy?" Rowan asked, grabbing his arm. "You want to jump in the middle of a police operation? We wait here."

The three of them watched as the officers divided into two teams. The first surrounded the van and motioned the driver and another man from the front seat to get out. Then the back door was opened, and six young women and two young men stepped out. Two of the women looked very weak and stumbled as they walked.

"Those must be the people who were supposed to be transported," Rowan whispered. "At least they're safe."

"But what about Dmitri?" Albin said.

"Hold on. The police are going into the house. They'll find him." The second team ran toward the front door. Rowan thought he recognized Rochambeau's voice as the lead officer spoke through a megaphone toward the house.

The front door opened, and Demidov appeared framed in light, with Boris behind him. Both of them had their hands up.

"Where is Dmitri?" Albin asked. Again he tried to go toward the house, and again Rowan had to grab his arm.

"He should still be locked up in the house," Rowan said. "Unless you saw them take him somewhere else?"

Taylor shook his head. "I watched the house from the time you left until the time the police picked us up. Did the policeman tell you that Demidov left while we weren't watching?"

"He wouldn't have told me anything."

Two officers led Demidov and Boris toward a squad car which had pulled up into the driveway, while the other four entered the house, weapons drawn. "If Dmitri's in there, they'll find him," Rowan said.

They waited. Rowan could sense the tension coming off Albin in waves, and his own heart beat rapidly. What if Dmitri was dead, and Rowan had abandoned him? Taylor took his hand and squeezed it. "Dmitri will be all right. I know it."

The car with Demidov and Boris drove away, and an ambulance arrived for the two weakest women. The other women and the two men were bundled into additional police cars.

"What if they don't find him?" Albin said. "Suppose they just give up and he is still inside?"

"Rochambeau knows he's supposed to be there," Rowan said. "We just have to wait."

The two ambulances pulled away, followed by two police cars. There were still two cars in the driveway, a patrol car and a Citroën DS5 sedan. "There must still be officers in the house," Rowan said.

They watched. After another ten minutes, a plainclothes officer stepped out the front door, escorting someone small, wrapped in a towel. "It's Dmitri!" Albin said.

Rowan could feel relief coming from both Albin and Taylor. He took a deep breath. At least Dmitri was safe. He picked up the goggles and peered through them. "That's Rochambeau with him. But Dmitri's not carrying anything. Where is the painting?"

"I must go to him." Albin started to move forward.

This time rather than stopping him, Rowan said, "If you want to see him, go to the *Police Judiciare* offices on the Rue de Roquebilliere. I'm sure that's where Rochambeau will take him."

"Will they arrest him?" Albin asked.

"I told Rochambeau that Dmitri stole the painting." He kept the goggles trained on Rochambeau, who led Dmitri to the sedan. A uniformed officer got in the back with Dmitri.

"What!" Albin said. "But what if they put him in prison? Why would do you do such a thing?"

"Before I knew about the smuggling operation I thought that would encourage Rochambeau to rescue Dmitri." He put the goggles down and looked at Albin. "Remember, I work for the people who own the half-million-dollar painting Dmitri stole. It's my responsibility to get it back. If he has to go to jail for the theft, then that's his problem."

Albin tried to punch Rowan, but he ducked, and Taylor grabbed the Frenchman's arms from behind. "No, no!" Albin said, and he began to weep.

Taylor turned him around and hugged him, throwing an angry glance at Rowan. "You have to be strong, Albin," he said. "Go to the police. Find out about Dmitri."

Rowan handed him one of the GPS devices. "Go back to your car and drive into Nice. Taylor's right. Go to the police. Take Taylor with you."

"What will you do?"

The Russian Boy

"I need to find the painting." Rowan looked back at the villa. "I wonder if they're going to send an evidence team right away, or wait until morning."

"This is France," Albin said.

Two more officers stepped out of the front door of the house, closing it behind them. They walked to the remaining squad car, and followed Rochambeau's sedan down the driveway.

Rochambeau's car left along the Chemin des Douaniers, but the squad car remained in front of the gates, which swung closed.

"Go on, Albin," Rowan said. "Take Taylor, and go to the police. They probably won't let you see Dmitri for a while, but at least they can tell him that you're waiting there. Rochambeau doesn't seem like a bad guy. Maybe he'll even tell Dmitri that you're there."

"I'm going to stay with you," Taylor said. "You're going to break into that house, aren't you? You can't do that alone. You can't even get over the fence by yourself."

"Of course I can."

"You can get in but you can't get out. No arguments." He started down the hillside, and Rowan followed, as Albin turned around to return to his car.

"Wait for me, Taylor," Rowan grumbled. Then he lost his footing, slipped, and went skidding down the hill, knocking right into Taylor and sending both of them sprawling to the ground. He ended up on top of Taylor, his dick pressed through his pants against Taylor's leg. To his horror he felt it growing.

"Jesus," Taylor said. "Hold your horses, Mr. Horny. There'll be plenty of time for that after we find the painting and get back to the hotel."

"Sorry." Rowan was sure his face was red. He stood up.

"Take my hand," Taylor said. "It's obvious my balance is better than yours."

"I'll be fine."

"Take my fucking hand," Taylor said, and Rowan heard something in his tone that said maybe Taylor was starting to feel over his head.

He reached out for Taylor's hand and squeezed it. "You're amazing, you know that?"

"So I've been told. Though not by you until just now."

Rowan laughed. At the edge of the woods, they paused. The squad car was facing them, with its headlights lit. "We'll have to go around," Rowan said.

They walked carefully through the woods, passing the squad car, and it was only when they were past it that Rowan realized he'd been holding his breath.

For good measure they walked another hundred feet until the road curved, then hurried across it. They were exposed along the side of the road for that same hundred feet until they could dart into the cover of the olive groves surrounding the villa.

They walked along the fence, searching for the tree with the overhanging branch. But it was hard to find in the dark, and the night vision goggles only showed tree after tree, none of them leaning in the right direction.

"I don't ever want to climb a tree after we get finished with this," Rowan grumbled. "Where is that goddamn tree?"

"It didn't pick up and walk away," Taylor said. "It's got to be here somewhere. Just keep walking."

Rowan bumped right into it, banging his head. "Shit."

"Well, at least you found it," Taylor said. "You first. I'll spot you."

Rowan felt self-conscious as he hoisted himself up. What was he doing, imagining a future with a twenty-something guy? He was too old to keep a young buck interested. Hell, he was too old to be climbing trees in the dead of night. He scraped his shin on the tree's rough bark, and made a very ungraceful dismount to the inside of the fence. He was nursing his ankle when Taylor dropped down beside him. "You all right?" Taylor asked.

"I'll survive."

"Well, then, lead on, Macduff," Taylor said.

"Cute and talented and he quotes Shakespeare," Rowan said. "I think I'm in love."

He said it jokingly, but Taylor leaned over and kissed him on the lips. "The feeling is mutual."

Rowan felt as if he'd stuck his finger in an electric socket. Taylor pushed the small of his back and he began moving across the darkened lawn, toward the back of the house.

"How are we going to get inside?" Taylor asked.

"We're going to have to play it by ear."

They prowled around the rear of the house looking for a way in. The windows were too small, and only doors were sliding glass ones. Shining a flashlight in, Rowan could see that there were bars on the inside preventing the doors from being opened even if the lock was picked.

The Russian Boy

"Fuck me," Rowan said, when they had examined the last door.

"Later," Taylor said. "What about the front?"

"What if the cop at the front gate is watching?"

"Do we have a choice?"

Rowan sighed. "You're right."

They crept around to the front of the house. The squad car was still parked at the gate, its headlights facing parallel to the gate rather than inside. "Stay here," Rowan whispered. He pulled a pair of rubber gloves from his pocket and slipped them on, then walked carefully up to the front door.

He tested the knob—and it turned. Thank God for small favors, he thought. He looked back to Taylor and nodded, and as he pushed the door open and stepped inside, Taylor followed him in.

Taylor closed the door behind them. The only illumination was moonlight from the sliding glass doors, but with the night vision goggles the room was lit with an eerie green glow.

"Look at the walls," Taylor said, his voice catching.

Even in the green glow, Rowan recognized that he was in the presence of great art. The Chagall painting they had seen earlier had pride of place in the center of the wall, with a short stepstool next to it. It was surrounded by other paintings by Russian masters—Goncharova, Kandinsky and Bakst, among them.

"I could just stay here and study," Taylor said.

"Take a good look, because I'm sure all of these will be confiscated by the police in the morning," Rowan said. "Or even in the next few hours, if Albin's wrong about the efficiency of the evidence collection team."

He knew that he should look for *The Russian Boy*, but he couldn't stop staring at one particular portrait, a Valentin Serov portrait of a young man in military garb. Suddenly the room was strobed with light so bright that Rowan had to shut his eyes. "The police must be back," he said. "Dmitri said he saw the cardboard tube on the bureau in Demidov's bedroom. We'd better hurry if we expect to get the painting and get out before they come in."

He hurried to the staircase, Taylor behind him, and climbed to the second floor as they heard the sound of a car engine outside, then doors slamming. Rowan looked into the first room they came to. It was an office. The second was a small bedroom. It wasn't until the third that they found the master bedroom.

They heard the front door open. "Why don't we just let the police retrieve the painting?" Taylor asked. "Now that they're here."

"If the painting's in a cardboard tube, the police may not recognize it for what it is. I need to make sure that it stays safe."

He spotted the cardboard tube on the long, low bureau and crossed the room to it, as he heard voices in French downstairs. He picked up the tube. It felt heavy, which was a good sign."

"We'd better get out of here," Rowan whispered.

"Aren't you going to open it?"

"Not here. Not now. We've got to get out before the police find us."

He grabbed the tube and slung it over his shoulder, just as he figured Dmitri had carried it, then walked back to the bedroom door, listening. There were more voices downstairs now. "How are we going to get out of here?" Taylor asked.

Rowan looked around the bedroom. Tall French doors opened out onto a balcony overlooking the ocean, and remembered the circular stair they'd seen when they walked around the house in daylight. He hurried across the room and tried the latch.

It wouldn't turn. He undid the bolt and the doors swung open. The surf was quiet, the sea a dark void ahead of them. To one side was a gate that led to the stairs. He lifted the latch, which creaked so loudly he was sure it was audible throughout the house.

He held his breath. No one on the ground floor had raised an alarm, so he nodded to Taylor to follow him and he began going slowly down the stairs. The lawn below him was lit with a glowing rectangle of light coming from the living room.

He paused once he could peer in the living room. There were four men inside, all of them staring at the art around them. But at any minute, one of them could glance out the window and see Rowan and Taylor. He stood there, paralyzed.

"Swing and drop," Taylor whispered.

"What?"

"Step aside."

He shouldered past Rowan, grabbed the railing, and swung out into space, dropping to the ground on the far side of the staircase, out of view of the living room. He landed on his feet, but then fell to the ground.

"Taylor!" Rowan said. He gave up on caution and raced around the stairs, disregarding the chance that anyone would see him from inside. The cardboard tube banged against his arm. He raced around to

The Russian Boy

Taylor.

"I'm fine," Taylor said, sitting up. "Just landed funny."

They were both in the shadows and no one inside seemed to have raised an alarm. "Let's get out of here," Rowan said. He helped Taylor to his feet, both of them shaky, and began the long journey through the woods.

Discovery

Nice, March 1913

Alexei was in awe as he watched Fyodor's painting of him develop. It was early March, and most of the Russian nobility were preparing to return to Moscow and St. Petersburg, so Fyodor had to hurry to put the finishing touches on various portraits. Alexei was kept busy ferrying paintings to and from the framer, as well as his regular duties at the studio. So there was not much time to pose, but Fyodor was determined to carve out a half hour or so at first light, almost every day.

Alexei had always loved Fyodor's work, but he could see that the painter was doing something new and different with this portrait. There was an animation and a palpable sense of desire that had not been previously evident in Fyodor's paintings.

One morning in mid-March, a week before Orthodox Easter, Alexei brought up the question he had been longing to ask. "Will I be able to stay with you, Maestro, when my family goes back to Russia?"

Fyodor looked up from his easel. "That is up to your father."

"Will you ask him for me?"

"You must do that yourself, my little one. Show him your work, how much you have improved. See what he says."

"Do you want me to stay?"

Fyodor put down his paintbrush. "Of course I do. I love you. But you are dependent on your father, and I rely on the good will of the Russian community. We must not do anything to jeopardize either. If you must go back to St. Petersburg, you must. I usually go to Russia myself, in the summer. We can be together then. And you will come back next winter."

Alexei pouted, and Fyodor said, "Please, resume your position. I am almost finished for today."

That afternoon Gavril appeared at the studio door as Fyodor was finishing a portrait of an older Russian woman with double chins. "Go, enjoy your afternoon with your brother," Fyodor said. "I will clean up myself."

"I must change my clothes." Alexei ducked behind the screen, and once again Gavril attempted to follow him.

"Gavril! This is private!"

"You are my brother. Nothing is private from me." Gavril pushed

The Russian Boy

him lightly in the chest, and Alexei stepped back. Then his brother repeated the gesture, until both of them were protected from the studio by the screen.

Alexei looked at him in alarm. At least he had made the bed that morning, so there was no clear evidence that he and the maestro slept together.

Gavril stood at the entrance to the sleeping chamber, his arms crossed. "Go on, you said you have to change."

Alexei had become shy around Gavril when his body began to change, when he sprouted hair under his arms and felt his dick stiffen. He was embarrassed that Gavril might see some change in him and comment on it. But his brother appeared implacable, so Alexei pulled off his shirt, folding it carefully.

"I have to talk to you," Gavril said in a low voice. He pointed to the bed. "It is just as I heard. You sleep in here with him, don't you?"

Alexei struggled to remain calm. "There is only one bed." He wanted to pull his pants off but was embarrassed, so he stood there half-clothed. "People sleep together all the time without anyone taking notice. You and I shared a bed when we were children."

"People are talking," Gavril said, looking away from his brother and toward the screen separating them from the studio. "The Baron Pshkov has been making crude jokes about the services you provide to Luschenko."

"The Baron Pshkov!" Alexei said, a little too loud. He lowered his voice. "They say he has one valet to bugger him and another to suck his dick."

Gavril looked horrified. "How can you even speak that way?"

"If you are going to quote the Baron Pshkov to me you should know what kind of source he is."

"Obviously he is a source who knows what he is talking about." Gavril turned around the room, surveying it. He noticed the canvas of Alexei, covered with an old sheet. "What is this?" he asked.

"No!" Alexei said reaching out for his hand. "That is private. You must not look at the maestro's work until it is finished."

Gavril shook off his arm and pushed him aside. He lifted the cloth, and his mouth dropped open. "It is you!"

"Yes, it is," Alexei said crossly. "Put the cover down."

Gavril dropped it, as if it was diseased. He looked back at his brother. "But you are naked."

"You have seen me naked since we were children and we were

bathed together."

Gavril backed away. "It is true, then, what they say. That he is buggering you." The horror shone on his face, and he glared at his brother.

"Gavril, please," Alexei said, reaching out toward him. "You must not tell anyone, especially not Papa. The maestro is teaching me a great deal about painting. I must be able to stay with him."

"You most certainly must not! The honor of our family is at stake, to say nothing of your own standing as a man."

Gavril turned and rushed away from the sleeping quarters. Alexei wanted to run after him, but he couldn't appear half-naked in the studio with the portrait subject there. By the time he had pulled his shirt on, Gavril had gone out the front door.

Alexei chased after him, running down the twisting stairs to the ground level, his pulse racing. When he burst out the front door he found Gavril leaning in the door of the Lancia Epsilon, speaking with his father in the driver's seat. The sun glinted off the car's rounded hood, so bright that it brought tears to Alexei's eyes.

His father jumped out of the car, wearing his driving coat, with his goggles hanging around his neck like a second set of eyes. He stalked around the front of the car and grabbed Alexei by the shoulder. "Is this true? That you are this painter's catamite?"

Alexei didn't recognize the word. He struggled to contain his sobs. "I am his apprentice. He is teaching me to paint."

"He is corrupting you. Get in the car. I am taking you home."

"No! You can't take me from him." He tried to back away from his father, but the older man had an iron grip on Alexei's shoulder. Gavril grabbed one arm, and the Count the other, and they pushed Alexei into the back of the car.

"You can't take me away from the maestro!" Alexei struggled against Gavril, who got in beside him to hold him down. The count put his goggles on his face, looking like a giant insect, and got into the front seat. The car came on with a roar, and the Count reached over to the horn mounted on the side and blasted it twice at a horse and carriage ahead of them. Then he swerved around them and drove past, as Alexei huddled in the back seat and cried. His brother sat opposite him with his arms crossed.

When they reached the Villa des Oliviers, the Count shut the car off and stalked toward the stables. Gavril took Alexei by the arm and pushed him toward the house, where he was locked in his room. He

The Russian Boy

did not even have his paints to occupy him. All he could do was lie on his bed and cry.

His bedroom window looked out over the front of the house, and late in the afternoon Alexei saw Fyodor Luschenko arrive in a hired horse and carriage. The valet, Leo, answered the door, but would not allow Luschenko to enter. Alexei watched from his window, tears streaking his face, as his maestro walked slowly back to his carriage, his head and back bowed.

He tried to open the window, but it was locked. He banged on it, but Luschenko either did not hear, or would not look up. Alexei placed his palms flat on the window as he watched Luschenko drive away, and the tears streamed down his face.

Leo was sent to the studio the next day to retrieve Alexei's clothes, with specific instructions to leave all paintings and art supplies there. Two days later, Alexei returned to St. Petersburg with his parents, his brother and sister, and his grandmother.

He never saw Fyodor Luschenko again.

A Two-Man Operation

Nice, Saturday night

Rowan and Taylor retrieved the motorcycle and went back to the Negresco. Rowan was exhausted and knew that he should go to the police station to check on Dmitri—but that would have to wait until morning.

The streets of Nice were busy even at that hour, and Rowan kept looking behind him to see if the police had realized he and Taylor had been in the house and were chasing them. But they made it back to the hotel without incident, and climbed wearily up to Rowan's room.

Once there, he unscrewed the plastic cap from the tube. Then he reached inside and felt canvas. Taylor stood beside him, watching his every move.

Slowly and painstakingly he pulled the canvas from the tube, and then unrolled it onto the bed. There, below him, was the painting he had loved for so long. The edges of the canvas were rough, and there was some damage to the curtains behind the boy, but *The Russian Boy* shone.

"It's amazing," Taylor said. "To be able to paint like that."

"You watch," Rowan said, staring at the canvas. "Someday people will be saying that about your work." He turned to the young man next to him and they kissed, with the watchful eye of the young Russian staring up at them.

When he felt Taylor's body sagging beneath him, Rowan pulled away. He lifted the painting carefully from the bed and carried it to the large table where they had been eating. His body ached and he was so tired he could barely see straight. He and Taylor both discarded their clothes and collapsed into bed together. Just before he fell asleep he thought of Dmitri, and hoped that he was all right.

Rowan woke to sunlight streaming in the room. It was just before six on Sunday morning, and he and Taylor had only had a few hours' sleep. He picked up his cell phone and carried it into the bathroom with him. After he'd relieved himself, he called Albin.

"Rowan? You are with the police?" Albin asked.

"No, not yet. How about you?"

"I went there last night but they would not let me see Dmitri, or remain there. I am to call later to see if I may post bail."

"But Dmitri's all right?"

"They would not say."

"Taylor and I are going over there as soon as he wakes up. We'll call you later."

Taylor was awake when Rowan left the bathroom, and they both showered quickly and then rode to the *Police Judiciare* offices on the Rue de Roquebilliere. It was seven in the morning, but despite the hour, there was a buzz of activity at the offices. Rowan asked to speak to Claude Rochambeau regarding the raid on Demidov's home, and this time he only waited a few minutes before the inspector came out to the waiting area. "This is my associate, Taylor Griffin," Rowan said, introducing them.

"You know that we were successful last night?" Rochambeau asked.

"Yes. We came to ask about Dmitri Baranov."

Rochambeau nodded. "Follow me." He led them into the same interview room where he and Rowan had spoken on Thursday. It seemed like such a long time had passed since then.

"So what are we to do about M. Baranov?" Rochambeau said, when Rowan and Taylor were seated at the scarred metal table. "Interpol would like to speak with him about the stolen painting."

"I have it right here," Rowan said, holding up the cardboard tube. "Dmitri risked his life to help me retrieve it. I hope that will be in his favor with Interpol."

"How do you come to have it in your possession? I thought you believed it was in Demidov's house."

"I was hired to retrieve the painting. I did."

Rochambeau frowned, but he didn't push the issue. "May I see?"

Once again, Rowan opened the cardboard tube and carefully withdrew the painting. With Taylor's help he spread it out on the table. In the bright fluorescent light, *The Russian Boy* glowed with vibrant color and effusive brush strokes. Looking at it up close, Rowan could see both the influence of the Impressionists, but also something more, something unique to Fyodor Luschenko. There was a passion in the application of the paint, along with a deliberateness. He found himself drawn to the pearl of precum at the tip of the young man's penis. It was a microcosm of everything the painting stood for, a combination of color that created an effect of light, shadow and beauty.

"This is the painting? You are sure?" Rochambeau asked.

"I'm sure."

Rochambeau nodded, and Rowan rolled the painting up and put it back in the tube.

"I will take charge of it now, please." Rochambeau held out his hand.

Rowan began to protest, but Rochambeau said, "This painting is evidence in a case of theft. While I appreciate your help and your role in its recovery, I must insist."

"Will you speak to Interpol about Dmitri?" Taylor asked. "Tell them that he feels bad and he did everything he could to get the painting back."

"You may do that yourself. Please return here on Monday at nine a.m. I know you have all put yourselves at risk to retrieve the painting-- but you understand, these things are out of my hands." He took the painting and left the room.

"Well," Taylor said.

Rowan looked at his watch. It was still early in the morning, and he realized that he was still very tired. "I don't know about you, but now that we know Dmitri is safe, I am very much looking forward to getting back to the Negresco."

Taylor yawned, and Rowan followed. "I guess that's a yes," Rowan said.

Rowan struggled to stay awake on the brief trip back to the hotel. He left the motorcycle with the valet at the front door, and they collapsed back in bed. He woke to Taylor nuzzling his neck. "What time is it?" he asked.

"Nearly noon. We've slept away half the day." He leaned down and kissed Rowan on the lips, then ran his hand down Rowan's chest to his crotch.

Rowan's dick was achingly hard with the need to urinate. "I have to use the restroom," he said, sitting up.

"You mean that isn't for me?" Taylor sat back against the pillows and smiled.

"It's for you, all right. Just give an old man a couple of minutes to get his act together."

"We've got all day," Taylor said.

Pissing was painful, Rowan pressing down on his stiff dick until the urine streamed out. He was hungry and thirsty and horny all at the same time.

When he got out of the bathroom, Taylor was on the phone. "I ordered us some room service," he said, as he hung up. "I hope that's OK."

The Russian Boy

"A man after my own heart," Rowan said, smiling.

"Among other body parts." Taylor patted the bed next to him. "I figure we have at least fifteen minutes before the food gets here."

"What I have in mind for you will take a lot longer than that," Rowan said, sitting down next to Taylor. "But fifteen minutes is a start."

He leaned down and kissed Taylor, who sprawled back against the heaping pillows. Both of them had grizzled chins, though Rowan's was rougher and grayer than Taylor's. Rowan was struck again by how beautiful Taylor was, and how young.

"How old are you anyway?" he asked.

Taylor smiled. "Does it matter?"

"I'm fifty." Rowan swung his leg over so he was straddling Taylor. "I don't have a lot of money, and I don't even have a steady job. All the money I bring in from this case is going to send my son to a painting course in Italy. I can't offer you what you deserve."

He leaned down and kissed Taylor again. The young man's smooth full lips felt soft and yielding beneath his own. "You can offer me this," Taylor said, reaching down to Rowan's stiff dick.

Rowan groaned. "I'm serious."

"So am I." Taylor smiled. "I'm twenty-six, Rowan. I don't need money; I've been living on rice and vegetables and the occasional glass of cheap wine since I was old enough to drink. And the better I get, the more I can charge tourists for my paintings. You don't need to pay a dime for me. All you have to do is love me."

There was a sharp rap at the door. "Hold that thought," Rowan said. "And cover yourself up." He stood up and grabbed a bathrobe, then went to the door. He was surprised to find Albin there.

"What are we to do about Dmitri?" he asked.

"Come on in." Rowan saw the room service waiter just behind Albin, and while Albin sat down at the table with Taylor, Rowan signed for the food.

"We'll go to the police together tomorrow," Rowan said, sitting down and picking up a *tartine*, a slice of baguette that had been spread with raspberry jam. "Mmm, this is delicious," he said, after he bit into it. "Help yourself, Albin."

"I cannot eat for worrying about Dmitri."

Rowan put the tartine down. "Dmitri committed a crime, Albin. If he has to pay for what he did, he will. But I promise you I will do whatever I can to help him." He held up the platter of chocolate croissants. "Now eat something. You can't help Dmitri if you're so hungry you can't think."

Albin grudgingly accepted a croissant, and Rowan poured hot chocolate from the pitcher, and all three of them ate a midday breakfast.

When the food was finished, Rowan sat back. "There's nothing more we can do today, Albin. You should go home and get some rest. You'll feel better in the morning."

"I will stay with you," Albin said. "You are my only connection to Dmitri."

Rowan pushed back his chair and stood up. "Sorry, Albin, what Taylor and I have planned for this afternoon is strictly a two-man operation."

Albin looked confused, but then he looked from Rowan to Taylor and understanding dawned on his face. "Eh, bien, I will go home. But if you hear anything about Dmitri you will call me?"

"Yes. And we'll see you tomorrow morning at the Police Judiciare."

Rowan ushered Albin to the door, and closed and locked it behind him. He turned back to Taylor and shucked his robe, tossing it over a chair. "Where were we?"

Taylor stood up, dropped his own robe, then sprawled back on the bed. "I was here, and you were on top of me."

"I remember that," Rowan said, climbing on to the bed. "But I'd rather have you on top of me. You're a lot more limber than I am."

"I can show you how limber I am."

Rowan lay back against the pillows and Taylor climbed on top of him, facing Rowan's feet. He presented his naked ass to Rowan, who reached up and pried the globes apart and stuck his tongue into Taylor's pink hole.

Taylor groaned as he leaned down and began to suck Rowan's dick. Rowan slicked Taylor's hole with this tongue, then began tracing his index finger in ever-narrowing circles around it.

Rowan felt an orgasm rising from his balls to his belly, and Taylor must have felt it too because he pulled off and turned around to face Rowan again. He pressed his lips against Rowan's and reached behind him, pulling a condom out from under the pillow. He opened it and slipped it on Rowan's dick. Then he turned to face the door and slid his ass down over Rowan.

Rowan groaned beneath him. "You are amazing," he said.

"You ain't seen nothing yet." Taylor twisted around so that his face was back at Rowan's and kissed him again.

It was an amazing feeling, having Taylor slide up and down on his dick as they kissed. He felt so connected to Taylor, more than he had felt to any man in a long time.

The sensations were too wonderful; he couldn't hold back. He reached around to Taylor's dick and began jacking him as Taylor rode up and down on him. His pulse quickened and it was hard to breathe as the power of his orgasm surged inside him. Taylor howled and Rowan ejaculated into the condom as Taylor's dick spurted in Rowan's hand.

"I'd say that's pretty limber," Rowan said, panting, as Taylor slid off him and lay down next to him.

"Just one of my many talents," Taylor said. He yawned and nestled up against Rowan.

Flights

Nice, Monday morning

After a few hours in bed with Taylor, a great dinner, and a good night's sleep, Rowan woke for the last time to the glorious Mediterranean sunrise. They shared another room service breakfast, both of them lingering over the last dregs of hot chocolate even though Rowan was sure Taylor was as eager as he was to see Dmitri and know first-hand that he was all right.

"A boy could get spoiled by this," Taylor said, sighing, as he nibbled a chocolate croissant. "But I can see this fairy tale is coming to an end. If I don't want to lose my fellowship at the Institute I should get the train back to Paris later. And you'll go back to New York, won't you?"

"Let's see what happens today," Rowan said, though he felt his heart sinking at Taylor's matter-of-fact prediction. He tried to think of their time together as an amazing fling, separate from his dull real life, but that was hard to do when the gorgeous young man was still naked in his bed, with a dab of chocolate on his chin just waiting to be licked off.

Albin was waiting at the police headquarters when Rowan and Taylor arrived. Rochambeau only kept them waiting for a few minutes before ushering them back to the interview room, where they met a gruff, heavyset Frenchman from Interpol named Duclos. "The museum in New York has declined to press charges as long as the painting is returned to them," he said.

"So Dmitri is free to go?" Albin asked.

"He is on a student visa," Duclos said. "The Institute des Artistes in Paris has revoked his fellowship. Without it he must return to Russia."

Albin looked at Rowan for help.

"Is there no way he could stay in France?" Rowan asked. "He risked his life to get the painting back."

"The painting he stole," Duclos said.

"He was desperate," Taylor said. "He's an amazing painter, you know. That's all he cares about. France has a great tradition of supporting artists. Can't you continue that for him?"

Duclos looked at Rochambeau, who shrugged. "How will he support himself?" Duclos asked.

The Russian Boy

"I will take care of him," Albin said. "I have an apartment and a job. I promise he will not be a burden to the state."

"The paperwork will have to go through the proper channels," Duclos said. "But for now I believe M. Baranov can be released." He opened the door. "If you will come with me, Monsieur?"

Albin stood up to follow him. "You will come to my apartment tonight?" he asked Rowan and Taylor. "We will celebrate?"

"Of course," Taylor said, and Rowan nodded.

When Duclos and Albin had gone, Rowan asked Rochambeau, "What about the painting?"

"I have spoken with the director of the Institute des Artistes. He would like you to return the painting to Paris so the restorer can finish his work."

"I can do that," Rowan said. At least he would be able to go to Paris with Taylor. Rochambeau left, and returned a few minutes later with the painting in the battered cardboard tube. Rowan opened the plastic cap and peered in, just to be sure.

"It is the same painting," Rochambeau said.

"You understand I have to be careful," Rowan said. "This painting has been through a lot since it left Paris."

Rochambeau shook their hands and ushered them back out to the lobby. "I may need to contact you for further statements," Rochambeau said. "We found Henri Scarano's fingerprints at Pascal Gaultier's home, and Gaultier gave us a statement that puts Scarano together with Yegor Rostnikov."

"You found Gaultier?" Rowan asked.

"Yes. We will keep a closer eye on him now that we know where he is." Rochambeau gave them both a brief bow, and left.

"I need to call my boss," Rowan said, as they walked out the door of the police station. "And make arrangements for Paris."

"I'd like to paint, if I can," Taylor said. "If I only have one more day in this amazing light."

"Fine with me. Just take your cell with you." They took a cab back to the Negresco, and Taylor took his easel and canvas out to the Promenade to work on the painting he had begun on Friday.

Standing at the window overlooking the ocean, Rowan looked at his watch. If it was eleven in the morning in Nice, it was only six AM in New York. But he knew Ron Kramer was an early riser, and sure enough, Kramer picked up his cell after only a single ring.

"I have the painting, and I'm taking it back to Paris," Rowan said.

"Then I'll come back to New York."

"Good job," Ron said. "I knew you could handle this. But I don't want you to hold that painting any longer than you have to. Can you get to Paris tonight?"

Rowan felt his stomach drop. He had been hoping to have one more night with Taylor.

"Let me see what I can work out," he said.

There was a 6:05 flight that evening that got into Orly at 7:30, and he booked two tickets, one for himself and one for Taylor. Fortunately Taylor had left his passport in the hotel room and Rowan was able to enter all the necessary information.

When he had made all the arrangements, he went back to the window overlooking the Promenade and the ocean, and spotted Taylor at his easel. Should he go out and tell Taylor that they were leaving, give him the opportunity to spend time with Dmitri? Or let him stay on the Promenade and paint?

Though it was selfish of him, he decided to let Taylor finish his painting. He packed for both of them, and as he was finishing Taylor returned to the room. "We're leaving already?" he asked.

"My boss wants the painting back in Paris. I booked us tickets on the 6:05 flight to Orly."

"Did you call Albin and tell him we're not coming for dinner?"

"I thought I'd let you tell Dmitri yourself. You have enough time to run over there if you want."

Taylor shook his head. "I'll call. It's easier."

Rowan stepped out onto the balcony and closed the door behind him to give Taylor some privacy. He saw Taylor sprawl on the bed, his phone to his ear, and noticed again how young he was. It wasn't fair to saddle him with an attempt at a long-distance relationship, with Taylor back in school in Paris and Rowan in New York.

They would have one more night together in Paris, and then Rowan would go home and Taylor would go back to his painting classes at the Institute.

Sooner than he expected, Taylor was opening the balcony door. The young man stepped out next to Rowan and leaned forward on the balcony railing, inhaling the fresh air. "It's gorgeous here," he said. "I think Dmitri is going to flourish with Albin, with this light."

"Will you miss him back in Paris?" Rowan asked, looking straight ahead, not at Taylor.

"Probably. But that's life, you know? People come and go."

Rowan swallowed hard. He had believed the same thing when he was Taylor's age. Now, it seemed, he mourned every loss—his marriage, his relationship with his kids, now this brief connection to Taylor.

"Speaking of which," Rowan said. "Time for us to go." He turned to walk inside but Taylor caught his arm.

"One more kiss by the Mediterranean?" he asked.

He pulled Rowan close to him and wrapped his arms around Rowan's back. Rowan closed his eyes and pressed his lips against Taylor's. Every sensation was heightened as their bodies touched and their lips locked. Taylor's were soft and wet, as if he'd licked them just before.

Rowan could hear the traffic noise below, the sound of the waves on the rocky beach, the cries of children at play. The air was redolent with automobile exhaust mixed with salt air and the faintest scent of coconut tanning lotion. Taylor smelled of sweat and traces of the vanilla soap from the hotel bathroom.

They both leaned against the iron balcony railing as they kissed, and Rowan felt it pressing against his hip. He tightened his grip on Taylor as their tongues dueled. When he finally pulled away to gasp for breath, he opened his eyes and found Taylor watching him. "You don't close your eyes to kiss?" Rowan asked.

"I want to memorize every detail of your face," Taylor said. "I have a feeling you'll be in my dreams for a long time."

"We'll have one more night to share dreams. I booked us at a hotel by the airport."

"No, I want to take you to my apartment," Taylor said. "I want you to see it. I want you to sleep in my bed with me so your scent will be on the sheets." He gripped Rowan's hand and squeezed. "Please?"

"Of course." Rowan was touched by the romantic gesture, and he had to admit he liked the idea of leaving his imprint at Taylor's apartment.

They carried their luggage downstairs, where Rowan checked out, putting the bill on his corporate credit card. He hoped Ron Kramer would be able to pass the bill off to the NYMFA without problems. The bellman hailed them a cab, and they rode to the airport in silence.

The flight north was much better than Rowan's southbound one had been, and they deplaned in Paris without incident. Taylor gave his address to the cab driver and he took Rowan's hand once again as they sat back and watched the city appear.

The cab driver pulled up at the foot of a staircase in Montmartre. "We get out here," Taylor said. It was dark and cold, with tiny snow flurries swirling as they climbed.

"Big change from the Riviera," Rowan said, as they climbed. He felt every one of his fifty years as he trudged up the stairs towing his rollaboard bag.

"Let me carry that for you," Taylor said, as the bag bounced over the cobbled steps.

"I can manage." Rowan gently pushed Taylor away. "How many more flights?"

"At the top of this staircase we turn and walk down an alley to the building. Then there are four flights inside."

Rowan groaned. "We could have just stayed at the hotel where I made a reservation. The things I do for love."

Taylor stopped. An elderly woman coming down the staircase hurried past them. "That's what this is, isn't it?" he said to Rowan when she had passed. "Between us. Love."

Rowan had meant his comment as a joke. But seeing the seriousness on Taylor's face, he said, "Yes. I love you."

"Good. Because I love you, too," Taylor said, then turned and continued to climb.

Not a Problem Here

Paris, Monday night

By the time they reached the door of the apartment, Rowan was exhausted. "We should have stopped for dinner. I can't make that trip again."

Taylor pulled a heavy key from his pocket and opened the door. "I can cook for you."

The room was tiny, with one big double bed in the center, and a sharply sloping roof with a dormer window cut into it. Through an open door, Rowan saw a tiny bathroom, barely big enough for a toilet, a sink and a stall shower. There was a half refrigerator along one wall, with a hot plate and a coffee pot on a counter.

"You live here?" It made his own apartment in New York look like a palace.

"Yup," Taylor said, dropping his duffle on the bed. "But I won't be able to manage the rent on my own. I'll have to look for a room somewhere, or a share where I can have my own bed."

He walked over to the cupboard above the counter. "Great, we have some pasta," he said. "Macaroni and cheese all right for dinner?"

"Have any wine?"

"Yup. It's just plonk, though." He pulled a box out of the refrigerator, and handed it to Rowan with a glass. "Help yourself."

While Taylor cooked, Rowan sat at the tiny table and opened his laptop. He drank his wine and wrote up his report for Ron Kramer. He had been in France for a week and he was surprised at how much had happened in that short time. Two men had died, a smuggling ring had been broken up, a stolen painting retrieved. And Rowan had fallen in love.

That part didn't make it into the report. He finished his narration and closed the laptop just as Taylor brought two plates of steaming pasta, topped with shaved parmesan cheese, to the table.

"It's not gourmet, but it's filling," Taylor said.

"We ate a lot of pasta when I was in school," Rowan said.

"We?" Taylor speared a forkful of elbow macaroni.

"I was married then, to Elizabeth."

"What's she like?"

Rowan shifted uncomfortably on the hard chair. He rarely spoke about Elizabeth or his kids with men he dated; it was like they belonged to an earlier part of his life, when he was a different man. But he wanted Taylor to know, to understand him.

"She's a very strong woman," he said. "She sees what she wants and she goes for it. We met in college, and after we graduated she became a paralegal, and then worked while I finished my PhD. When I got the job at St. Michael's she went to law school as part of my employee benefits."

"She lives in New York, too?"

Rowan shook his head. "She stayed in Virginia with the kids when I moved out. She was already a partner in a firm there."

"You don't like talking about her, do you?" Taylor asked.

Rowan put his fork down. "I didn't know what I wanted when I was your age. I didn't know if I was straight or gay. I just knew that I liked to study art. Elizabeth made all the decisions—that we should get married, that I should take the job at St. Michael's. As soon as she finished her degree she got pregnant with Nick, and arranged a part-time job for herself with a sole practitioner in town. She ran the house, raised the kids. I kept my head in the clouds."

"And then?"

"And then I met Brian Wojchowski."

The sound of his name surprised Rowan. He hadn't said it out loud in years, though he had often thought of him.

"He was my student, though he wasn't in my class any more by the time we started… I don't even know what to call it."

"Having sex?"

"Well, yes. It was more than that for me, though. It was like a door opened to a whole new world, and I realized who I was and what I wanted."

"How old were you then?"

"Forty-five."

Taylor's fork clattered to the plate. "Forty-five?"

"I was a late bloomer. But in short order I lost my job and my marriage. Brian left for San Francisco and made it clear he didn't want me to follow. So I moved to New York and started over again."

Rowan took another forkful of pasta. The cheese tasted sharp in his mouth but he kept on eating.

"My generation has it so much easier than yours," Taylor said, picking up his fork. "I knew I was gay when I was thirteen and I realized I was getting boners from looking at naked boys in the locker room. My mom was cool about it, and I had a boyfriend in high school, but he was on the down low so it's not like we went to the prom together."

It was such a foreign idea to Rowan that he had trouble grasping it. How different would his life be if he had known what Taylor did at thirteen?

"I'm sorry there's no dessert," Taylor said, standing up to take away the empty plates.

"So what, we just go to sleep? Nothing else?"

Taylor laughed. "Well, I guess you could call that dessert."

Rowan stood up. There wasn't enough room for both of them to move around the tiny room, so he crossed to the bed, and as Taylor washed the dishes Rowan stripped off his clothes, folded them, and put them on top of his suitcase. He hadn't been to the gym since he left New York, but he figured all his running and tree climbing had to count for something. He was glad there wasn't a full-length mirror in the room, so he was spared the sight of his own naked body.

It was chilly, so he got into bed as Taylor was finishing, pulling the down quilt up to his chin. This was where Dmitri had slept, where Taylor and Dmitri had made love. The idea was a bit creepy—but in the years since he'd come out of the closet, he'd had sex in worse places.

Taylor dried his hands on a cloth towel and turned to the bed. "You look cozy."

"I'd be cozier if you were under here with me."

"That can be arranged." Taylor pulled off his T-shirt, dropped his jeans to the floor and stepped out of them.

"Stay like that for a minute," Rowan said. "I want to look at you."

Taylor's arms and legs had darkened from his exposure to the sun, and his white briefs shone against his skin. His long, hairless legs had a coltish grace, and his nipples stood out on his smooth chest.

Taylor vogued for him, turning slowly and making poses. Then he began to slink his briefs down, inch by inch. Rowan felt his mouth go dry. His dick rose against his abdomen as he glimpsed Taylor's half-hard dick in the striptease.

"Fuck this." Taylor dropped his briefs as his stiff dick sprung free, and he jumped on the bed, scrambling under the covers. "I'm not wasting any time with you here in my bed."

He climbed onto Rowan and pressed his body down, and they kissed. He rubbed his dick against Rowan's leg, and Rowan's own dick rubbed against Taylor's smooth belly. Then Taylor pushed the covers back and climbed up Rowan's body, positioning his dick at Rowan's mouth.

Rowan leaned down and sucked him, as Taylor flexed his ass cheeks and pumped his dick in and out of Rowan's mouth. Then he pulled out and moved back down to suck Rowan's dick. They went back and forth like that—Taylor sucking Rowan, Rowan sucking Taylor—until both of them were sweaty and Rowan's dick was aching for release. Taylor finally scrambled around so that they were in a sixty-nine position, and took Rowan's dick in his mouth.

Rowan sucked Taylor's dick in a frenzy, losing all finesse, just desperate to get his handsome young lover off, even as his own passion rose. They came almost at the same time, both of them spewing cum. Showing more energy than Rowan felt, Taylor turned himself around and nestled up against Rowan's hairy chest.

"Just in case you were wondering," Taylor said, tickling his hand down Rowan's chest. "That was the best sex this bed has ever seen."

"Good to know." Rowan yawned and leaned back, and he was asleep almost immediately.

When he woke the next morning, Taylor was already dressed. "Sorry there's nothing here for breakfast, and there's no room service," he said. "But there is a nice café across from the Institute."

Rowan stretched and groaned. The bed was old and worn, and his muscles ached. He stumbled through a quick shower—the water was cold—and then got dressed. "You paint outside in this weather?" Rowan asked as they walked through the narrow streets of Montmartre to the Institute. It was bitter cold, though the snow flurries of the night before had not stuck.

"You get used to it. Only for a couple of hours a day in the winter, though."

Rowan carried the cardboard tube with the painting over his shoulder and thought he'd be glad to be rid of it. It was gorgeous, but too much of a burden.

In the café across from the Institute, they ordered steaming cups of hot chocolate and a basket of chocolate croissants. "I have a meeting with the director at nine," Rowan said, looking at his watch. "You have class?"

"Studio," Taylor said. "From nine to twelve. Will you still be around when I finish?"

"I will. I need to book a ticket back to New York but I haven't

The Russian Boy

done that yet."

Rowan paid for breakfast and they walked across the street to the Institute. It was a huge stone building with a mansard roof, a central atrium and a massive marble staircase. Impossibly young students milled around the ground floor, chattering and talking on cell phones. The walls were hung with student art, and Rowan thought a lot of it looked pretty good.

"Meet me here at noon?" Taylor asked.

"OK."

Taylor leaned over and kissed Rowan's cheek, then hurried up the staircase. Rowan crossed the lobby to the director's office, and introduced himself to the man's secretary.

He sat in the outer office for nearly forty-five minutes. *I guess this painting isn't as important to them as I believed*, he thought, as he watched people come and go. But at least he would have the money for Nick's course. He sent his son a brief text, and smiled when a few minutes later the reply appeared. "Awesome!"

He sat back. Even though he'd taken the job for the money, he was very happy to have helped bring *The Russian Boy* back to safety. It was a painting that had meant a lot to him in the past, and he empathized with all the drama behind it. Even though Luschenko's affair with Alexei Dubernin had ended in flames, with the lovers separated and both of them dying soon after the painting was created, at least it had resulted in a piece of great art.

Now that art would be back in a museum, where everyone could appreciate it, because he had pushed himself and worked his butt off to retrieve it. Knowing that made him feel like all the years he had spent, in school and working for Ron Kramer, had paid off in a big way.

He remembered the phrase "the more things change, the more they remain the same." Attitudes in the 21st century toward homosexuality were much more enlightened than they had been back in 1912. Would Luschenko's life have crashed and burned if a similar scandal arose today?

Rowan had lost his job because of his affair with Brian only a few years before. But Taylor's attitude was so much more open than Rowan's had been at his age. Perhaps there was hope for the future.

Finally the director's door opened and he stepped out. "I am Paul Matignon. Please accept my apologies for keeping you waiting. We have had an emergency this morning and I am at a total loss."

His eyes lit up as he saw the cardboard tube. "That is *The Russian*

Boy?" he asked.

"Yes." Rowan handed him the tube.

"Please, come in." Matignon led Rowan into a high-ceilinged room with canvases on easels around the room, and bookshelves full of art texts. He felt a momentary pang, missing the teaching environment. But that door had closed to him the first time he kissed Brian Wojchowski.

Matignon opened the tube and pulled out the painting, and Rowan helped him lay it out on a slanted table. Matignon inhaled deeply. "It is a beautiful painting, no?"

"It is. I'm glad to have it back where it belongs."

"At least this is one crisis resolved," Matignon said. "One of my professors, who teaches the history of art courses, suffered a heart attack last night. He will be unable to return to teach for the rest of the term, and he will most likely retire. I have been trying to find someone to replace him."

He looked up at Rowan. "I have spoken about you with Mr. Kramer, in New York. You have taught, have you not?"

"Yes. I spent fifteen years teaching art history in Virginia."

"But you are not teaching now?"

"No. I lost that position."

"So you are available?" Matignon's eyes lit up. "Your French is very good. You could teach here?"

Rowan shook his head. "My teaching career is over. An unfortunate incident with a former student."

"A *former* student? And that was a problem in Virginia?"

"A male former student. Yes, it was a problem."

Matignon walked around to his baroque wooden desk and motioned Rowan to a seat across from him. "That is not a problem here."

Rowan felt his heart jump. Then he remembered Taylor. "There is another complication, however."

"You have the proper credentials?" Matignon said.

"Yes. But I've begun a relationship with one of your students. So I couldn't teach here."

"Who?"

"Taylor Griffin."

Matignon nodded. "A very talented painter. But he is not technically a student, you know. He is on a fellowship, and does not take courses in the history of art. So there would be no circumstance in

The Russian Boy

which he would be in your class."

Rowan's pulse accelerated. "It wouldn't bother you—that Taylor and I..."

"Not at all. And you would do me the greatest favor by taking this job, Dr. McNair."

For the first time in years, Rowan felt like he deserved that title.

"And you, Dr. Matignon, would do me the greatest favor by hiring me," he said.

He spent the next few hours with the department secretary, filling out paperwork, including an application for a *carte de séjour* and a work permit, then reviewing the syllabi and teaching materials for the classes he would be picking up. When he looked at his watch, it was quarter past noon, and he jumped up and ran out to the lobby.

Taylor was standing all alone in the center of the lobby, looking downcast. Rowan raced across the marble floor, darting past clusters of students. He grabbed Taylor at the waist and pulled him close for a kiss.

"You're awfully happy," Taylor said.

"You will be too, too, when I tell you what's happening." He told Taylor about the offer from Dr. Matignon. "I filled out all the papers, but I didn't sign anything. I wanted to check with you first. Is it OK with you if I stay in Paris?"

"It's better than OK. It's amazing!" Taylor kissed him again, both of them oblivious to the students around them.

"There's one condition, though," Rowan said, pulling back. "We find a new apartment with fewer steps – and hot water."

"I can live with that," Taylor said.

ABOUT THE AUTHOR

Neil Plakcy is the author of the *Mahu* mystery series, about openly gay Honolulu homicide detective Kimo Kanapa'aka. They are: *Mahu, Mahu Surfer, Mahu Fire, Mahu Vice, Mahu Men, Mahu Blood* and *Zero Break* (2012).

He also writes the Have Body, Will Guard adventure romance series, *Three Wrong Turns in the Desert, Dancing with the Tide* and *Teach Me Tonight.*

His other books are the Golden Retriever Mysteries *In Dog We Trust* and *The Kingdom of Dog*, as well as the novels *GayLife.com, Mi Amor*, and *The Outhouse Gang* and and the novella *The Guardian Angel of South Beach.*

Plakcy is a journalist and book reviewer as well as an assistant professor of English at Broward College's south campus in Pembroke Pines. He edited *Paws & Reflect: A Special Bond Between Man and Dog* and the gay erotic anthologies *Hard Hats, Surfer Boys, Skater Boys, Model Men* and *The Handsome Prince.* His erotic stories have been collected in four Kindle editions: *Tough Guy Erotica, Mr. Surfer and Other Gay Erotica, Three Lambs*, and *Pledge Class and Other College Boy Erotica.*

His website is www.mahubooks.com.

Made in the USA
Lexington, KY
25 January 2012